THREE PLAYS:
PIAF, CAMILLE, LOVING WOMEN

Pam Gems began to write plays as a child, encouraged by the staff of the Priory Church School in Christchurch, Dorset. She wrote for some years, without achieving production, and it was not until she was in her forties, having worked at many different jobs, and reared four children, that she began to find work in fringe theatre. This was particularly accessible as, happening during the day, it was possible to combine production with school hours. Since then she has had a number of productions in London, three with the Royal Shakespeare Company, and many productions abroad, most particularly of *Dusa, Fish, Stas and Vi* and *Piaf*. She is on the steering committee of the Women's Playhouse Trust, which seeks to support women in the theatre.

Her plays are *Betty's Wonderful Christmas* (1972), *After Birthday* (1973), *My Warren* (1973), *Miz Venus* (1973), *Go West Young Woman* (1974), *My Name is Rosa Luxemburg* (1975, translated from French), *Up in Sweden* (1975), *Rivers and Forests* (1976, translated from French), *Guinevere* (1976), *Dead Fish* (1976), *Dusa, Fish, Stas and Vi* (1976), *Queen Christina* (1977), *Franz into April* (1977), *Piaf* (1978), *Lady-bird, Ladybird* (1979), *The Treat* (1982), *Aunt Mary* (1982), *Loving Women* (1984), *Camille* (1984) and *Pasionaria* (1985). She has also produced her version of *Uncle Vanya* (1979), *A Doll's House* (1980) and *The Cherry Orchard* (1984).

PAM GEMS

THREE PLAYS:

PIAF

CAMILLE

LOVING WOMEN

PENGUIN BOOKS

Penguin Books Ltd, Harmondsworth, Middlesex, England
Viking Penguin Inc., 40 West 23rd Street, New York, New York 10010, U.S.A.
Penguin Books Australia Ltd, Ringwood, Victoria, Australia
Penguin Books Canada Ltd, 2801 John Street, Markham, Ontario, Canada L3R 1B4
Penguin Books (N.Z.) Ltd, 182–190 Wairau Road, Auckland 10, New Zealand

Piaf first published by Amber Lane 1979
Revised version published in Penguin Books 1985
Camille and *Loving Women* first published 1985

Copyright © Pam Gems, 1985

All rights whatsoever in these plays
are strictly reserved and applications for
performance, etc., should be made before rehearsal
to Actac, 16 Cadogan Lane, London SW1.
No performance may be given unless a
licence has been obtained.

Made and printed in Great Britain by
Cox & Wyman Ltd, Reading
Filmset in Aldus (Linotron 202) by
Rowland Phototypesetting Ltd,
Bury St Edmunds, Suffolk

CONTENTS

‖ PIAF ‖

CHARACTERS

EDITH PIAF
TOINE
JOSEPHINE
MANAGER
LOUIS LEPLÉE
ÉMIL
LEGIONNAIRE
JACQUES
LOUIS
EDDIE
POLICE INSPECTOR
PAUL
2 GERMAN SOLDIERS
GEORGES
BUTCHER
PIERRE
SAILOR
MARCEL
2 AMERICAN SAILORS
BARMAN
MADELEINE
LUCIEN
JEAN
NURSE
DOCTOR
PIANIST
ANGELO
PHYSIOTHERAPIST
DOPE PUSHER
THEO

Piaf was first presented at The Other Place, Stratford-upon-Avon, by the Royal Shakespeare Company on 5 October 1978. It was directed by Howard Davies and designed by Douglas Heap.

The cast was as follows:

PIAF	Jane Lapotaire
TOINE	Zoe Wanamaker
MADELEINE	Carmen du Sautoy
NURSE	Susanna Bishop
INSPECTOR GEORGES BARMAN	Conrad Asquith
LOUIS BUTCHER LUCIEN DOPE PUSHER	Bill Buffery
MAN AT REHEARSAL PIERRE	Ian Charleson
MANAGER	Geoffrey Freshwater
LOUIS 'PAPA' LEPLÉE JEAN	James Griffiths
ÉMIL JACKO EDDIE	Allan Hendrick
ANGELO GERMAN SOLDIER	Anthony Higgins
PAUL AMERICAN SAILOR PHYSIOTHERAPIST	Ian Reddington
LEGIONNAIRE JACQUES GERMAN SOLDIER MARCEL AMERICAN SAILOR THEO	Malcolm Storry
MUSIC/DIRECTOR PIANO	Michael Tubs
ACCORDION	Roy Stelling

SYNOPSIS OF SCENES

ACT I

ACT II

Set and staging are non-naturalistic throughout, with scenes indicated by minimal prop and furnishing changes.

ACT I

The MANAGER *enters, with a Thirties' floor microphone.*

MANAGER [*testing*]: One, two, three . . . [*To audience*] ladies and
gentlemen . . . ladies and gentlemen . . . I give you . . . your
own . . . Piaf!
[*Musical introduction:* La goualante du pauvre Jean.
He gestures, with a sharp glance off, and goes. A pause.
PIAF *enters.*

She sings the first few lines of La goualante du pauvre Jean,
falters and stops, swaying at the microphone.

The MANAGER *runs on, and tries to assist her off. But* PIAF
resists. There is an undignified fight.]
PIAF [*struggling*]: Get your fucking hands off me, I ain't *done*
nothing yet . . .
[*Blackout. Straight into*]

SCENE II

The young PIAF. *She sings part of* Les amants d'un jour, *in French,
artlessly, sans mike, in the street.* LOUIS LEPLÉE, *the club owner,
arrives, in evening clothes, pauses to listen. She sees him.*

PIAF: Get your fucking hands off me, *I* ain't done nothing.
LEPLÉE: All right, kid . . . all right!
PIAF [*reassured*]: Oh, sorry guv. [*Cheeky*] What can I do you for?
[*This makes him laugh.*]

No, well, if I knew you was coming I'd have shaved me legs.

LEPLÉE: Never mind the legs . . . where did you get that big voice?

PIAF: It's only so's they can hear me over the traffic.

LEPLÉE: How long have you been singing?

PIAF: Coupla minutes, that's all.

LEPLÉE [*assessing her shrewdly*]: Extraordinary.

PIAF: I said sorry!

[*He takes out his wallet and gives her some money. She is dumbfounded.*

Light change.
As LEPLÉE *goes,* PIAF *turns towards her friend,* TOINE, *who enters, throws down her large Thirties' clutch bag, and sits heavily, taking off her shoes and massaging her feet, wincing.*]

PIAF: Toine – here – guess what!

TOINE: Fuck off.

PIAF: Wassa matter with you?

TOINE: Fucking pimp's had me on that corner, I thought my bleeding toes would burst. I haven't seen more than a couple of fellers all night . . . he's gotta change my shift.

PIAF: Here, listen –

TOINE: Him with his bloody favourites, think I don't know?

PIAF: Listen! You're never going –

TOINE: That fat Hélène, sits in the fucking caff half the time, I'm not going to stand for it –

PIAF: This bloke . . . !

TOINE [*irritable*]: What?

PIAF: Me big chance! – you know, like on the movies.

TOINE [*baffled*]: Eh?

PIAF: This bloke comes up to me – hey! Remember what the fortune teller told us –!

TOINE: Hang on . . .

PIAF: *You* remember! I was standing outside the Cluny Club, singing –

TOINE: Singing?

PIAF: Yeah, you know . . . for a lark . . . I'm just getting going when up he comes . . . real swell . . . top hat, silk scarf, silver cane, the lot. Next thing I know he asks me inside.

TOINE: Iyiy!

PIAF: Toine, you've never seen nothink like it – white tablecloths, little velvet chairs with gold tassels, anything I wanted to drink –

TOINE: Hah, I get it – another fucking funny, Christ he must be hard up . . . here, can you see any crabs?

PIAF [looks perfunctorily]: No, listen! He says to me, he says 'You've got a good voice, kid . . .'

TOINE: Hah!

PIAF: Shut up . . . 'I want you . . .' [She fixes TOINE with a magnetic stare.] . . . 'I want you to star in my club!' Whatcha think of that!

TOINE: Oh Christ, she's away.

PIAF: It's true!

TOINE: Ede –

PIAF: Look, I'm not saying he's young or goodlooking or any-thing –

TOINE: Ede, have you gone off your head or something?

PIAF: I keep trying to *tell* you! [Her rage subsides as she concedes the unlikeliness of the tale.] He wants me to sing . . . in his show . . . Cluny Club.

TOINE: Where all the swells go? Get away.

[But PIAF is counting the money.]

Listen . . . where did you get that?

PIAF: He *gave* it me . . . honest. For nothing!

[They both look at the money. TOINE shakes her head slowly.]

TOINE: Nah.

[PIAF waits patiently for the verdict.]

Nah . . . sounds funny to me. Look, kid, I wouldn't have nothing to do wiv it. He's got a little business going, he's short of girls – [she laughs] haha, hahaha . . . he must be!

PIAF: Speak for your bloody self!

TOINE [threatening]: Get off.

[PIAF backs away prudently.

13

Hiatus.
She scuffs moodily . . . picks up the dress TOINE *has taken off.*]

TOINE [*without raising her eyes from her magazine*]: It's too big for yuh.

[PIAF *hums moodily, ruining* TOINE'S *efforts to read.*
She puts down her book with a martyred sigh.]

Oh all right. You can have this. [*She proffers her long, thin, dark-purple Thirties-style scarf.*]

PIAF: Thanks! [*She arranges it around her neck.*] Here, don't laugh. He told me to have a bath . . . wash me hair.

[*They laugh, jeering.*]

TOINE: Tell you what, though. [*She finds a comb in her bag . . . tidies* PIAF'S *hair, arranges a spitcurl on her forehead.*] That's better – we-ell, you wanna look decent.

PIAF: Thanks. [*She makes to go . . . pauses.*]

TOINE [*without looking up from her book*]: OK, what is it now?

PIAF: Can I have a lend of your handbag?

TOINE: No.

[*But* PIAF *knows the value of fidgeting.*
TOINE *grinds her teeth, hurls the bag at her.*]

PIAF: Thanks! [*She tucks the unsuitably large poche under her arm and struts off proudly, causing* TOINE *to grin.*]

TOINE: Take it easy, squirt. [*To the audience, tired*] Well, can't be for the fucking singing, can it – he can hear that for nothing in the street. Be Tangier for you, I shouldn't doubt. [*She picks up her things and goes.*
Music.]

SCENE III

The Cluny Club. Chairs on tables. PIANIST *strums,* PAPA LEPLÉE *waits with his* MANAGER. PIAF *runs on.*

LEPLÉE: You're late.
PIAF: Sorry.

LEPLÉE [*looks at her, then, to* MANAGER]: Ee-dith. We'll have to do better than that.

MANAGER: What about the one you said before?

LEPLÉE: Tich? . . . Nipper? . . . what was it?

MANAGER: Tich Sparrow.

[PIAF, *now sprawled on the top of the piano, rears up in horror.*]

LEPLÉE: What do you think?

MANAGER: 'S all right – no good going for something glamorous.

PIAF: Whaddya mean?

LEPLÉE [*musing*]: The little sparrow . . . La Môme Piaf . . . The Kid Sparrow . . . Piaf . . .

[PIAF *mimes being sick over the keys.*]

MANAGER: Piaf . . . Piaf . . .

PIAF: Piaf? What sort of a name's that?

LEPLÉE: Better than Edith Gassion – it's not a stage name, kid.

PIAF: Oh. Oh . . . well . . . I know, what about Lola Fairbanks?

MANAGER: Piaf – yeah, that's OK.

PIAF: Zozine Heliotrope . . . Claudette Cunningham . . .

LEPLÉE: Piaf . . . Piaf . . . Piaf . . . Piaf? [*With conviction*] Piaf!

PIAF [*desperate*]: Desirée de la Renta . . . Desirée!

LEPLÉE: Piaf!

PIAF [*leaps down in fury*]: Piaf? Where am I going to get with a name like that?

[*The* MANAGER *gestures to* LEPLÉE . . . *Who needs such a scruff? But* LEPLÉE *laughs.*]

LEPLÉE: Let her sing.

[PIAF *sings* Les amants d'un jour, *in English. The* MANAGER *and* LEPLÉE *exchange a glance . . . the* MANAGER *shrugs – not bad, and goes.* ÉMIL, *the young waiter, sets a table.*]

OK, kid. OK.

PIAF [*not sure what he means*]: Yeah?

LEPLÉE: Are you hungry?

PIAF: Not 'alf. [*She crosses to table, set for dinner, sits. Then she sips delicately from the finger bowl.* ÉMIL *guffaws.*]

What's the matter?

ÉMIL: That's the finger bowl, scruff – for washing yer 'ands.

PIAF: Where's the soap? All right, clever cock. Seen me drink –
now you can watch me piss. [*She does so. And marches off, to*
PAPA LEPLÉE's *laughter.*

> *Light change. Low light.*
> LEPLÉE *stacks a last chair. A noise. He jumps, alarmed . . .*
> *and sees* PIAF *at a distance.*]

LEPLÉE: Oh, it's you. I thought you'd pushed off . . . what do you
want?

PIAF: I thought you'd want to see me.

LEPLÉE: What for? Come on, I'm tired, I've had a long day.

PIAF: Up to you, innit?

LEPLÉE: What do you mean?

PIAF: I thought you might wanna – well, after all, I mean . . . you
did give me my big break – I mean, it's OK by me.

LEPLÉE: What?

PIAF: Well you must have done it for something. If you want
sucking off or anything, just say the word – no skin off my nose.

LEPLÉE [*dry*]: Oh . . . I see. Are you ready, my dear? [*But
addressed to* ÉMIL, *who appears, bearing* LEPLÉE's *coat, hat,
scarf. He robes him reverently.*

> LEPLÉE *puts his arm across the boy's shoulders.* ÉMIL *smiles,
> malevolent.*]

As you see . . . little fish.

PIAF: Oh. Oh! . . . why didn't you say! [*She gives him an
affectionate and familiar dig in the ribs.*]

LEPLÉE [*to* ÉMIL]: What do you think?

ÉMIL [*shrugs*]: They seemed to like her – at least you can hear her
over the cutlery.

> [LEPLÉE *and* ÉMIL *leave . . .* PIAF *crosses.*]

SCENE IV

The street . . . The music is Un sale petit brouillard. PIAF *is getting it
from a* LEGIONNAIRE.

LEGIONNAIRE: And sun and sand and sea and sand and sand and
sand and sand and sea . . .

[PIAF *simulates noisy and joyous ecstasy.*]

. . . and flies, flies, flies, flies, flies!

TOINE [*enters*]: Ede! Ede, is that you? We can hear you half way down the street, you're s'posed to be down the Club, Papa's screaming blue murder!

PIAF: Hey, Toine . . . cop on to this, will you? [*disengaging herself*]

TOINE: What, for nothing?

PIAF: Do us a favour . . . I'm pegged out.

TOINE: Oh all right. But not for nothing.

[*He pays. She takes over.*]

PIAF [*going*]: He's a legionnaire.

TOINE: Oh, why din't you say? [*She livens it up a bit.*]

LEGIONNAIRE: And sea and sand and sand and sea and sand and sand and . . .

TOINE: What's he on about?

PIAF: He's a fucking Algerian!

TOINE: Oh. Hang on . . . hang on . . . holdee on a bittee, matey – here, you wouldn't like to lie down, would you . . . only I got bad feet, see?

[*Lights down on* TOINE *and* LEGIONNAIRE *as* PIAF *crosses to* PAPA LEPLÉE, *who sits at a table drinking brandy. She throws herself on his lap.*]

LEPLÉE [*as he sees her*]: You're late! Steady on, my head's not too good.

PIAF: You know your trouble, too much of the other.

LEPLÉE: You're a familiar little devil. You're going to have to settle down, you know, if you want to make something of yourself . . . you won't always have me.

PIAF [*cheeky*]: Why, where you going?

LEPLÉE: I don't know, I've been feeling a little odd for the last two days.

PIAF: A little who?

LEPLÉE [*laughs*]: I should miss you. Ever get nightmares?

PIAF: Nah.

LEPLÉE: I had a funny dream about my mother last night. She seemed to be beckoning me.

PIAF: Lucky you. Mine took one look and pissed off.

LEPLÉE: All on your own, are you?

PIAF [*sturdy*]: Yeah. [*Casual afterthought*] I did have a little girl once.

LEPLÉE [*surprised*]: You?

PIAF: Yeah. Cunts.

LEPLÉE: I beg your pardon?

PIAF: The people looking after her. Only never told me! Somebody down the road said, 'Hey, d'you know your kid's ill?' I was round there the same week, they wouldn't let me in – 'Ew new, it's not convenient, anyway, she's dead, died six o'clock this morning.' I wasn't having that. [*Laughs, in fond reminiscence*] Nah, we had a real old punch-up. Hey, did you know something? When people die they go all *stiff*! She was sliding about the parquet in the end . . . talk about shove-ha'penny, we had a right old fracass! [*She laughs, in fond reminiscence.*

But he stumbles to his feet, almost backing away from her.*]
Look, it's not unreasonable. I only wanted a bit of her hair, for me locket.

[*He looks down at her, then turns, moving even further away.*

Music . . . sombre. PIAF turns to her three friends, JACQUES and EDDIE, who look tough, and LOUIS, younger. PIAF throws her arms about JACQUES, who throws her off irritably.*]

JACQUES: Get him over here. [*He twists her arm cruelly.*]

PIAF: Ow! Hey, Papa, come and have a drink.

[*PAPA approaches, genial.*]

PIAF: Jacques . . . Eddie . . . and little Louie.

[*JACQUES digs her in the ribs.*]

PIAF: What do you think of little Louis?

LEPLÉE [*with a quick glance at* LOUIS]: Not just now. I'll get Émil to give you a drink.

JACQUES: Busy counting the takings, eh Papa?

LEPLÉE [*jovial*]: Never you mind about that.

EDDIE: Go on, you must be rolling in it.

LEPLÉE: That's what they all think.

[LEPLÉE *takes another look at* LOUIS.

The others move away discreetly, but PIAF *blows it, in a moment of panic.*]

PIAF [*returning*]: Hey . . . hey, d'you hear the story about the man with cock trouble?

[*They turn on her murderously.*]

JACQUES [*to* PIAF]: Shut up.

PIAF [*unable to stop*]: He goes to the chemist and says, 'Look, there's something the matter with my cock' . . . no, listen and the chemist says, 'For fuck's sake, man, can't you see I got a shop full of ladies, you'll do me out of business.' Ah . . . 'Take these tablets three times a day and if you have to come back for Christ's sake call it your elbow.' So he comes back the next week and the chemist says, 'Tablets any good, how's your elbow?' And he says, 'Oh, much better, but I still can't piss out of it!' [*She shrieks with laughter.*

LEPLÉE *laughs and goes . . . the moment has been lost.*

Music of La ville inconnue.]

JACQUES [*grabbing her*]: You messed it up, didn't you?

PIAF: No I never.

JACQUES: All right, where'd you say he kept it?

PIAF: What?

JACQUES: His money, you twot . . . the cashbox!

EDDIE: Edie, look, why don't you and me get together . . . eh?

PIAF [*drunk*]: Yeah . . .

EDDIE: What about poor little Louis here, though?

JACQUES: Does he keep it in his room?

EDDIE: Little Louis could go up there, proposition him . . . you never know, might work out for them, then you and me can enjoy ourselves.

PIAF: Yeah.

[*Music.*]

JACQUES: Where's the safe, you bitch?

[*They cross, in the direction of* LEPLÉE.

PIAF *makes to follow but* LOUIS *puts out a restraining hand, then melts away.*

A shot.

PIAF *sits, white-faced, at the table.*

PIAF *sings* La ville inconnue.]

SCENE V

PIAF *and Police* INSPECTOR.

INSPECTOR: Come and sit down. Let me see . . . ah . . . Edith.
   [PIAF *fidgets, as he writes.*]
   Name?
PIAF: You got it. [*nodding at his papers*]
INSPECTOR [*glares, and then decides to be foxy*]: That's right.
   Edith Gassion . . . known as La Môme Piaf. [*writing it down*]
PIAF [*nervous*]: What am I supposed to have done . . . I ain't done
   nothing –
INSPECTOR: Address?
PIAF: Haven't got one.
INSPECTOR: No fixed address?
PIAF: I ain't *done* nothing –
INSPECTOR: Right. We will now proceed with your involvement
   in –
PIAF: Eh?
INSPECTOR [*sudden frontal bark*]: What was your involvement in
   the Leplée affair?
PIAF: What?
INSPECTOR: Name?
PIAF: Oh Christ.
INSPECTOR: I seriously advise you to co-operate.
PIAF: I ain't *done* nothing!
INSPECTOR: That is what I am here to find out. [*Slight pause*]
   Father's occupation?
PIAF: Street acrobat. And businessman.
INSPECTOR: What was your relationship with the deceased?
PIAF: Who?
INSPECTOR: With Louis Leplée.

PIAF: Oh, he weren't no relation of mine. He was a big shot!

INSPECTOR: You were with Leplée the night he was murdered.

PIAF: Not only me . . . other people.

INSPECTOR: Including friends of yours.

PIAF: People I know, yes.

INSPECTOR [*showing her a paper*]: These names? You were seen
   together.

PIAF: Just having a laugh.

INSPECTOR: Planning to rob your patron, Louis Leplée.

PIAF: No!

INSPECTOR: You told them where he kept his money.

PIAF: No.

INSPECTOR: Where did he keep his money?

PIAF: In his room. [*And could bite her tongue out.*]

INSPECTOR: You told them.

PIAF: They ASKED me!

INSPECTOR: Edith Gassion, I ask you, formally . . . what was
   your implication in the Leplée affair? [*He stands over her,
   slapping his leg lightly with his right hand.*]

PIAF: I ain't done nothing!
   [*He slaps her face.*]
Leave me alone . . . he was my guvnor . . . he give me my big
break, I'm not gonna want to –
   [*He hits her again.*]
. . . I'm . . . I'm not gonna do him in, am I?
   [*He hits her again and this time she breaks down, sobbing
   noisily.*]
. . . I keep seeing him . . . with his face . . . all over his chops
. . . all . . .
   [*She continues to sob. Then it subsides. She pulls herself
   together with a tremendous effort, squints up at him
   mutinously.*]
I ain't done nothing.
   [*He goes.*
   PIAF *relaxes in her chair. She hums snatches of* Tu me fais
   tourner la tête . . . *stretching out her legs, and then her
   arms.*]

21

[*murmurs to herself*]: Ah, what a shame . . . what a shame.

[TOINE *bursts in, carrying a newspaper.*]

TOINE: Ede, you're famous!

[*She is followed by the* MANAGER.]

PIAF: Eh, what's going on? [*bewildered*]

MANAGER: Piaf, I've got you a booking.

TOINE: Tonight!

PIAF: Eh?

MANAGER: You'll be doing a guest appearance at the Pickup Club . . . give her the piece to read over . . . it's all about your life with Papa, *ménage à trois*, that sort of thing.

TOINE [PIAF *leans over her shoulder*]: 'Club singer in Alleged Gangland Slaying' . . . they think you done him in!

MANAGER: But they can't prove anything, you're in the clear . . . sign there.

TOINE: Go on, Ede.

PIAF: What's he talking about . . . push off.

[*The* MANAGER *hits her in the face, just like the* INSPECTOR.]

MANAGER: Now listen, squirt. You – are money. And while you're money you'll do as I say. Here's five hundred. Get yourself toffed up . . . I want you soignée, sophisticated and elegant . . . oh, and get rid of that. [*pointing to* TOINE]

TOINE [*as he goes*]: What do you mean, I'm her partner – anyway, where's that fifty you promised me? [*To* PIAF] How much?

[PIAF *counts, then examines a note.*]

PIAF [*awed*]: Hey . . . hey . . . [*She suddenly smacks herself in the face with the money, letting it fly.*]

TOINE: What you doing! [*She grabs it up.*] What you wanna do that for?

PIAF: OK, quick, let's push off before he sobers up –

TOINE: No, look . . .

PIAF: You nuts? He's gonna be back, bloody cops on his tail –

TOINE: Neow! Didn't you get it? He's working for *you*! He's your agent – I mean, once he knows you can't sing . . . but while it lasts . . .

PIAF [*warming*]: Yeah . . .

TOINE: We could BUY things!

PIAF: Yeah . . . nah, he's gone daft, pinched it out the till . . . he'll be in the wagon by now.

TOINE: He bought me a brandy. For nothing. You're in the papers, Ede! You're famous!

PIAF: Yeah?

TOINE: Yeah.

PIAF: Right. In that case . . . I'm gonna get myself one of those little black skirts with the diamond panel down the front . . .

TOINE: Ooh . . . can I come?

PIAF: You found him, mate . . .

TOINE: Only I didn't know . . .

PIAF [*firmly halving the money and giving* TOINE *her share*]: We're in this together!

TOINE: Thanks! What about shoes?

PIAF: Five-inch courts . . . crocodile. We'll have to entertain, you know . . . soda syphon . . .

TOINE: Ice bucket . . .

PIAF: Toilet roll . . .

   [*They caper, screaming with delight.*]

   Proper furniture! Fridge . . . telephone . . .

TOINE: Telephone . . .

PIAF: Bar stools . . .

TOINE: Bar stools . . .

PIAF: With squashy seats . . .

TOINE: Made out of elephants' testicles . . .

PIAF: Eh?

TOINE: It's what I heard.

PIAF: Oh well, if it's the fashion.

TOINE: What about gloves?

PIAF: Gloves? What you want gloves for?

TOINE [*hard and bright with excitement, as always, a beat behind*]: Dunno!

PIAF: Waste of money innit, don't tell me you're gonna start using gloves – oh, I get it . . . you're getting classy ideas!

TOINE: All I need's the gear!

PIAF: Yeah, you could get one of those gold lamé skirts – hang on . . . you're working for me now . . .

TOINE: Yeah?

PIAF: Fuck the gloves!

TOINE: Yeah!

PIAF: Christ, kid, have you realized . . . we can have all the fellers we want . . . the ones we want.

TOINE [*sour*]: So what?

PIAF: There's the little guy down the garage. I could get him a lovely blue suit, camel coat, cuff-links, silk shirts – you could find him a coupla girls so's he can make a living, feel independent . . .

TOINE: Yeah.

PIAF: We could have a party! Whee! [*And she throws the money into the air again.*]

TOINE: Edith! [*She bends, groping.*] Oh, honest . . .

[PAUL *enters, handsome and well-dressed.*

PIAF *looks across the room and falls in love.*]

TOINE [*scrabbling*]: Ooh, I do feel funny.

PIAF [*mutters*]: Shut up.

[*He takes her in his arms, and they dance. He bends her backwards, as in the movies, and kisses her. She totters as he releases her abruptly, moves away, turns, and throws the carnation from his buttonhole at her. She ducks, then grins soppily and bends to pick it up.*]

PAUL: You . . . you . . . only you. [*He returns, kisses the palm of her hand, the inside of her wrist.*

She comes on the spot, as he kisses up the inside of her forearm.]

The Restaurant des Fleurs. Ten o'clock. I shall squeeze time till then. [*He kisses his hand at her and goes.*]

PIAF: Ooh!

TOINE: Oo-erh . . .

PIAF: Did you see him!

TOINE: My stomach feels like a box of budgies!

PIAF: Eyes like a shopful of irises . . .

TOINE: I'm a bit constipated.

PIAF: Oh Christ. Look at this place. Two squashed Gitanes and a packet of Cream Crackers! You're gonna have to pull your socks up, mate, I don't call this putting on the style.

TOINE: Sorry, Ede, I been a bit off-colour.

PIAF: All you do is let down the whole feel of it!

[*She grabs a wandering mike and breaks in* Tu me fais tourner.

PAUL *sits, in white tie . . . and she crosses, and bends over the table, singing into his face. At the end of the song he rises to greet her. She gives him a quick feel.*

He extricates himself with a furious frown, looking to see if they have been observed.]

PAUL [*furious hiss*]: Piaf . . . !

PIAF [*innocence*]: What's the matter?

PAUL [*vicious mutter*]: You *know* how I hate to be touched.

PIAF [*slight pause*]: How about the song?

PAUL: I thought you were over the top a bit.

PIAF: Me . . . never!

PAUL: Piaf, your private life is your private life. Don't mix it.

PIAF: Come on, they love me singing to yuh . . . everybody knows! [*She heaves a happy sigh.*] I used to see meself off every night on tour, dreaming about you in that blue dressing gown.

PAUL: Piaf, your voice!

PIAF: Oh Christ, nothing's right. I wish I was back with Toine and the boys.

PAUL: You don't have to stay in the gutter just because you were born there.

PIAF: I feel out of place! I'm doing like what you said . . . trying to be a lady . . . [*She becomes aware of her own voice, and shrivels in her seat.*] . . . sorry, love . . .

PAUL: After all . . . [*takes a fastidious sip from his glass*] . . . after all, they don't want rubbish at the Palace.

PIAF [*screams*]: The Palace? The Palace? You rogue . . . you devil! He never said! He's bloody gone and done it and you never said! Is it true? Have I got it? The Palace? No . . . I don't believe it . . .

[*But he leads her to the microphone.*

She sings L'Accordéoniste.

At the end, the MANAGER *runs on and* PIAF *realizes that there is something wrong.*]

PIAF: *Arrêtez* . . . stop, stop the music.

[*The* MANAGER *comes to the microphone.*]

MANAGER: Ladies and gentlemen . . . ladies and gentlemen . . . countrymen . . . countrywomen . . . I have to tell you . . . it is war . . . war!

[*He breaks momentarily into a large white handkerchief.*
PIAF, *excited, grabs the microphone.*]

PIAF: Bloody Boche . . . not a good prick among 'em and I should know . . .

MANAGER: Piaf, please! Ladies and gentlemen, in this solemn moment in the history of our –

PIAF [*crowding the mike*]: They do it all by numbers you know!

MANAGER: Piaf, let go of the mike . . . ladies and gentlemen . . . our National Anthem . . .

PIAF [*to the tune of* King Farouk]: 'Make 'em squit, make 'em puke, hang their bollocks on a hook . . .'

MANAGER [*losing his cool*]: Look, will you shut your fucking mouth . . . I've got the fucking King of Rumania over there! [*And dies as he realizes that he is on sound.*]

SCENE VI

PIAF'S *apartment, sumptuous whorehouse furniture.* TOINE *enters, wearing clothes in the style of France in the Forties . . . huge hat, a sling bag, square-shouldered suit and wedge-heeled shoes.* PIAF *follows her on, removes a bottle of whisky from under her coat and puts it on a tray with two glasses.*

TOINE: Yeah, he said he couldn't come on account of me not having big tits . . . he said if I had big tits he could come whenever he wanted.

PIAF: Give him the push.

TOINE: Funny, I like him. Usually I only like men with big feet . . . hey, that's real whisky, where'd you get it?

[PIAF *gestures, tantalizing.*]

TOINE: Is it a celebration or something . . . I know . . . some-body's having a birthday upstairs.

PIAF: It's nothing to do with Madame and the girls . . . [*a knock*] . . . listen . . . keep your trap shut and no messing about.

[*Two* GERMANS *enter and click heels.*]

PIAF: Help yourselves . . . [*gestures at whisky*] . . . make yourselves comfortable.

[*The* GERMANS *fall with delight on the whisky.*]

TOINE [*cross*]: I wondered what you wanted me for.

FIRST BOCHE: Mademozelle Piaf, you are – *gut* singer!

SECOND BOCHE: *Fabel hov!* [*He makes the girls jump.*]

FIRST BOCHE: You are first wiz me. My friend also. We are seeing you in Amsterdam in '37.

PIAF [*politely*]: No shit?

[*The* SECOND BOCHE, *having no French, murders a Piaf song . . . the girls grimace puzzlement.*]

PIAF [*interrupting*]: Yeah, well, wish we could offer you some grub . . . something to eat. Only we ain't got nothing. Nothing to eat . . . skint . . . hungry. [*She makes chewing motions.*

TOINE *points graphically into her mouth.*

PIAF *digs in an elbow to quieten her.*]

PIAF: Aren't you in the catering corps then? I thought you were in the catering corps . . . [*She snatches the drink from him, gives it to* TOINE, *who knocks it back.*] . . . share and share alike, that's our motto.

[*The* GERMANS *confer hurriedly.*]

FIRST BOCHE: Ach, I am the small gift forgetting.

[*He lumbers off, returns staggering under an enormous crate of tins and bottles.* TOINE *is rabid with excitement,* PIAF *cool.*]

SECOND BOCHE [*plunging in and bringing out bottled fruit*]: Gut? Gut?

PIAF: *Gut.*

TOINE: *Gut!!*

[*The* SECOND BOCHE *takes off his belt and kneels to join* TOINE, *who is already at the bottled peaches.*]

PIAF: Hey, tell you what . . . why don't you two boys nip upstairs? Madame and the girls are dying to give you a good time.

FIRST BOCHE [*his jacket already unbuttoned*]: Oh, but we was thinking –

27

PIAF [*with awesome dignity*]: Oh no. Me and my friend nottee whorees. We just live here because the old slag upstairs gets coal and grub from the Boche . . . I mean, our German allies . . .

TOINE: So's we don't freeze to death.

[*The disappointed* GERMANS *are thrust out, arguing to each other in German.*

The girls shriek with laughter and fall on the tins.]

[*mouth full*]: I've never seen so much grub in me life . . . peaches!

PIAF: Hey, hey . . . don't be so fucking greedy.

TOINE: I've only had two bits!

PIAF: You've had three!

TOINE: I haven't!

[*They pull the jar between them.*

GEORGES *runs on, holding on to his trousers.*]

GEORGES [*furious*]: Did you send those bloody Boche upstairs?

PIAF: Christ, I forgot it was Monday.

TOINE: What?

PIAF: She lets the Resistance in, for nothing.

TOINE: What's happened to your mates?

GEORGES: Gone out the window. I hope that bloody glass roof holds.

[*A sound of smashing glass . . . ending in a tinkle.*]

TOINE [*slight pause*]: They've fallen through.

GEORGES: Sharp as ever, Einstein.

PIAF: Oh, d'you want the photos?

GEORGES: What photos?

PIAF: The pictures . . . of me with the boys, you twit . . . from the prison camp. [*She hands them to him.*] You nearly got us into trouble . . . Jerry started getting nasty.

TOINE: Yeah, tell him where we hid the film! [*She cackles.*]

GEORGES [*riffling through shots*]: These are no fucking good.

PIAF: Why not?

GEORGES: They're all smiling, aren't they? We need mug shots. You'll have to go again.

PIAF [*groans*]: Oh Christ.

GEORGES: Get your agent to fix another tour – as far as Jerry's concerned you're clean. I want plenty of pictures with the boys, but steady face shots . . . and for Christ's sakes cut the funny stuff. There's half a million Frenchmen behind wire . . . how we s'posed to spring 'em without papers?

PIAF: All right, all right.

GEORGES: Well don't fuck about – it's people's lives!

PIAF: I know.

GEORGES: Fine bloody way to win a war.

TOINE: We got to eat.

PIAF [*giving him a generous bag of the tins*]: More than one way of winning, love.

GEORGES: Fuck 'em to death, you mean? [*He goes.*]

TOINE: How many you give him?

[*A man (*BUTCHER*) tries to enter.*]

BUTCHER: Hello, my lovelies . . . you gonna give me a good time?

PIAF [*laconic*]: Piss off.

TOINE [*laconic*]: You heard.

BUTCHER: I'm a wholesale butcher, love! Now you're not going to turn down a nice boy in the meat business, are you now?

TOINE [*helping herself liberally to tins*]: Oh well, time I was getting back anyway, Ede – you know, the war effort.

[*She goes off with the* BUTCHER, *his hand on her behind.*]

PIAF [*laughs*]: Honest, what you'll do for a bit of offal.

[GEORGES *enters.*]

PIAF: The answer's no – oh, it's you.

GEORGES: I thought, seeing as how I was here . . . one for the road?

PIAF: You gotta nerve.

GEORGES: Comforts for the troops, love. Don't want to go empty-handed, do I.

PIAF [*as they both begin to undress*]: Thought I was supposed to be rotten at the war effort.

GEORGES: Did I say that? [*He falls on her.*]

PIAF: Ouf . . . Christ . . . champagne and orchids with it!

[*They roll, laughing.*]

PIAF *sings* Hamburg.

End of song. A young man, PIERRE, *cycles across the stage.*

He wheels, and calls to PIAF.]

PIERRE: Hey . . .

PIAF: Yeah?

PIERRE: You're Edith Piaf, aren't you?

PIAF: D'you know, ever so many people say that!

PIERRE [*beginning to ride off*]: You really look like her . . . no kidding!

> [PIAF *laughs.*
>
> PIERRE *wheels round and skids back alongside her.*]

You A R E Piaf!

PIAF: How d'you know?

PIERRE: The laugh!

PIAF [*worried*]: Here, what are you doing out on the streets?

PIERRE [*touching the side of his nose, conspiratorially*]: Ahah . . .

PIAF: You wanna be careful, kid. They'll pick you up.

PIERRE: I'm O K. [*Gets on his bike.*] Hey Piaf, after the war, can I be your agent?

PIAF [*laughs*]: What a nerve! Got any experience?

PIERRE: No, I've never worked . . . couldn't get a job. Does that rule me out?

PIAF: From being an agent? No.

PIERRE: Right then – see you after the war.

PIAF [*touching him up*]: Mind you, I got me own conditions.

PIERRE [*cheeky*]: Good! [*He goes.*]

PIAF: Bloody cheek.

SCENE VII

PIAF's *apartment.* PIAF *is on the phone.*

PIAF: Look, I'm not touring with a bunch of hopheads . . . get a replacement!

> [*She is distracted by* TOINE *who runs on, waving her arms.*]

What's the matter? – no, not you, hold on . . .

TOINE: Piaf, the war's over!

PIAF: No shit . . . [*Into the phone*] . . . and listen, I want a fire in

30

my dressing room . . . I'm getting those pains in my wrists again. Bad enough having to sit up all night in freezing cold trains. [*To* TOINE, *who stands in front of her, grinning foolishly*] What's the matter now? . . . not you, hang on . . .

TOINE: The war's over. Aren't you going to say nothing?

PIAF: What the fuck am I supposed to say? [*Into the phone*] Here, Henri, the war's over . . . so *she* says . . . [*To* TOINE] satisfied? [*To* HENRI, *on the phone*] Yeah, that's right, war's over – [*To* TOINE] Who's that little bloke plays sax . . .

    [TOINE *shakes her head* . . . PIAF *speaks into phone.*]

Hullo . . . hullo . . . [*To* TOINE] . . . he's gone mad! Hullo . . . Henri . . . what's the matter with you all? . . .

TOINE: Piaf, the –

PIAF: . . . did you get my fags?

TOINE: I was going to but I couldn't get through the crowds, they're all cheering and singing out there –

PIAF [*puzzled*]: Singing? Honest, fuck good you are . . . least thing and she sits on her ass – look, I'm trying to get a TOUR together! Why don't you just push off, you useless, washed-up whore?

TOINE: Edith . . .

PIAF: What?

TOINE: I don't want to say this, but you can be ever so rude sometimes.

PIAF: Oh Christ, now she's got the hump – and get my fags! [*Calls*] Singing? . . . who's singing?

TOINE: I keep trying to tell you . . . the WAR's over!

PIAF: No shit! Why ever didn't you say!

    [*They run screaming into each other's arms . . . and then off. Sounds on the p/a . . .* La Marseillaise *. . . rifle shots . . . bells . . . singing and cheering.*

    Enter PIAF, GEORGES, MANAGER, TOINE, *a* SAILOR, *arms linked . . .* PIAF *wears the* SAILOR's *hat. They sing* Milord. *At the last chorus they lurch off.*

    Their voices, off, on the fade to black.]

SCENE VIII

Josephine's nightclub. Placards, glamorous, of JOSEPHINE . . . *one in army uniform.* JOSEPHINE, *in glamorous, narrow-skirted evening dress, appears at the microphone. She sings* La petite Tonkinoise.

At the end of the song, she joins PIAF . . . PIAF *pours her a drink.*

JOSEPHINE: OK?

PIAF: Fine, Dusky.

JOSEPHINE: Couldn't get above an E this morning.

PIAF: No, well, I've never believed in keeping the throat covered . . . weakens it.

JOSEPHINE: Can't say I've noticed!

PIAF [*laughs her throaty, inviting laugh*]: I can always make a sou fog-hailing, eh?

    [*They laugh.*]

JOSEPHINE: So, how goes it?

PIAF: Great. Fine. [*But she is flat.*]

JOSEPHINE: I heard about your fee for the tour . . . good for us all, kid.

PIAF: When I get it.

JOSEPHINE: You'll love the States. [*No response.*] Wanna do a spot – come on, give me a break.

PIAF: Nah, you do your own singing.

JOSEPHINE: Like that, is it? [*Looks at* PIAF *shrewdly*] Uh-uh. I get it. Where's Gérard?

    [PIAF *shrugs, pulling a face.*]

    Look, I thought you two were supposed to be serious!

PIAF [*mutters*]: Who needs a fucking Duke?

JOSEPHINE: Don't be such an inverted snob! Listen, Gérard's good for you . . . you go to the country together, you're both off the juice, you were saying how much better you felt.

PIAF [*miserable*]: Well, you know how it is, Dusky.

JOSEPHINE: No, I don't . . . what you want to fuck up for? Look, Piaf, take it in your stride, girl. You're up there now. You've earned it . . . lie back and enjoy it.

[PIAF *shakes her head.*]

Look, you're not shit. Am I shit? When I first got taken to restaurants I'd piddle myself, *never* knew when they were gonna show me the door, you think *you've* had it rough . . . sister!

PIAF: Sure.

JOSEPHINE: Presidents . . . Princes . . . who gives a fuck, they're all made the same, I've known some serious men in my time, I'm telling you. Believe me, they appreciate being treated like human beings.

PIAF: Trouble with you, Dusk, is that you always see the best in people.

JOSEPHINE: Listen, Gérard's a great guy.

PIAF: Ever been to his place in the country – you've seen it . . . all the . . . books . . . furniture . . . paintings . . .

JOSEPHINE: Fantastic.

PIAF [*small pause*]: Most mornings . . . when we're down there . . . get up about two . . . he has some champagne and a shower . . . shaves hisself. Then he comes down to the big drawing room, the one with the blue Aubusson . . . rings the bell – and I come in dressed as the housemaid with me tits hanging out.

JOSEPHINE: Sounds like fun.

PIAF: I give him his coffee. Then he craps on the carpet.

JOSEPHINE: You're kidding!

PIAF: No I'm not . . . big deal it's not on my face. Some poor sod of a gardener comes in to clean up after him, get the stains out . . . he spends the rest of the afternoon on his knees, praying. The maids hoover round him.

JOSEPHINE: Is he nuts?

PIAF: You wouldn't think so, watch him playing the market. No, I've never been taken with the so-called aristocracy – not since an old mate of mine come up before a bloke she'd been with the night before and he gave her thirty days.

JOSEPHINE: You did the right thing. He should use the john.

PIAF: Yeah. I'm on me own again, though.

JOSEPHINE: Listen, who needs it?

PIAF: I do. You must have somebody – what's it all for?

JOSEPHINE: You wanna meet some real class?

PIAF: Who?

JOSEPHINE: Marcel.

PIAF: Marcel? Not Mar– you mean you know, him . . . you know the Champ?

[JOSEPHINE *takes* PIAF's *wineglass from her, smiles and leaves.*

Light change.

PIAF, *downstage, on her feet, like a boxer.*]

. . . kill him, kill him . . . give it to him, let him have it . . . oh no . . . oh no . . . stop him . . . Marcel! Come on . . . come on . . . get back in there . . . come on, love . . . let him have it . . . go on . . . go on! Ah! . . . that's it . . . that's it . . . you're on the way . . . the Champ! The Champ!!!

SCENE IX

PIAF's *bedroom. The music of* Mon Dieu . . . *soft.* PIAF *and* MARCEL *in friendly, post-coital mood.*

PIAF: I wish you could have seen me when I was a kid, I had lovely little tits.

MARCEL: They look all right to me.

PIAF [*touching her jawline*]: I'm losing me teeth, too . . . and I'm going here . . . [*touches under her chin*]. Let's see yours. [*She inspects his mouth.*] Christ, Aladdin's cave! Ain't you got none of your own, Marce, must have cost you a fortune!

MARCEL: You're better without 'em . . . take 'em out, put 'em in a glass, I'm not going to get me cheeks cut, am I?

PIAF: Yeah, like the little daft kids, in the home I was in. They pull out all their teeth, so's they won't bite each other.

[*They nod, dwell for a beat.*]

They can't enjoy an apple, you know. [*She feels his arm.*] Champ.

MARCEL: I'm just a guy with a fist, Edith.

PIAF: No, you're not. You're the best – oh, I've helped fighters

spend it. Not you though, eh? We go shopping, it's for your old
lady and the kids, I don't know why I put up with it.

MARCEL: I'd marry you if I could, Edie.

PIAF: You're the faithful sort, love.

MARCEL: I don't feel too good about it. Well, what sort of a life is it
for her, stuck at home with the kids?

PIAF: Better than any woman in the world. Except me. I've got
this, haven't I? I think I will have these lifted . . . all the stars are
doing it.

MARCEL: What you want to get cut for, why take the risk?

PIAF: You do.

MARCEL: That's different. Mind you . . .

PIAF: Mmm?

MARCEL: We-ell, they think you don't give a bugger.

PIAF: What do you mean?

MARCEL: I had a guvnor once . . . greedy bugger . . . I was only a
lad . . . put you in anything. Somebody down the gym said . . .
he'd fixed up this bout for me . . . 'his face is going to be plum
jam, you know' – 'Oh, we don't care what we look like,' he says,
'just so long as the money's right.' 'We.'

PIAF: Christ.

MARCEL: He was right about the money.

[She looks at him.]

You don't do it for love, kiddo. On your own there all right . . .
in the ring, I mean.

PIAF: Yeah, I know.

[He looks at her.]

Well, I don't mean I'm gonna get me head bashed in . . . not
unless I'm dead unlucky . . . still . . . it's the same every time
. . . just before you go on. Never mind what they've said to you
in the dressing room – your mates . . . that walk to the fucking
mike . . . it's from here to Rome. [Slight pause] And if you fuck it
– well, you can't say . . . hang on, loves, mind if I have another
go – well, I have been known to.

[They laugh.]

No. Even worse if it's gone off well.

MARCEL: How do you mean?

PIAF: You don't want it to end. Show over . . . you're on your own again.

[*They have both expressed more than is usual for them. Baffled, they are silent. He plays with her fingers.*]

PIAF [*low*]: Don't go.

MARCEL: I must, love.

PIAF: Get an earlier plane back. For me. Please?

MARCEL [*kisses her*]: All right, kid. Just for you.

[*He kisses her again, a long, loving embrace.*
The music of Mon Dieu *becomes very loud, ending in a drumroll.*
MARCEL *leaves abruptly.*
Light change.
PIAF *stands alone, to the reverberation of deep notes sustained on piano and accordion.*]

PIAF [*dazed, as if waking from a dream*]: Marcel?

[PIAF *sings* La belle histoire d'amour.]

ACT II

PIAF's *dressing room in New York.* PIAF . . . *off* . . . *singing* Si tu partais. *Some applause. Pause.*
PIAF *enters, fast, whisky bottle in one hand, slopping glass in the other.*

PIAF [*on the move, muttering to herself*]: . . . fuck me . . . I don't fucking believe it – OUT! . . . oh, it's you.
    [PIERRE *appears.*]
Don't say anything.
PIERRE: Piaf, there's nothing that can't be fixed. A change of repertoire, that's all.
PIAF: OK, so they play off the fucking beat, that's all they can do . . . it's like singing in a morgue –
PIERRE: I think you should –
PIAF: I'm going home. I must have been daft – why the fuck d'you put me up for it? I should have listened to Maurice, I should have done that film. We're going to be right down the sluice.
PIERRE: Not necessarily.
PIAF: Don't be so daft.
PIERRE: We've got signed contracts . . . coast to coast – and a return spot here.
PIAF: Bollocks.
PIERRE: We're contracted, Edith!
PIAF: When were you born, kid?
PIERRE: I'm telling you –
PIAF: No, no, no . . . listen . . . look . . . look, love, it's not worth – asspaper!

37

PIERRE: If the Yanks want to renege on their contractual obligations it's going to cost them money. They're legally contracted!

PIAF [*short laugh*]: You got a lot to learn. Look, Pierrot, what do you think the law is? What do you . . . who do you think it's for? People like us? People who make the laws do it for their own use. The contract that can't be split down the middle doesn't exist. They don't want us, we don't play. Believe me. Fact of life.

[*A knock.*]

I don't want to SEE anybody!

[*It is* JOSEPHINE, *shining, glamorous, and full of vitality.*]

PIERRE: It's Jo . . .

[*She waves to* PIERRE, *swoops on* PIAF, *embraces her, then inspects her.*]

JOSEPHINE: Fuck up, huh?

PIAF: Are you kidding?

JOSEPHINE: Sure, we have to go to work.

PIAF: I'm going home. [*To* PIERRE] Book the flights, love.

JOSEPHINE: Over my dead body. [*She jerks her head at* PIERRE.]

PIERRE: Piaf, I think you should listen. [*He goes.*]

JOSEPHINE: We'll talk about it.

PIAF [*drinking*]: I don't know what I'm supposed to be celebrating. Long time since I got the bloody bird – shave under me armpits next time.

JOSEPHINE [*laughs*]: That's better!

PIAF: They don't know what I'm singing about half the time. Anyway, who wants to see some little cunt looking like a war widow when they can have Doris Day.

JOSEPHINE: Stop putting yourself down.

PIAF: Perhaps I should sex it up a bit.

JOSEPHINE: Over my dead body.

PIAF: All right for you, Dusky, you don't have the same problems.

JOSEPHINE [*dry*]: You think so?

PIAF: Let's face it, I didn't start out with what you've got.

JOSEPHINE: Neither did I, kid. Come on . . . you don't have to fall for all that glamour stuff . . . you're the real thing!

PIAF: Oh, sod that . . . where's it got me?

JOSEPHINE: You're not out of a sixpack – mind your language.

PIAF: Sorry.

JOSEPHINE: And lay off that.

PIAF: Keeps me going.

JOSEPHINE: Not for long.

PIAF: Anyway, what's the point? One sentence. 'Get an earlier plane.'

JOSEPHINE: Honey, you have to get over it. You know you do.

PIAF: Yeah. [*But she turns her head away.*]

JOSEPHINE: Now don't start crying again. Tich – come on! You'll ruin your eyes for the late show.

PIAF: I'm not going out there again! I'm all on me own, you know.

JOSEPHINE: That's not true and you know it. [*She hands* PIAF *a handkerchief.*

PIAF *snivels and sniffs, then blows her nose with a snort into the handkerchief and hands it back to* JOSEPHINE.]

PIAF [*tragic*]: I wasn't always on me own.

JOSEPHINE [*apart, she knows what's coming*]: Oh shit. [*To* PIAF, *soothing*] I know, baby, I know.

PIAF: I ever tell you about my little girl?

JOSEPHINE: Sure. Lotsa times. Poor little Georgette.

PIAF [*firmly*]: Natalie.

JOSEPHINE: Didn't you tell me –

PIAF [*a quelling glance*]: Died in my arms. Didn't cry! – well, she was a real little lady, genuine *Marquis*, her father . . .

JOSEPHINE: No kidding. [*Accepts* PIAF's *fanciful mood.*]

PIAF: Over a year I nursed that kiddie . . . like a little angel, she was . . .

JOSEPHINE: Ah . . .

PIAF: . . . blue eyes . . . fair curly hair . . . like Shirley Temple only . . . you know – pretty. [*Sighs*] I was only a slip of a thing meself . . . barely out of convent.

JOSEPHINE: You're not kidding.

PIAF: Never left her side – well, except to go to the lav, of course.

JOSEPHINE: Sure, sure.

PIAF: I mean . . .

JOSEPHINE: Oh sure.

PIAF: Only just made it back when she snuffed it.

JOSEPHINE: My God . . .

PIAF: I mean . . . you'd never forgive yourself.

JOSEPHINE: Right. [*Lifts her glass.*] Here's to little Natalie!

PIAF: Who? [*Caught out, she breaks up.*
   They laugh.]
   [*Growls*] Well, what did they expect? I know what they wanted –
   some crap with a feather up its ass. Like hell – I'm Piaf!

JOSEPHINE: That's better!

PIAF: When I go on to do a song, it's me that comes on. They get
   the lot.

JOSEPHINE: Sure.

PIAF: They see what they're getting – everything I got.

JOSEPHINE: Sure . . . but learn how to save it.

PIAF: Nah.

JOSEPHINE: Kid, you can't have an orgasm every single time you
   walk on stage.

PIAF: *I* can.

JOSEPHINE: No you can't. Nobody can. Nobody peaks all the
   time. Technique, baby! Trust it. Let it work for you. That way
   you don't exhaust yourself all the time. You're going to do great
   here – OK, some changes . . .
   [PIAF *shakes her head.*]
   . . . they want you! Highest paid woman singer in the world,
   that talks!

PIAF: Oh, fuck the money.

JOSEPHINE: Oh, sure we go out there because we want to be loved
   . . . like all those other myths from people who never gave one
   ounce of themselves . . . what do they know?

PIAF: They know when they want you. [*Slight pause*] Nah, it's not
   the money . . . they couldn't PRINT enough for the way we
   feel – I've seen you shaking away in the wings. Singing ditties?
   That's just the fucking tourist trade. No . . . when I'm out there
   – it's got to happen. Doesn't happen . . . terrible.

JOSEPHINE: I know what you mean.

PIAF: The trouble is, I'm off my own patch here . . . that's where
   it's going wrong.

JOSEPHINE: Good . . . you're beginning to work, that's my baby.

PIAF: OK . . . give it a whirl . . . just for you, Dusk.

[*They embrace to seal the deal.*]

JOSEPHINE: Listen, promise me something.

PIAF: For you, anything.

JOSEPHINE: I'm serious. This is a big country. Take care of yourself.

PIAF: OK.

JOSEPHINE: I mean it.

PIAF: Sure . . . Mom.

[*They laugh.*]

JOSEPHINE: We'll do the town . . . have a great time – hey, would you like to meet Harry Truman? He's about your size.

PIAF: So I noticed.

JOSEPHINE: Listen, he's a sharp fellow and tells a mean story, no flies . . .

PIAF: Sure . . . bring on the natives!

SCENE II

A bar. Two American SAILORS, *in their cups, and a* BARMAN. PIAF *sitting between the* SAILORS *on a bar stool . . . she is wearing a cocktail hat and a short silver-fox jacket over her black dress.*

PIAF: Hi boys . . . what are you drinking?

FIRST SAILOR: Shorty! Where've you been all my life?

PIAF [*blenching good-naturedly at the whisky on his breath*]: Make it doubles.

[*The* BARMAN *obliges.*]

FIRST SAILOR: Thanks, ma'am.

SECOND SAILOR [*a very loud whoop*]: Whoo-hoo!

FIRST SAILOR: So what's a fancy little lady like you doing in a joint like this?

PIAF: You'd be amazed.

SECOND SAILOR: Here's looking at you, kid.

PIAF [*to* BARMAN]: Got a room upstairs?

[*He nods, she throws a note on his tray.*]

So, how about it, boys?

SECOND SAILOR: Anything you say, little lady, anything you say.

FIRST SAILOR: Lead me, lady . . . lead me.

[PIAF *gets up . . . the* FIRST SAILOR *follows her. The* SECOND SAILOR *lags, rejected.*]

PIAF: What are you waiting for?

SECOND SAILOR: You mean, me too, ma'am?

PIAF: If I'm giving lessons I may as well take the whole class.

[*The* BARMAN *puts down his cloth and follows them off purposefully.*]

SCENE III

PIAF's *apartment in Paris. Partly furnished . . . there is a sofa, a small table, two usable chairs . . . and furniture unpacked.*

MADELEINE *enters stage left as* PIAF *enters stage right, a mink coat over her shoulder and carrying a bouquet of flowers. She is followed by* LUCIEN, *much younger than* PIAF. *He wears clothes* au courant *for the Fifties. His manner is wire tight.*

MADELEINE: Piaf . . . you're back! We were coming to meet you!

PIAF: Caught an earlier plane.

[*She takes off her coat, drops it on the floor . . .* MADELEINE *picks it up.*]

Nice place. I like it.

MADELEINE: It *was* jolly difficult finding an apartment with *seven* bedrooms – you did say seven?

PIAF: Sure – Lucien here likes a change of view every night.

MADELEINE [*baffled*]: Oh I see.

PIAF: . . . Nah, it's for his group. There's seven of them, eight including me . . . I'm gonna put these boys on the map! Did you get that big fridge?

MADELEINE [*faintly*]: Will you *all* be dining at home?

PIAF: Nah, just for snacks . . . cheese, hamburgers, Seven-Up, they're growing lads – oh and cornflakes . . . they're *very* into cornflakes. Go on, Lucien . . . read me the notices . . . ah, look at his dear little bum.

> [MADELEINE *goes.*
> PIAF *sits, helping herself to a drink.*
> LUCIEN *picks up the papers and reads.*]

LUCIEN: 'At first sight you wonder . . . this dumpy little woman with the big forehead . . .'

PIAF [*growls*]: It's not that big . . .

LUCIEN: '. . . black dress, pale, agitated hands . . .'

PIAF: Christ . . .

LUCIEN: '. . . then she opens her mouth . . . sounds like you never heard . . . a cat mewing on the tiles . . . the ecstasy of morning . . . they are all here.'

PIAF: Do you wanna touch me up?

LUCIEN [*putting a hand inside her dress and reading a new notice*]: 'How is it possible to listen to one woman singing twenty songs in a foreign language, and find one's face wet with tears at the end? There is only one word for it – genius. And that genius is Piaf.'

PIAF [*growls*]: That'll be Alain, bugger owes me money. Go on.

LUCIEN [*a new notice*]: 'The voice, rising like the slanting sun from the floating bric-à-brac of the Seine on a warm spring morning, fuses the backbone. She sings of love. She sings of sexual treachery . . . of unhappiness . . . of being made helpless by love. She sings of being alone, and of feeling bad . . . and we can't bear it for her.'

PIAF [*abruptly*]: Who wrote that? [*She jerks round, slopping her drink.*

> *He fumbles with the page.*]

Christ, can't you read now? [*Gets up and stumps off.*] Bloody kids . . . can't even get myself a decent man.

LUCIEN [*mutters*]: Piaf, you know how I feel about you.

PIAF: Yes, I'm your fucking meal-ticket. Well, where would you be without me . . . eh?

LUCIEN: Nowhere.

PIAF: Right . . . and don't you forget it.

LUCIEN: Piaf, let's not get in a fight . . .

PIAF: Who said you could call me Piaf? Who said you could call me Piaf?

LUCIEN [*totally confused*]: What do you want me to call you?

PIAF: It's Madame to you, and don't you forget it.

LUCIEN: Even when we're fucking?

PIAF: Especially when we're fucking. Madeleine . . . Madeleine! Where is that middle-class bitch?

MADELEINE [*behind her, good-humouredly*]: Piaf, I wish you wouldn't speak to me like that.

> [LUCIEN *grimaces behind* PIAF's *back and makes his exit, taking the bags.*
>
> PIAF *catches his exit.*]

PIAF [*calls after him*]: Hey, park the car! And don't forget to give the dog his enema! [*To* MADELEINE] What do you think of him?

MADELEINE: The young man?

PIAF: Yeah . . . Lucien . . . me new feller.

MADELEINE: He's very good-looking.

PIAF: You can say that again. We really get it on together. Cold little prick. I said –

MADELEINE: I heard you, Piaf.

PIAF: Yeah, well, he'll do till I trade him up. Always set up your next trick before you shove in the icepick.

MADELEINE: Come and lie down.

PIAF: There was a guy on the plane I fancied but he was Australian – you gotta draw the line.

> [*She allows* MADELEINE *to tuck her up on the sofa.*]

MADELEINE: You'd be much more comfortable in bed.

PIAF: Nah, can't sleep if I try – got any tablets?

> [MADELEINE *already has the bottle in her hand. She tips out two tablets but* PIAF *reaches up, snatches the bottle and tips it into her mouth, taking a swig of whisky.*]

MADELEINE: Piaf, that's too many!

> [*Too late. She makes* PIAF *comfortable and walks off.*]

PIAF: Madeleine?

MADELEINE: Yes?

PIAF: I want full coverage for this opening . . . I'm gonna put these boys on the map.

MADELEINE: It's all taken care of. [*She makes to go.*]

PIAF: Rub the back of me neck for me.

MADELEINE: Do you want Gordon?

PIAF: I don't want to know how many times he's been raped this month . . . you do it.

[MADELEINE *returns and massages* PIAF's *shoulders.* PIAF *winces.*]

MADELEINE: Try to relax. [*She continues.*]

PIAF [*after a pause*]: I still miss him, you know.

MADELEINE: I beg your pardon?

PIAF [*angry*]: I said I still miss him . . . Marcel! [*She rises.*]

MADELEINE: I know, Piaf . . . I know.

PIAF: Not that we'd have made it. He'd never have left his wife. He was lovely. Hate being on me own, without a feller. What do you do?

MADELEINE: Sorry?

PIAF: You're on your own, what do you do, d'you see yourself off?

MADELEINE: Do I have to answer that?

PIAF [*raps*]: Yes.

MADELEINE: Very well. I have a little dog.

[PIAF *laughs.*]

PIAF: St Bernard?

MADELEINE: Chihuahua.

PIAF: Serves me right, eh?

MADELEINE: Come and lie down.

PIAF: No, I asked for that. You got a right to your own life, love.

MADELEINE: Let me tuck you in.

PIAF: Sure. You got a lot to do.

[MADELEINE *tucks a rug over* PIAF *and goes.*]

PIAF: Madeleine!

MADELEINE [*reappears*]: What's the matter?

PIAF: I'm lonely!

[MADELEINE *crosses, sits with* PIAF.
PIAF *falls asleep.*
MADELEINE *rises carefully, but* PIAF *grabs her.*]

Caught you out . . . where you going?

MADELEINE: I *must* get some sleep.

PIAF: You must, what about me? Get somebody on the phone . . . get Eddie.

MADELEINE: Piaf, it's five o'clock in the morning.

PIAF: So what? Get Jean-Claude.

MADELEINE: He's on tour.

PIAF: What about Guy . . . Eddie . . . get Lucille, I must have somebody.

MADELEINE: I could try Hélène.

PIAF: That fat bitch. I know, get old Toine, she's good for a laugh . . . my old mate from Belleville – get Toine.

MADELEINE: Before my time, I think.

PIAF: Well find her. Fucking friends, never here when you want them . . . find old Toine . . .

[*She is confused with drowsiness.*

MADELEINE *turns, as* PIAF *falls asleep again, to welcome* TOINE, *who enters in coat and headscarf.*]

TOINE: Ede?

MADELEINE: Oh please don't wake her, she has such trouble sleeping.

TOINE: Who, Ede? Sleeps like a horse.

MADELEINE [*low*]: Would you care to wait . . . I know she's dying to see you.

TOINE: What for?

MADELEINE: After all the trouble we had finding you.

TOINE: You wouldn't have got me usually, but I'm on the early shift. Then I had to wait for a train.

MADELEINE: I'll get you something.

[*She goes.*

TOINE *crosses to* PIAF, *looks down at her before sitting.*]

TOINE: Christ, what's happened to you?

[*She looks round at the apartment in aggressive awe, jumps slightly as* MADELEINE *returns with a tray.* TOINE *knocks back a glass of wine in one.*]

MADELEINE: Would you care for some coffee?

TOINE: No thanks, upsets me liver. Who are you, then?

MADELEINE: I'm Madame's secretary.

TOINE: Christ. Not the hostess?

MADELEINE: Ah, no – not the hostess.

TOINE: How many rooms she got here?

MADELEINE: This floor and the one above.

TOINE [*outraged*]: Two whole floors?

[MADELEINE *refills her glass.*]

MADELEINE: You and . . . ah . . . Madame are old friends, I believe?

TOINE: Yeah. We was on the road together. I'm a . . . performer.

MADELEINE: I see. What do you –

TOINE [*quickly*]: Well, I'm retired now.

MADELEINE: I see.

TOINE [*quickly*]: So you wouldn't have heard of me. [*Expands, undoes her coat*] So, you're the secretary?

MADELEINE: Ah, yes.

TOINE: Typing, that sort of thing?

MADELEINE: I look after Madame's affairs.

TOINE: Christ. [*She appraises* MADELEINE.] Been here long?

MADELEINE [*hesitates*]: No, not long.

TOINE: Hmm. Get on with her all right, do you?

MADELEINE [*fatal slight pause*]: Oh yes.

TOINE: Humph.

[PIAF *stirs, coughs, sees* TOINE.]

PIAF: What the fuck are you doing here?

TOINE: She said you wanted to see me.

PIAF: Christ Almighty! [*Glaring up at* MADELEINE] I must have *some* fucking privacy!

[*Glares at them both, exits, coughing.*]

TOINE [*to herself, ironic*]: Thanks.

MADELEINE: Tch, I'm *so* sorry.

TOINE: Ah, don't worry about it, she can be *ever* so rude some-times – look, are you gonna pay my fare?

MADELEINE: Of course. [*Exits for money.*]

PIAF [*enters*]: And where's the fucking gargle? Where's she gone? And where the hell did you spring from?

TOINE: I got off early to see you.

47

PIAF: Well, you might as well sit down now you're here. [*Takes a drink, feels better.*] How's the kiddie?

TOINE: I got two more now.

PIAF: You got three kids . . . never . . . I don't believe it!

TOINE: You would if you 'ad 'em.

PIAF: What's your husband do now?

TOINE: Warehouseman. Sanitary supplies.

PIAF: All right for hygiene then?

[*Hiatus. They don't know what to say to each other.*]

TOINE: Course what he'd really like is a little place of his own. There's a little bar down the road going cheap.

PIAF: Oh yeah? [*She can see it coming.*]

TOINE: Yeah . . . guy shot hisself. All it needs is a coat of paint.

PIAF: I'll come round and have a look.

TOINE: Would you? I been following you in the papers. I cut it out.

PIAF: You don't want to believe all that. It's not all fun and games.

TOINE: Go on, you must be rolling in it.

PIAF: D'you want to meet Errol Flynn?

TOINE: Get away!

PIAF: No, I mean it. He's taking me to the ballet – I'll introduce you.

TOINE: No! Really? I'll have to go home and change – get a babysitter . . .

PIAF: Oh, never mind all that. Come on, I'll drive you round there in me new Porsche.

TOINE: Yoohoo! Hang on. You can't drive.

PIAF: Who says I can't . . . haven't tried yet, have I? Here . . . [*To* MADELEINE] you gonna lend her that fur jacket I give you? [*Calls, going off with* TOINE] Bring it!

[MADELEINE *stands, the money in her hand.*]

SCENE IV

A hospital waiting room, festive and expensive. A young man (JEAN) *in a bright blue suit walks up and down impatiently. He carries a huge bunch of flowers, a bumper box of chocolates and an enormous pink teddy bear.*

A NURSE *enters . . . he approaches her urgently.*

JEAN: How is she, how is she?
NURSE [*arch*]: Patience, patience!
JEAN: When can I see her?
NURSE: It won't be long now. [*She goes.*
    He walks up and down, smoking, agitated. He turns as
    PIAF *enters, assisted by the* NURSE. *Her head is swathed in*
    bandages and she has two sticks.]
PIAF: Oh, look who's here . . . only the pisser who tried to finish
    me off . . .
JEAN: Darling!
PIAF [*swiping at him with stick*]: Get him out!
NURSE: Steady, Madame, steady . . .
PIAF: Fucking murderer!
JEAN: What do you mean! You're the one told me to step on it!
PIAF: Got it all worked out, have you? He thought he was going to
    cop the lot, the dibs –
JEAN: Are you joking, I was making more in hotel-management!
    [PIAF *takes another swipe at him and they both howl with*
    pain.]
NURSE: Madame . . . Madame, please . . . !
JEAN: I got rights, you know, I am your husband!
PIAF: Don't you start! [*And she grapples with him, going for him*
    with fists and feet.]
NURSE [*trying to intervene*]: Madame – Monsieur!
PIAF: Piss off! [*to* NURSE]
JEAN: Stay out of this!
    [*He starts to beat* PIAF *up. She makes a terrible noise and the*
    NURSE *runs for the* DOCTOR. *A melee.*]
DOCTOR: Madame, control yourself!
PIAF [*turning on him*]: Fucking do you, for a start!
DOCTOR: Ow! Out . . . out, the pair of you . . . what do you think
    this is, a giraffe-pit?
    [*The* NURSE *and the* DOCTOR *attempt to remove* JEAN *and*
    PIAF.]
JEAN [*nursing his wounds*]: Aw!

PIAF: Get off, you fucking poxer – [*reels, in pain*] Christ, my head!
[*Instinctively, the* DOCTOR *and* NURSE *go to her assistance.*]
You'll have to give me something . . . [*collapsing on to her bum
on to the floor, legs splayed.*
They help her to a seat.]

JEAN [*still in pain, but disregarded*]: Aw!

DOCTOR [*to* PIAF]: Sit down. [*But he sighs sentimentally over*
PIAF's *furious visage, and kisses his fingers to her.*] You may,
Madame, be a vicious and foul-mouthed slut . . . but I salute the
artistry – ow! [*as* PIAF *clouts him*]

PIAF [*to* JEAN, *who guffaws at the* DOCTOR's *discomfort*]: Out!

JEAN [*to* DOCTOR]: Salute who you fucking well like, mate . . .
I've just lost me bloody investment . . . aw . . . [*Groans as he
hobbles off.*]

DOCTOR: I think she's broken my finger.

PIAF: Up yours, are you gonna give me – oh . . . [*mollified as the*
DOCTOR *injects her*] . . . aw . . . ahhh . . .

DOCTOR: Feeling better?
[*He helps her to her feet . . . the lights begin to go as they
leave, the* NURSE *following with the sticks.*
PIAF *pauses.*]

PIAF: Hey, d'you hear the one about the man who won an elephant
in a drinking contest? He takes it home, ties it up outside his
house, next morning, bang-bang on the door – neighbour. 'Hey,
is that your elephant?' 'Yer.' 'Well it's just fucked my cat.'
'What, you mean like this?' [PIAF *mimes screwing, rocking her
hips.*] 'No, like this.' [PIAF *stamps one foot.*
She and the DOCTOR *laugh heartily on the fade . . . not so the*
NURSE *who is shocked at this* lèse majesté *with the* DOCTOR.]

SCENE V

Rehearsal studio. A PIANIST *strums.*
PIERRE *and the* MANAGER *enter separately.*

MANAGER: Good to see you.

PIERRE [*puts hat and briefcase on piano*]: Long time.

MANAGER: Sit down, take the weight off your feet. Any idea of
. . . only I said ten-thirty because naturally I didn't expect to see
you till about now.

PIERRE: She'll be along. Car's probably on its way. She was up
when I rang.

[*Slight pause*]

MANAGER: So, how's it going?

PIERRE: Very well, very well.

MANAGER: Plenty of money coming in?

PIERRE: Oh yes.

MANAGER: I should think you earn your screw, son. You've stayed
the distance – how d'you manage it?

PIERRE: We get along all right.

MANAGER: She does what she wants, you mean.

PIERRE: No, no . . . there's give and take.

MANAGER: Wouldn't do for me. There's only one thing to do with
a woman who makes trouble.

PIERRE: What? . . . make love to her, you mean?

MANAGER: No. Hit 'em in the face.

PIERRE: What?

MANAGER: They don't like that.

PIERRE: I see.

MANAGER: Couple of clips round the kisser, kid, you'd have no
trouble at all.

[PIERRE *gets up, moves away.*]

What about songs?

PIERRE: Couple of new ones. Really good.

MANAGER: Hmm. Now, about this latest idea . . .

PIERRE: Oh come on . . . you know how she is. It's worked before.
She *is* a professional – where the work's concerned she's the best
in the bloody world, now you know that. Where else could you
fill this bloody barn without back-up artists . . . she's always
been a good thing from that point of view.

MANAGER: I pay for it . . .

PIERRE: Sure, sure. We can come to an agreement. Look, if it keeps
her happy, that's all that matters.

MANAGER: Yeah, well, I was sorry to hear about the latest accident. Did she get my flowers?

PIERRE: Yes. Thanks.

MANAGER: You were lucky, that lad might have killed her. How's she looking, by the way . . . has she recovered?

PIERRE [*carefully*]: Oh yes. She's looking fine.

MANAGER: No scars?

PIERRE: No, no, she looks great. She's in love again . . .

MANAGER: Only I must have sophistication . . . my audiences demand it –

> [PIAF *enters at the rush, a bulging handbag under one arm. She wears an untidy, very dirty bandage around her head, from under which her hair pokes, greasy and ludicrous. She is slightly pot-bellied in a dirty pink jumper. The* MANAGER *blenches.*]

PIAF: Hello, Henry, me old fruit . . . still the stiffest prick in Paris?

> [*The* MANAGER *is entirely unable to answer.*]

How am I? Go on – say it . . . I look like an old ratbag! Never mind . . . wait till you see what I got for you! . . . where is he? . . . where's he gone? Angelo . . . Angelo! – oh, there you are. The audition's in here, love, not in the bloody lav. He's a bit nervous.

> [ANGELO *has entered. He is tall and handsome, despite the cowboy suit and boots.*
> PIAF *throws herself down . . . leaving* ANGELO *stranded centrestage.*]

How about *that*, then!

> [*The* MANAGER, *lost for words, turns his back for a moment.*]
> [*To* ANGELO]: Go on, love . . . go on.

ANGELO [*slight Italian accent*]: You want I should sing?

PIAF: Yeah.

ANGELO: Sing now . . .

PIAF: Well that is the general idea.

> [ANGELO *takes a creased brown paper bag from his pocket, removes a battered piece of sheet music, crosses, hands it to* PIANIST, *who looks at it with a sneer . . . turning it*

over dismissively. He chews gum as ANGELO *whispers instructions.*]

PIERRE: When you're ready, kid.

[ANGELO *takes centrestage. He takes a stance, Italian fashion . . . nods wildly at the* PIANIST *and launches into* Deep in the heart of Texas, *with an attempt at an American accent, and gestures. The* PIANIST *finishes, but* ANGELO *does a repeat phrase, so the* PIANIST *tries to pick it up, a fatal beat behind.* ANGELO *finishes, holding a 'yippee' stance.* PIAF, *grinning broadly, claps enthusiastically.*]

PIAF: What did you think of that, Henry!

[*A silence. The* MANAGER, *caught between shock and hilarity, can find no words. He bends his head, shakes it wisely . . . looks back and forth, avoiding her eye.*]

Well?

MANAGER [*another pause*]: Piaf . . . Piaf – he's a nice-looking boy. Have him. You deserve a break – no, I really mean that.

PIAF: And?

MANAGER: Oh please . . . [*And hilarity overcomes him . . . laughs, wiping his eyes.*

PIAF *turns to find* PIERRE *and the* PIANIST *doubled over with laughter.*]

PIAF: Pierrot?

[*But* PIERRE *bursts out laughing.*]

What's the matter with you all . . . what's so fucking funny? [*Makes to attack* PIANIST] I'll do you for a start . . .

[*He ducks . . .* PIERRE *restrains her.*]

PIERRE: Piaf . . . you promised!

PIAF: All right! All right. But you're wrong . . . the lot of you.

PIERRE: He can't *sing*, love!

PIAF: What's that got to do with it?

MANAGER: Piaf, we're not talking about his cock.

PIAF: Aren't you? Aren't you? Then you bloody well should be.

ANGELO: Darling . . . please . . .

PIAF: Shut up. Look at him, take a look! Six foot tall, good hairline, good nose . . . look at his thighs! OK, the suit's a joke, even I can see that. But put him in something decent . . . give him the right material, the girls'll go mad. He's a fucking Eyetie, for God's sake! I know – ballads . . . he needs *ballads*! *O Sole Mio . . . O Sole Mio*, pet . . .

ANGELO: No, no . . .

PIAF: Come on, love . . . give 'em the old *bon giorno*.

ANGELO: Is not right . . . is too square.

PIAF: Nah, nah, come on, trust me . . . I know what I'm doing!
[*She begins to hum it.*
He breaks into the song . . . and sings gloriously. When he reaches the high bit she cuts him off.]
OK, OK – there, you see . . . see what I mean? When he forgets to perform, he's *lovely*! He's a winner! [*But there is no response.*] Oh, fucking men. [*No response*] All right, if it's down to me . . . I'll whack in thirty per cent. [*No response*] Fifty.

PIERRE: Piaf!

PIAF: Shut up . . . whose side are you on!

PIERRE: All right. OK.
[*He leaves, with the* MANAGER.
Light change.
PIAF *helps* ANGELO *into a new jacket, changes his tie.*]

PIAF: What's the matter?

ANGELO [*restless*]: I don't know.

PIAF: I do. You feel out of place.

ANGELO: I don't belong here.

PIAF: Nobody does, love.

ANGELO: What am I doing here . . . I'm a labourer!

PIAF: This is work, too, you know – we've worked hard, haven't we?
[*He shrugs, unconvinced.*]
I bet your stomach never felt like that on the building site, eh?
[*He grins briefly.*
She pursues her advantage.]
Look, all those bloody union meetings you go to . . . make a name, you can use it how you want . . . but you got to make a name first.

ANGELO: As a singer?

PIAF: Yeah, daft innit, but that's how it works.

[*He shakes his head.*]

And don't stand there feeling guilty because you're in the money . . . sort it out for yourself – anyway, wait till you've seen as many damp, shitty dressing rooms as I have, *and* all the rest.

ANGELO: I miss my mates.

PIAF: Me too . . . me too. Sometimes I nip out, do a bit of street singing . . . just to keep me hand in. I heard a woman say once: 'Hey, she sounds like Edith Piaf' and the other one said, 'Trying to.'

[*This makes him laugh.*]

ANGELO: I owe you everything.

PIAF: You're lovely.

P/A: Your call, please, Madame Piaf and Monsieur Angelo, your call, please. Thank you.

PIAF: Don't forget the plot on number three.

[*He nods.*]

Double intro . . . second pause . . . bam-bam . . . you come in.

ANGELO: Thanks.

PIAF: And remember not to waggle your head. Keep still. Make THEM come to you . . . make THEM talented. Let's have a look at you . . . no, over here.

[*He stands before her.*

She grasps his thighs with fierce adoration.]

Wah, they'll come in their knickers. But don't forget the men . . . they've got to like you, too . . . they've got to want to BE you. And listen. Stick to the gestures we worked out . . . don't drift into things of your own.

ANGELO: OK.

PIAF: Come off cleanly, big strides . . . but slower, like we rehearsed. Don't lift your chin up, it makes you look ugly. And don't hunch your shoulders – what are you looking like that for?

ANGELO: Nothing, nothing.

PIAF: What have I done now? I'm only trying to –

ANGELO: I know, I know. [*He turns away, clutching his stomach.*]

PIAF: I get it. I'm sorry, love. It's going to be all right . . . I promise. Listen, I'll be there. It's together from now on, you and me. [*She dives into her bag.*] Here, I was going to give you this after. [*She dangles a bunch of keys.*]

ANGELO: What is it?

PIAF: What do you think . . . vrmmm . . . vrmmmm!

ANGELO [*smile of pure happiness*]: Edith! But you shouldn't!

PIAF: Just this once! [*Kisses him.*
They embrace.]

P/A: Your call, Madame Piaf . . . your call, Monsieur Angelo.
[PIAF *moves away, takes a long scarf from her bag.*]

ANGELO: Darling . . . what are you doing?

PIAF: Oh, just something for the rheumatism, love.
[ANGELO *goes.*
PIAF *injects herself.*
PIAF *sings* Bravo pour le clown.]

SCENE VI

PIAF's *apartment. At the end of the last scene there is a musical link, using the music of* Misericorde, *and introducing the powerful sound of a car being driven very fast. There is a crash .., which reverberates in and out of the music, ending with the music of the phrase 'quand un homme vient vers moi' from* La belle histoire d'amour.

In PIAF's *apartment,* PIERRE *confers with a* PHYSIOTHERAPIST.

PIERRE [*writing a cheque for the fee*]: So, you'll be coming to do the treatments daily.

PHYSIO.: Yes, though I entirely agree with the hospital – it's madness for Madame to discharge herself.

PIERRE: I know. However, she insists.

PHYSIO.: There is still glass to be removed from her forehead – by the way, how did she come to lose the three ribs?

PIERRE: A previous car accident.

PHYSIO.: Obviously she should give up driving.

PIERRE: No, no, she doesn't drive. She tends to be driven by young men.

PHYSIO.: I see.

PIERRE: Look, we fully accept the risk, but we need to get Madame working again. When can she sing?

PHYSIO.: I don't think you understand! The mouth is badly torn – ripped! We can't start on that sort of scar-tissue for months – she mustn't even speak!

PIERRE: No, no, that's impossible, she has a big concert in six weeks.

PHYSIO.: I've obviously not made myself clear. This patient is lucky to be alive. Most women of her age would have been dead from shock on arrival. There's severe internal injury . . . laceration. She's probably only alive because she's a singer – we got very good response from the diaphragm. There'll be a lot of pain, for some time. Of course, she can be helped with that.

PIERRE: You mean, morphine?

PHYSIO.: Yes. [*He catches some anxiety in Pierre's voice.*] Why, has she been on –

PIERRE [*giving him the cheque*]: No, no, no – it's nothing. Just . . . there was a lot of pain *last* time, that's all.

[*PIERRE goes.*
The PHYSIOTHERAPIST *prepares for the treatment.*
PIAF *enters, looking very much the worse for wear.*]

PHYSIO.: Good morning, Madame Piaf.

PIAF [*evilly*]: Oh Christ, here it comes. [*A little, winning smile*] Are you going to give me a shot?

PHYSIO.: I'm sorry, Madame, you've already had the prescribed dose.

[*Her face becomes a vicious glare. But he will not budge.*
She slumps into the chair.]

Try to relax. [*He begins to work on her face.*]

PIAF: Christ Almighty! Madeleine! [*She catches the* PHYSIO-THERAPIST'*s eye.*] Oh. All right, get on with it.

[*He begins again.*]

Ow! Oh!

PHYSIO.: Madame, please. You say you want to sing in six weeks . . . it's impossible, but at least I'm trying.

[PIAF *submits, grasping the arms of her chair in agony.*

MADELEINE *enters, dressed for travelling, with her suitcase and a travelling bag and handbag. She stands.*

PIAF *ignores her.*]

MADELEINE: Piaf . . .

[PIAF *ignores her.* MADELEINE *puts out a hand.*]

I've come to say goodbye.

PIAF: Piss off.

MADELEINE [*low*]: Please, Piaf . . .

PIAF [*low mutter*]: Fuck off . . . that's my answer to you, mate.

MADELEINE [*upset*]: Very well. [*She takes a large envelope from her bag.*] You've given me too much. I can't accept it.

[PIAF *spits on the proffered envelope.*

The PHYSIOTHERAPIST *and* MADELEINE *exchange a small glance, then* MADELEINE *gently puts the envelope at* PIAF's *feet. She picks up her suitcase.*]

Goodbye then.

[*With a witchlike gesture* PIAF *wipes the envelope on her ass and throws it in* MADELEINE's *face.*]

[*quietly*]: Goodbye then. I wish you the very best. I really mean that.

[*There is no response.*

She goes.]

PIAF: Go on . . . piss off after her.

PHYSIO.: I beg your pardon?

PIAF: You heard. Florence Nightingale! 'Ew, I'll never leave you, Piaf . . . I'll do anything!' Like fuck . . . they'll have your blood for breakfast. And sick it up all over your shoes – 'Yew don't appreciate me!' Who the fuck do they think YOU ARE?!

What goes on here, mate, is the rest of me. And it's not worth knowing, I can tell you. Come here, looking for glamour. They want glamour, they can pay to see me, at the Olympia . . . and I don't mean shoved-up tits, neither.

PHYSIO.: Could you put your head straight, please?

PIAF: Nah, they all want a slice, even the bloody managers. Will they take the rough with the smooth, will they hell! They want the bloody product, they want that all right, all wrapped up with a

feather in its ass, but *songs* – what do they know about songs!
'What rhymes with June, lads?' I said to him, 'No, I'm sorry . . .
don't like it.' 'Oh, I thought you'd reckon it, Piaf . . . it's a love
song.' Love!

Nah, pretty soon they're not going to want my stuff. My sort's
dying out. Going extinct. What they want now is discs. Canned.
In the can – well, real thing, dodgy, innit? I mean, you can *count*
discs . . . stack 'em . . . put 'em in containers. They don't bloody
answer back! [*Again it seems as if she will settle, but no.*] Love.
I'll tell you about fucking love. [*To the audience*] Friend of mine
. . . tart . . . dropping a kid. We get an old nurse to her in the end
. . . dear little baby boy. And the old girl's washing her down
with Dettol after. 'Hullo . . . where is it?' 'Where's what?' says
me friend. 'You know, your bits and pieces,' says the old biddy
'. . . your Thingme!' 'Oh . . . that . . .' says me friend.
'Chewed off long ago.'

That's fucking love for you.

PHYSIO. [*unmoved*]: It's not uncommon, I'm afraid.
PIAF [*sourly*]: Oh well, you'd know, working in hospitals.
[*Brightens*] Hey, I bet you've seen a thing or two!
PHYSIO.: Could you keep your head still, please?

   [JACKO, *pageboy, enters with flowers.*]

JACKO: Hi, Piaf!
PIAF [*unable to see him as* PHYSIOTHERAPIST *tries to work on her
face*]: Don't think we've had the pleasure.
JACKO: You will, love, you will.
PIAF: Cheeky with it . . . how d'you like to be in pictures?
JACKO: Knock it off, I'm a singer. [*She takes a look.*]
PIAF: Are you now?
JACKO: Well, trying to be.
PIAF: Going to have to do more than try, love. [*She gets up, gives
him the once over.*] Not bad . . . not bad at all. Just my size, in
fact.
JACKO: That's what you think!

   [PIAF's *throaty laugh rings out.*]

PIAF: What's your name?
JACKO: Jacko. [*She kisses him.*

Music.

PIAF *crosses to her dressing table. Applies make-up . . . pulls down her corset nervously.*]

P/A: Your call, Madame Piaf. Madame Piaf, your call, please.

PIAF: Jacko!

[*He appears . . . wearing a Piaf blue suit . . . they embrace.*]

PIAF: What's it like out front?

JACKO: Electric.

PIAF: Buggers think I can't make it.

JACKO: Not a bit. They love you, same as ever.

PIAF: Well, I don't give them no shit – remember that, kid, give 'em the real thing. Mm, you're lovely – you can sing too!

JACKO: I don't know about that.

PIAF: Now don't piss on yourself . . . plenty do that for you – how do I look?

JACKO: Bloody good . . . will that stuff stay on?

P/A: Madame Piaf . . . your call, please . . . your call, Madame Piaf . . . thank you.

[PIAF *panics.*]

JACKO: OK, love, it's OK.

PIAF: You'll be there?

JACKO: Right where you can see me.

PIAF: Sure. [*Pulls herself together*] Go on. I just need a minute to . . . get it together.

[*He gives her a sharp look, but goes.* PIAF *injects herself. Big musical build . . . Hymne à l'amour.*]

P/A: Under the direction of Michel Desmoulins . . . with the Orchestre Bourre . . . we proudly present . . . Edith Piaf!!

[*music changes to her signature tune . . .* La goualante du pauvre Jean.

PIAF *moves to microphone. She acknowledges applause, laughing her throaty, inviting laugh. She announces the name of composer and lyricist . . . and then sings* Hymne à l'amour.

At the end of the song PIAF *accepts applause, bowing, and waving with a warm smile.*

Sharp light change.

PIAF's *manner changes in mid-smile. The radiant charm disappears and she looks up, her face murderous.*]

PIAF: Kill the fucking lights! And where was the follow spot . . . I'm not that small! Just do what you're fucking paid for. [*She turns to a young man (PUSHER) who has appeared at her side.*] Have you got it?

[*He nods.*

She opens her hand . . . but he does likewise.]

PIAF: Look, I haven't got any money on me, I'll see you tomorrow.

PUSHER: Sorry, Piaf, I daren't, you know that.

PIAF: But I can fix it tomorrow, no trouble.

PUSHER: Can't you get it from the box-office?

PIAF: No, he won't have it.

[*The PUSHER moves off.*

PIAF becomes frantic.]

Look, I must have a delivery.

PUSHER: I'll be round in the afternoon.

PIAF: No . . . no . . . [*She hangs on to him. He extricates himself sadly.*]

PUSHER: Piaf, you know better than that. We're in the same boat, remember. I'll see you tomorrow. [*He goes.*

PIAF becomes agitated. She begins to shake.]

PIAF: Oh God . . . oh God . . .

[*Her mania increases. She plucks at her clothes . . . scratches . . . shivers . . . heaves as if to be sick . . . whimpers. She crouches . . . howling . . . then goes into a violent fit.*

An ATTENDANT enters. She fights him off savagely, screeching and terrified. He cuffs her and carries her off.]

SCENE VII

A room at the Ritz. JACKO *onstage.* PIAF *enters . . . in a new jacket . . . her hair combed.*

PIAF: How do I rate?

JACKO: Fan-bloody-tastic!

PIAF: So you'd pay for an all-nighter?

JACKO: You can have one now if you like . . .

　　　[*They embrace.*

　　　PIERRE *enters.*]

PIERRE: I like it, keep it in.

　　　[PIAF *screams welcome,* PIERRE *picks her up, swings her round.*]

　　Has she been a good girl?

PIAF: Cross me heart.

JACKO: A very good girl. Champagne?

PIERRE: What the hell are you doing in a hotel? I went to the apartment.

JACKO: Slight problem with the bills . . . no gas.

PIAF: And I wanted an omelette.

PIERRE: So you move into the Ritz?

PIAF: Only while we're broke!

　　　[JACKO *pours the drinks.*]

　　OK, Pierrot! What have you come up with? I can't wait to get started.

PIERRE: Piaf . . . I have to know. Is it finished?

PIAF: Yes, love. It's finished. All I want now is the work. When do we start, boss?

PIERRE: Piaf, it's bound to take a little time. [*Slight pause*] I can't get any bookings. They don't want to know.

PIAF: I've told you, I'm off the shit.

PIERRE: We've tried everything. Nobody's playing.

　　　[*Silence.*

　　　PIAF *mutters under her breath.*

　　　JACKO *proffers the champagne.*]

PIAF: No, love. OK, nobody's playing. Right. If that's the way they want it. If we have to prove it, we'll prove it. We'll do the provinces . . . fleapits, cinemas, holiday camps – feel like a tour. Lose the bottle, Jacko . . .

JACKO: Right, love.

PIAF: Give Michel a ring . . . Eddie . . . I'll need some songs – we'll start rehearsing tonight . . . OK, Pierrot?

PIERRE: I don't know. It may be difficult.

PIAF: Come on, I'll be a draw . . . they'll come to see if I can stay on me feet!

[*He doesn't respond.*]

We'll get all the publicity we want . . . the press are on my side. Come on, Pierrot . . . we've done it before, we can do it again!

PIERRE: One-night stands . . . fit-ups . . . travelling overnight . . . that was a long time ago. We're all older.

[*Silence*]

If we do it – I F we do it . . .

PIAF: Thanks, boss!

PIERRE: I said 'if' . . . I hold the purse. No running up debts, no freeloaders, no private shows, parties, subs, handouts . . . you've got to start holding on to something.

PIAF: I know, I know . . .

PIERRE: If you know so much, why don't you do something about it? It's just common sense, Edith!

[*A hush*]

PIAF: Sure. I know. I made a mess of it with the shit.

JACKO [*after a pause*]: You OK, love?

[*She nods . . . turns to* PIERRE.]

PIAF: Can't get me the bookings, eh? Been trying, have you, or is it second thoughts time?

PIERRE: What do you mean?

PIAF: Where were you when I was in the bloody bin?

PIERRE: Look, Piaf, I've explained to you –

PIAF: That's right . . . you had a lot on. What with your new apartment, your portfolio . . . not to mention all your new clients. I hear you're collecting glass now.

PIERRE: What's wrong with that?

PIAF [*to* JACKO, *jocular*]: Never asks us to his little dinner parties.

PIERRE: Only because I know you wouldn't come.

PIAF: Right. He can leave me out of it.

PIERRE: Look, I've never tried to –

PIAF: You never draw breath! Get it together, don't miss a trick, lunch with the accountant once a week. Fuck his own grand-mother to get that fur-collared overcoat.

PIERRE: Piaf, why pick on me? I'm just an ordinary guy –

PIAF: Oh sure. We know what you were. And we know what you
want. You're doing well. Only don't bother waiting down the
school gates for those two little girls of yours.

PIERRE: Why not?

PIAF [*vicious*]: Because you've made such fucking little ladies of
them, they're ashamed of you already!

[*A silence*]

PIERRE [*at last*]: Who told you that?

JACKO: Leave it, love.

PIAF: All right. I'm sorry. What you don't understand is that we're
not all into buying and selling.

PIERRE: Nothing wrong with honest trade. You sell your voice.

PIAF: That's a laugh.

PIERRE: Only because you fuck about. You've had the rate for the
job, you just don't hang on to it!

PIAF: No, well, I'm rubbish, aren't I?

JACKO: Don't worry, love. You'll never be a lady.

PIAF: Too right. I've seen them, the ladies. Get the hots for a feller,
they take it out on a day's *shopping*! Can't risk a bit of the other,
might give the old man an excuse, wreck their investments – put
theirselves to better use, there might not be so many wars, not
that they'd be any fucking good at it. They think they can take it
with 'em, like the man who goes to see his mate and a woman
comes to the door and says, 'You can't see him, he's dead.' 'Dead?
He can't be, he's got my big chisel!'

[*They laugh.*]

Nah, we'll go on as we are. Just get me the bookings.

PIERRE: Edith, I have to know. Is it over?

[PIAF *looks into his eyes candidly.*]

PIAF: Yes, love. It's finished.

[PIERRE *embraces her, kisses her on both cheeks and goes.*
She smiles up at JACKO, *he goes.*
She pushes up her sleeve for a fix.]

Open stage. The MANAGER *enters, crosses to microphone.*
Reprise of act one, scene one.

MANAGER [*testing the microphone*]: One, two, three . . . [*He
raises his head* . . .] Ladies and gentlemen, I give you . . .
your own . . . Piaf! [*He gestures, with a sharp glance off, and
goes.*
     PIAF *appears. She sings the first few bars of* La goualante du
     pauvre Jean. *And breaks down.*
     The MANAGER *appears.*]
PIAF [*struggling*]: Get your fucking hands off me, I ain't done
nothing nothing yet . . .
     [*Light change.*
     MANAGER *enters again, as before.*]
MANAGER: Ladies and gentlemen, I give you . . . your own . . .
Piaf!
     [*Musical intro* . . . Hamburg.
     PIAF *appears, assisted on by* JACKO. *She pauses, but makes it
     to the microphone. Then stands, as if unaware of her sur-
     roundings. Misses opening.*
     MANAGER *and* JACKO *run on to assist her off.*]
PIAF [*mumbles, as they lead her away*]: What is it . . . where's the
song?
     [*Blackout.*
     The MANAGER *appears, as before.*]
MANAGER: Ladies and gentlemen, I give you . . . your own . . .
Piaf!
     [JACKO *has to assist her onstage.*
     *Frail and trembling, she seems lost onstage, and terrified by
     the lights. Eventually she approaches the microphone, only to
     collapse on the floor.*
     JACKO *and the* MANAGER *run on.* JACKO *kneels beside her,
     his face alarmed.*]
PIAF [*looks up at him, returning to consciousness, murmurs*]: All
right, love . . . all right . . . I'm still here.

[JACKO *carries her offstage.*
Blackout.]

SCENE IX

PIAF's *room in a nursing home.* PIAF *sits in a wheelchair . . .* JACKO,
with flowers, at her side.

JACKO: How've you been?

PIAF: Not so grand.

JACKO: Did you get any sleep?

PIAF: I had to ask them for something.

JACKO: I'll have a word with them.

PIAF: I wish you would, I can't get any sense out of them. Any
more news of your tour?

JACKO: Yeah, but nothing come of it.

PIAF: Oh?

JACKO: The terms weren't right.

PIAF: Whatcha mean, it's a number-one tour, you nuts or something?

JACKO: I'm not going.

PIAF: You bloody are if *I* say so.

JACKO: I'm not leaving you in here.

PIAF: Oh . . . and who'll be the first to throw it in my face when the
time comes? Don't be a fool, cockie, they won't ask you
twice.

JACKO: I'm not leaving you!

PIAF: What's the matter, have they told you I'm going to die or
something – well, have they?

JACKO: No, of course not.

PIAF: What did he say?

JACKO: That you need a rest.

PIAF [*mutters*]: I'm rigid with rest. Look, it's a number-one tour!
D'you think that's nothing? I don't understand you, I really
don't. I put a bloody lot of work into you!

JACKO: I am not leaving you in the lurch. When you're better we'll tour together, like we said. I'm not leaving you in the shit and you can yell as much as you like, I shan't change me mind.

PIAF [*pause*]: Oh. Well. Well, as far as that goes, it'll have to come out in the open.

JACKO: What do you mean?

PIAF: It's the elbow, old son. Haven't you seen it coming?

JACKO: I don't believe you.

PIAF: Hard luck on you then. Get the message . . . you've had a good run for it.

JACKO: There's somebody else, you mean?

PIAF: Yeah . . . yeah. Now listen, don't forget. You've got a lovely tone, but lift. And don't forget the diction, never mind the A and R wizards. My God, those eyes of yours, you'll knock 'em cold. Here . . . something for luck. [*Gives him her cross of St Theresa. He cries.*]

All right, love, all right. Come on, give us a kiss.

[*He kisses her . . . she embraces him for a moment then withdraws.*]

Go on, off you go, I need a kip.

JACKO: If ever you need anything –

[*But she waves him off.*]

NURSE [*enters, looks round for* JACKO]: Oh! That was a love you and leave you! Ohh, look at these! [*She buries her face in the roses.*] I'll put them in water for you.

[*She hums, arranging the flowers.* PIAF *watches her.*]

There! [*She turns.*] Oh, by the way, *he's* here again. [*She giggles.*]

PIAF: What?

NURSE: The foreign boy.

PIAF: What does he want?

NURSE: Honestly, I don't know. We've been trying to find out, but he's so shy. I think what he really wants is to *see* you!

PIAF: Are you kidding?

NURSE: I said I'd ask.

PIAF: Oh, tell him me fanny's dropped off and I'm having a transplant.

NURSE: I shan't say anything of the sort. He's very good-looking. You could thank him . . . he's called every day.

PIAF: Oh, all right, just for a minute. Only if he's good-looking, mind!

[*The* NURSE *goes.*]

[*murmurs*]: Frighten him for life. [*She wheels the chair across . . . turns . . . aware of his presence, but without looking at him.*] Well, now you've seen me – what's the matter, died of shock? [*She turns to look at him.*

They look at each other. A pause.]

[*at last*]: What's in it for you, kid?

THEO: I don't want anything.

PIAF: Come on!

THEO: We-ell –

PIAF: Aha!

THEO: Perhaps . . . to be near you.

PIAF: What for?

THEO: I don't know. [*Slight pause*] I like it. [*Slight pause*] It makes me happy.

[*They look at each other. Then she gets a fit of coughing. At once he is at her side, attending to her.*]

PIAF: Thanks kid. What's your name?

THEO: Theo. Theophanis Lambouskas.

PIAF [*splutters, laughing*]: That'll have to go for a start. Tell me about yourself, Theo.

THEO: I have seen all your concerts. Olympia . . . Lyons . . . Bordeaux.

PIAF: Oh, Bordeaux . . . not so hot.

THEO: I wanted to come in America but that was not possible . . . actually it was the money.

PIAF: I sang thirty songs in the Carnegie Hall. They applauded for twenty minutes. That's a long time. [*She puts out a hand, touches his cheek.*] You're a nice-looking boy, Theo. [*She pats her hair, conscious of her appearance.*]

THEO: You want I should do your hair?

[*He takes out a comb and moves behind her, smoothing her hair with swift elegance.*]

PIAF [*in admiration*]: Oh, you're a hairdresser. There's not a lot left, I'm afraid.

THEO [*quiet and absorbed*]: We shall do it nice.
[*He bends over her, and they embrace.*
He helps her to her feet and she walks to the microphone and lifts her crippled hands, her eyes shining.]

PIAF: Ladies and gentlemen . . . ladies and gentlemen, I don't deserve such happiness. Ladies and gentlemen, I would like to present my husband . . . Theo Sarapo! [*She calls off, throaty and commanding*] Theo!
[PIAF *and* THEO *sing, together* . . . Chant d'amour. PIAF *takes the end of the song alone.*]

SCENE X

PIAF's *room in the South of France.* THEO *is tucking her into the wheelchair.*

PIAF: Who was it?

THEO: A visitor, darling. The nurse will see to it.

PIAF: Did she say who it was?

THEO: An old friend, from Belleville . . . 'Toinette?

PIAF: Toine . . . old Toine? Never. Where is she, fetch her in . . . Toine?

THEO: I think the nurse has sent her away.

TOINE [*enters*]: Ede? [*Bumping into* THEO] Where are you?

PIAF: Over here.

TOINE: Is it you?

PIAF: Well who the fuck d'you think it is, I'm not dead yet. Christ, you've put on weight. Let's have a look at you. How d'you find me?

TOINE: I took a train.

PIAF: Here . . . Theo. [*Takes his hand*] Well, what do you think of him?

TOINE: He's a bit young.

PIAF [*throaty laugh*]: Never think she was an old Belleville street-walker, would you?

TOINE: Edith!

PIAF: Oh Christ, you never could take a joke, give her a drink – you still *drink*, don't you?

TOINE: Only wine.

[*He goes.*

TOINE *comes and sits by* PIAF]: How old *is* he?

PIAF: Oh, don't you worry, he's old enough.

TOINE: You don't *do* nothing do you?

PIAF: Nah. Still . . . never know. Anyway, thanks for coming . . . see your daft face, cheer anybody up. What your old man say?

TOINE: Never told him, you know what he's like. He still thinks you ought to have set us up.

PIAF: Oh, you know me, never could hang on to nothing. Still, we had some good times, eh? Remember running in and out of Coco Chanel's buying two of everything. Never did pay that bill.

TOINE [*gets out Gitanes*]: Mind if I smoke?

PIAF: It's bad for yuh – read it in the papers.

TOINE [*cheerful*]: Oh well, you can only die once. [*And could bite her tongue off.*]

PIAF [*sardonic*]: Trust you.

[THEO *returns with wine.*]

TOINE: Aren't you having none, Ede?

THEO: Edith's on a diet just now.

TOINE: Oh? Oh, I bought you some apples. [*She gets in a muddle with her bag, fag, wine and the bag of apples.*

THEO *bends over her.*]

PIAF: Hey you two, no getting off! [*She laughs her deep, inviting laugh.*] We could tell him a thing or two, eh, Toine? Her and me, we had our own band at one time. Mind you, she spent more time seeing fellers off out the back than we ever copped in fees.

TOINE: Edith! We had to eat.

[*Pause.* TOINE *looks for topics.*]

Hey, remember that time in Milan?

PIAF: You never came to Milan.

TOINE: Yes I did.

PIAF: No you didn't.

TOINE: I did!

PIAF: You never!

THEO: Darling . . .

PIAF [*lies back, eyes closed*]: It's all right, love . . . yeah, I remember. Go on . . . tell him, Toine.

TOINE: We brought these Chinese acrobats back to the hotel where we was staying.

PIAF: Go on . . .

TOINE: There was ever so many of 'em.

PIAF: Tell him about the goldfish.

TOINE: I was going to! Anyway, they had this ornamental pond – you know, in the foyer. We got them all paddling . . . catching the fish in their little shoes!

[*She starts to laugh,* PIAF *joins in.*]

We . . . we went in the kitchens, making breakfast . . . we 'ad 'em on toast! . . . d'you remember, Ede?

PIAF [*doubled up*]: Yeah!

TOINE: Little bit of garnish . . . anchovies . . .

PIAF: And noodles!

TOINE [*shrieking with laughter*]: Oh Christ, I forgot about the noodles – they went too far there.

[*They both laugh, and subside together, clasping hands.*]

Oh dear!

PIAF: Oh dear!

[*They wipe their eyes and subside.*]

TOINE: I forgot what we did after that. Oh yeah . . . I remember. [*She smiles in fond remembrance.*] You tried to slash your wrists . . . Gawd, what a mess! I was so legless I nearly let her.

PIAF: Pity you didn't.

[*Slight pause*]

THEO [*murmurs*]: Darling . . . no.

PIAF: You're right. I wouldn't have met you.

TOINE [*fondly*]: We got thrown out.

PIAF: He's lovely. I don't deserve him. [*Her hands clench, picking at the rug which covers her knees.*] Go on, Toine, go on.

TOINE [*looks helplessly at* THEO . . . *she is stumped for a subject*]:

71

Oh, I know. My little girl, Janine . . . the youngest . . . she's ever such a good dancer, Ede. We're paying for classes – I mean, I don't know if it'll come to anything. Be nice though.

[PIAF *seems to be drifting off.*]

THEO: You want to sleep now?

PIAF: No, no, go on . . . you go on . . . [*To* TOINE] . . . go on, Toine . . .

[TOINE *searches for something to talk about.*]

TOINE: Um . . . yeah . . . um . . . ah! Remember the Boche, Edith? During the war? One of them looked me up once . . . I couldn't believe it! He was ever so well off. [*To* THEO] They shoved us inside . . . I thought our number was up, I can tell you – well, Ede was passing messages to our chaps in the prison camps . . .

[PIAF's *head is bent . . . she seems to have fallen asleep.*]

. . . is she all right?

[THEO *drops to his knees at* PIAF's *side.*]

Edith?

[THEO *puts his arms about* PIAF. *The music of* Non, je ne regrette rien.

Lights begin to fade.]

Ede?

[*Lights to black.*

Curtain call.

PIAF *sings* Non, je ne regrette rien.]

CAMILLE

based on *La Dame aux Camélias*,
by Alexandre Dumas *fils*

CHARACTERS

AUCTIONEER
ARMAND DUVAL
GASTON DE MAURIEUX
PRUDENCE DE MARSAN DE TALBEC
CLÉMENCE DE VILLENEUVE
SOPHIE DE LYONNE
COUNT DRUFTHEIM
LE DUC
GIRL
PRINCE BELA MIRKASSIAN
MARGUERITE GAUTIER
M. DE SANCERRE
JANINE/OLYMPE
JEAN
JEAN-PAUL
YVETTE
UPHOLSTERER
2 GRAVEDIGGERS
INSPECTOR
PIERRE
ARMAND'S FATHER, THE MARQUIS DE SAINT-BRIEUC
2 WAITERS
RUSSIAN PRINCE (SERGEI)
MAN
PRIEST

Camille was first presented at The Other Place, Stratford-upon-Avon, by the Royal Shakespeare Company on 4 April 1984. It was directed by Ron Daniels; Maria Bjornson was the designer and the lighting was by John Waterhouse. Guy Woolfenden arranged the music, choreography was by Anthony van Laast, fights arranged by Malcolm Ransom. Richard Oriel was the stage manager.

The cast was as follows:

MARGUERITE GAUTIER	Frances Barber
ARMAND DUVAL	Nicholas Farrell
PRUDENCE DE MARSAN DE TALBEC	Polly James
SOPHIE DE LYONNE	Alphonsia Emmanuel
CLÉMENCE DE VILLENEUVE	Rowena Roberts
JANINE/OLYMPE	Katharine Rogers
YVETTE	Sarah Woodward
GASTON DE MAURIEUX	Paul Gregory
LE DUC	Norman Henry
COUNT DRUFTHEIM	Charles Millham
M. DE SANCERRE	Arthur Kohn
PRINCE BELA MIRKASSIAN	Andrew Hall
JEAN	Peter Theedom
UPHOLSTERER	Andrew Jarvis
JEAN-PAUL	Brian McGinley or Richard Parry
GRAVEDIGGER	Peter Theedom
INSPECTOR	Norman Henry
PIERRE	Andrew Jarvis
ARMAND'S FATHER, THE MARQUIS DE SAINT-BRIEUC	Bernard Horsfall
RUSSIAN PRINCE (SERGEI)	Arthur Kohn

Other parts were played by members of the company.
The pianist was James Walker.

SYNOPSIS OF SCENES

ACT I

ACT II

ACT I

Marguerite's bedroom. White, with a white draped bed, and white silk damask cover. A few touches of blue. A dressing table, with crystal and silver appointments. A beautiful mirror in an ornate silver frame. Everything is labelled.

AUCTIONEER [off]: Lot one hundred and twenty-four . . . one steel fender, fire irons *en suite*, ditto firedogs – may I have your bids for this handsome lot, please? Note the chasing on the handles, ladies and gentlemen. Fifty francs? Fifty francs, Monsieur. Fifty-five . . . sixty – hold them up, boy, let them see the lot – there, fit for a gentleman's residence . . .
    [*Laughter.*]
    . . . sixty? I'm bid sixty. Yes, sir – sixty-five?
    [*A* MAN *in green baize lets a young man (*ARMAND*) through. He erupts into the room, brushing past the* MAN, *who closes the door behind him, cutting down the sound. Then he comes to a halt. He seems in a daze. He looks pale, but sweating, as though ill. The sight of the room seems to affect him. He looks about, at first confused, then, recognizing the room, he moves about, touching pieces of furniture with a locked, neutral expression. This goes on and he prowls, with increasing signs of agitation. He does not notice the* MAN *at the door receiving a tip from another, slightly older man (*GASTON*), who enters and strolls, curious to see the room. At a sound,* ARMAND *turns abruptly.*]
ARMAND: Who are you?
GASTON: Monsieur?

77

ARMAND: What do you want?

GASTON: I beg your pardon. I simply came to see.

ARMAND: See? [*He seems puzzled.*]

GASTON: Forgive me, I am intruding. I was enjoying the spring sunshine – a shower drove me in, the crowd intrigued me. Mere curiosity . . . I beg your pardon. [*He makes to go, but* ARMAND's *urgent sigh halts him.*] My dear sir – you're ill! Allow me –

ARMAND: It's nothing. Fever. I was in Egypt.

GASTON: Indeed? That would explain it. I am well acquainted with the rigours of foreign infection, I have been abroad myself . . . Persia, the Levant . . . for over a year. [*Slight pause*] I lost my dear wife.

ARMAND [*his voice thick*]: Lost?

GASTON: In childbirth.

AUCTIONEER [off]: *Chère Madame*, don't resist!
    [*Laughter, off.*]

ARMAND: And the child?

GASTON: My son?
    [*Laughter, off.*]
    Dead.

ARMAND: Dead?

GASTON: In the coffin with his mother.

AUCTIONEER [*now visible*]: Fifteen bonnets, all trimmed! Thank you – thank you! [*He bangs the gavel.*] Sold to the enchanting Mam'selle by the window. *Adieu* the bonnets, or may we hope *au revoir*?
    [*Laughter.*]

GASTON: You are not here to buy?
    [ARMAND *looks up at him uncomprehendingly.*]
    A remembrance, perhaps? The house is full of the most beautiful things. Quite lovely. Alas, all going at a price.

AUCTIONEER [*bangs gavel*]: And now, *mesdames et messieurs*, lot one hundred and thirty. A fine looking-glass, silver-gilt frame as described – fit for a palace. One thousand francs, ladies and gentlemen. For this fine mirror. May I say twelve hundred? And fifteen. Going at fifteen hundred –
    [ARMAND *crosses rapidly.*]

ARMAND: Two thousand!

AUCTIONEER: Two thousand behind me. And one? And two.

ARMAND: Three thousand.

GASTON: No . . . enough!

AUCTIONEER: Three thousand. And two-fifty. Three thousand five . . . and seven-fifty –

ARMAND: Five thousand!

AUCTIONEER: Monsieur?

ARMAND: Five thousand francs!

AUCTIONEER: At five thousand then, to the gentleman by the door! [*He bangs the gavel. Clapping.*] And now . . . the lot you've all been waiting for. Lot one hundred and thirty. The bed. Decorated with – ah . . . [*He consults his list.*] . . . camellias. What was it . . . twenty-three days of the month she wore white camellias and for the other five days she wore red . . .

ARMAND [*low*]: No.

AUCTIONEER: Truth of it, sir. [*Clears his throat again loudly.*] Well, ladies and gentlemen . . . there it is. The bed. What am I bid? [*A hush. Quietly*] I shall want a good price.

ARMAND: No.

AUCTIONEER: You bidding, sir?

GASTON: The gentleman is ill.

[*He assists* ARMAND *away from the door.*]

FIRST VOICE [*off*]: Two hundred thousand for the bed!

SECOND VOICE [*off*]: And fifty!

FIRST VOICE [*off*]: Three hundred thousand – are we bidding or not?

AUCTIONEER: Thank you, sir – three hundred thousand I'm bid, three hundred thousand –

ARMAND: No! No! No!

[*He leaps off. Sounds of a tussle.* GASTON *wrestles him back into the room. The auction continues in the background.* ARMAND *puts his hand on a piece of furniture, as if to prevent its being sold. The bang of the gavel. Applause.*
The noise rouses ARMAND. *He jumps up.*]

GASTON: You are too late – the bed is sold, the auction is over.

[ARMAND *staggers.* GASTON *helps him to sit.* ARMAND *seems in a daze.*

GASTON *sighs, a deep sigh.*]

You have had a loss.

[ARMAND *does not reply.*

Slight pause.]

GASTON: May I know the lady's name?

[ARMAND *looks up at him uncomprehendingly.*]

ARMAND [*rapid, normal tone*]: I was in a bad mood. The world seemed as full of rogues and charlatans as ever, the greatest, of course, being oneself . . . [*Silence.*]

I wasn't here.

[*He stumbles to his feet.*

GASTON *moves to assist him.*]

GASTON: What was the lady's name? May I know her name?

ARMAND [*as in a dream*]: Marguerite. Her name is Marguerite.

[*Aware of* GASTON *once more.*] At the opera.

[*They go.*]

SCENE II

In the foyer of the Opera House. The sound of a woman, live, singing Casta diva *from* Norma. *Onstage, two* WAITERS *prepare trays of drinks for the Entr'acte.*

Applause.

PRUDENCE *enters with* CLÉMENCE, *followed by* SOPHIE.

PRUDENCE: Thank God for that.

CLÉMENCE: Don't you like it?

PRUDENCE: The opera? Do you?

CLÉMENCE: Yes! I'm affected.

[SOPHIE *laughs loudly.*]

PRUDENCE: Rubbish, she weighs two hundred pounds and he's cross-eyed – well, we all know why.

CLÉMENCE: Why?

PRUDENCE: Never mind, it's medical.

[SOPHIE *accosts a young man* (COUNT DRUFTHEIM).]

SOPHIE: Count Druftheim?

COUNT: Excuse me, please, I must go with the opera, I am losing my hat. [*He backs away, bashful, and goes.*]

PRUDENCE: His hat!

SOPHIE: A serious matter. Known to cause impotence.

CLÉMENCE: What, losing your hat?

SOPHIE: Only in men.

[PRUDENCE *pulls a face at* SOPHIE, *then turns with a smile.*]

PRUDENCE: *Monsieur le Duc!*

[*All three curtsey as an elderly man* (LE DUC) *hobbles on, a very young woman* (GIRL) *on his arm. He swerves towards them, waving genially.*]

DUC: Ah, Prudence . . . fat as ever, eh?

PRUDENCE: Ah, *Monsieur le Duc*, always the wit.

DUC: D'you fancy the singing then?

CLÉMENCE: Ooh yes, especially the –

PRUDENCE: Sublime, sublime!

DUC: Absolutely . . . eh m'dear? [*Digs his companion in the ribs.*]

GIRL: What? Oh. Yes.

CLÉMENCE: Didn't you like the horses and the waterfall?

GIRL: Never saw them.

CLÉMENCE: But you couldn't –

DUC: Must be off, must be off . . . [*He steers his companion off, with a wave.*]

PRUDENCE: I bet you must.

CLÉMENCE: She won't have sat up once.

PRUDENCE: The old bastard.

CLÉMENCE [*flat*]: He's not bad. For a Duke. [*Her manner changes as* ARMAND *enters with* BELA.] Armand!

BELA: Seven on the black! Seven on the black, the odds must be millions!

PRUDENCE: What?

CLÉMENCE: You've been at the tables! Armand, we waited!

BELA: Seven . . . seven . . . seven! [*He turns on his heels in a Slavic dance, lifting his arms.*] Seven on the black!

CLÉMENCE [*flat*]: That's clever.

PRUDENCE: How much did you win, we must have a party . . . a trip to the sea, I'll hire coaches –

ARMAND: I shouldn't.

PRUDENCE: Why not?

[BELA *and* ARMAND *open their arms, to indicate that the money has been lost.*]

Oh! All of it? Oh!! [*To* ARMAND, *aside*] You never know when to leave off.

ARMAND: I?

PRUDENCE: Yes, you. [*As* ARMAND *whispers in* CLÉMENCE's *ear*] And you can stop that – she hasn't forgiven you, have you?

CLÉMENCE: What?

PRUDENCE: You've broken that poor girl's heart, she's been at the laudanum, I had to prise the phial from her hand, she was going to finish it all . . . weren't you?

CLÉMENCE: What? Yes.

PRUDENCE: She'd even made out her will – chosen the anthem and flowers for her catafalque.

CLÉMENCE [*soppy*]: I'm having white violets.

PRUDENCE: And tuberoses. For the smell. And her body's to be shipped to Lisbon.

CLÉMENCE: . . . to Lisbon.

BELA: Why Lisbon?

CLÉMENCE: Because I've never been there, silly.

[*But* ARMAND *has seen* SOPHIE.]

ARMAND: Mademoiselle de Lyonne? [*He makes an exaggerated bow.*]

SOPHIE: Monsieur Duval.

ARMAND: I thought we'd seen the last of you.

SOPHIE: Surprised?

ARMAND: By you?

PRUDENCE: Armand, that's enough.

ARMAND: Where have you been?

SOPHIE [*gazing at him insolently*]: I've been at the opera.

ARMAND: An elevating experience?

SOPHIE: No.

ARMAND: No?

SOPHIE: The bass was disappointing.

ARMAND: In what way?

SOPHIE: Insufficient. [*She continues to stare at him.*
He grabs CLÉMENCE *by the wrist.*]

CLÉMENCE: Armand . . . Armand, no!

PRUDENCE: She'll miss the last act! [*But he pulls her offstage.*]
That young man becomes more louche by the day.

BELA: Be good enough to confine your concern to the opera,
Madame.

PRUDENCE: Oh thank you very much! [*She walks away in a huff.*]

BELA: So you're back.

SOPHIE: Disappointed?

BELA: Where have you been?

SOPHIE: If you must know, I've been to Dieppe.

BELA: Dieppe? [*He bursts out laughing.*] Dieppe! The end of the
universe! A long way to buy a crochet hook . . . how very
discreet.

SOPHIE: Thank you.

BELA: And you're recovered?
[*She gestures dismissively and walks off.*
He pursues her.]

SOPHIE [*turns*]: Oh, you've no need to be anxious.

BELA: I? Anxious?

SOPHIE: As you see, he's left me.
[*He smiles.*]
As he will leave you, *Monsieur le Prince*.

BELA: Oh? You think so?

SOPHIE: Take my word. It's what he enjoys.

BELA: Armand? [*Laughing, takes her arm.*] Very well, let's make
him jealous.
[*She pulls free and walks away.*]
No? [*Catching up with her.*] Why not?

SOPHIE [*turning on him viciously*]: Because . . . 'Monsieur le
Prince' . . . I prefer my freedom.

BELA: Ah, a revolutionist! What are you going to fight with –
hatpins? Oh . . . [*As* ARMAND *returns, followed demurely by*
CLÉMENCE] . . . back again . . . so soon?

[ARMAND *grins, crosses to* PRUDENCE, *sits on the arm of her chair, stroking her arm.*]

PRUDENCE [*indulgently*]: Armand, why can't you treat us decently? You're no gentleman.

ARMAND [*ignoring her, to* BELA]: Have you ever noticed . . .

BELA: What?

ARMAND: . . . women's arms . . .

BELA: What about them?

ARMAND: . . . something honest . . . comfortable – [*He bends, bites* PRUDENCE *on the arm, making her scream.*]

PRUDENCE: Stop it! You're a brute.

ARMAND: Prudence . . . your flesh is so white . . . and so mature . . .

PRUDENCE: I mean it, Armand. You're too rough.

ARMAND: But worth your while. [*He reaches, lifts the necklace at her throat, lets it fall.*]

PRUDENCE: The pawnbroker doesn't think so. [*rising*]

ARMAND: What do you want then? [*He sits, taking her chair.*]

PRUDENCE: From you? . . . it won't be emeralds. And don't be in such a hurry. Go and make it up with Sophie.

ARMAND: No. We're enemies. [*He looks up at her, blank-faced.*]

PRUDENCE [*aside*]: What's the matter? [*Gently*] What is it?

[*He continues to look up at her inscrutably.*]

Home comforts? Is that it? [*She strokes his hair.*] All right, my dear. Old times' sakes, hmm? [*Brisk*] You can pay this for me.

[*She produces a bill. He whistles at the amount, but nods and rises.*]

Au 'voir, mes enfants. A little business to arrange for this young man . . . what I don't undertake for my friends! . . .

[*She and* ARMAND *move off together. The others laugh.*]

SOPHIE: She won't miss the finale either.

[*Laughter.*]

PRUDENCE [*apart*]: Armand, why must you be so cruel?

ARMAND: Cruel?

PRUDENCE: With women. Why?

ARMAND: They disappoint.

[MARGUERITE *appears, followed by an older man* (DE SANCERRE).

ARMAND *sees* MARGUERITE.

MARGUERITE *sees* ARMAND.

There is a long, still pause as they regard each other.

She inclines her head the merest fraction and walks away. He gazes after her then turns to PRUDENCE. *As he does so,* MARGUERITE *turns to see him go.*]

ARMAND: Who is that?

PRUDENCE: Marguerite.

[*He steps forward.*]

Come away, she's not for you.

ARMAND: Why not?

PRUDENCE: For one thing, you couldn't afford her.

[MARGUERITE *turns to her escort,* DE SANCERRE, *looking past him briefly towards* ARMAND.]

MARGUERITE: Will you forgive me, I'm feeling ill. No . . . stay. I'll see you later?

DE SANCERRE: Perhaps. [*He walks off.*

MARGUERITE *is left alone.*]

SOPHIE: Marguerite!

[MARGUERITE *and* SOPHIE *embrace.*]

MARGUERITE: How are you! . . . Bela − [*To* SOPHIE, *gaily*] − you're back!

[*as she gives* BELA *her hand in easy friendliness. He kisses it with dramatic ardour. She laughs, and sees* ARMAND *again, at a distance.*

ARMAND, *who has been watching her, immediately turns away.*]

Who is that?

BELA [*cool*]: A friend of mine.

MARGUERITE: Ah. [*She turns away.*]

BELA: Why, do you want to meet him?

MARGUERITE [*laughs*]: Certainly not, I wouldn't dream of depriving you.

[*She takes* SOPHIE's *arm, they walk apart.*]

Are you all right?

SOPHIE: Yes, I've stopped bleeding. She only left an arm in me. I was all festered!

[*They wave seductively at their friends.*]

MARGUERITE: Here. [*She gives* SOPHIE *her purse.*] No, take it, you'd do the same for me.

SOPHIE [*pocketing the purse*]: I doubt it.

[MARGUERITE *smiles, and moves away, to go.*]

ARMAND: *Mademoiselle* . . .

[MARGUERITE *turns.*]

Your flowers . . .

MARGUERITE: Yes?

ARMAND [*looking at her*]: They're beautiful.

MARGUERITE: Thank you.

[*She moves away, he follows. She turns.*]

Camellias.

[PRUDENCE *approaches.*]

PRUDENCE: Marguerite always wears them. My dear, may I present Armand Duval?

ARMAND [*bows*]: Why camellias?

MARGUERITE: Why not?

ARMAND: They have no scent.

MARGUERITE [*raising her eyebrows at his knowledge of flowers, then smiling*]: Ah, but you see, I'm an optimist. Please don't do that. [*As he blocks her path.*]

ARMAND: I must. When can I see you?

MARGUERITE: Please . . .

ARMAND: What do you want? Just tell me what you want.

MARGUERITE: From you, nothing. [*She attempts to pass.*] Don't do that.

ARMAND: What's the matter, don't you like me? Tell me what you want!

MARGUERITE [*to* BELA]: Your friend is impatient. [*She puts a gloved hand on* ARMAND's *cheek, speaks gently.*] Like a child. [*She goes.*]

ARMAND: No, wait! [*To* PRUDENCE] You, get her back for me!

PRUDENCE: She won't come.

ARMAND: Why not?

PRUDENCE: For one thing, I think she likes you.

ARMAND: What do you mean?

PRUDENCE: Armand, don't be obtuse. A woman in her position can't afford to like a man.

[*He goes abruptly.*]

PRUDENCE: I shall suspect that young man of a romantic disposition.

[*They laugh.*]

SOPHIE: Heart of stone. Prudence – supper!

PRUDENCE: Another time, my dears. [*She exits with* DE SANCERRE.

CLÉMENCE *gazes after* ARMAND. SOPHIE *joins her.*]

SOPHIE: Don't tell me you've lost your heart to Armand Duval. [*To* BELA] Only fools do that.

[*He turns on his heels and goes.*

The two women are left.

The old DUC *enters, helped by the young* GIRL, *who swerves away, guarding her prize. The old* DUC, *tired, waves vaguely, but is borne away.*

The sound of the music up as CLÉMENCE *and* SOPHIE *promenade, looking this way and that, displaying themselves.*

SCENE III

Marguerite's salon.
Screams. JANINE *runs on, pursued by* MARGUERITE.

JANINE: I never touched them!

MARGUERITE: Why were they under your bed then, you bitch?

JANINE: It wasn't me! Leave off! Marie!!

MARGUERITE: Nothing but trouble from the day you –

JANINE: It ain't fair! [*Sobbing noisily*] I was the one found Signor da Costa, if it was up to me he'd still be –

MARGUERITE: Well it ain't, so shut your gob –

JANINE: My nose is all swolled up –

MARGUERITE: The only trouble with your nose is the sodding great hole underneath it. Come on, where's the rest?

JANINE: Ow – what?

MARGUERITE: The moonstone collar and the pearls. If you've sold them –

[*She grabs* JANINE *by the hair and they fight, rolling on the floor.*

PRUDENCE *enters, followed by* JEAN, *the valet, with hatboxes. He grins at the fight, spits and goes.*]

PRUDENCE [*voice of brass*]: That's enough . . . that's enough! [*She lays about them with her parasol, parts them with expertise.*]

MARGUERITE: Robbing me from cellar to attic, you're going home to your pig-faced mother!

JANINE [*throwing stuff on the ground from her pockets*]: Go on, take it! I hope it sticks in your great mush and chokes you!

MARGUERITE: Hang on! Where do you think you're –

JANINE: I'm not staying here where I'm not appreciated! Who was it found Signor da Costa . . . me! [*She goes.*]

MARGUERITE: I'll bang her bloody head through that door.

PRUDENCE: They're all the same.

MARGUERITE: The linen slips through her hands like tiddlers, well, never met a laundress yet who wasn't light-fingered . . .

PRUDENCE [*sotto voce*]: You should know, dear.

[*Slight pause*]

She's right about da Costa, though.

[MARGUERITE *pulls a face.*]

My dear, the uglier the better . . . they pay up!

MARGUERITE: I hate her.

PRUDENCE: Well, that's because she's a little turd. But a good maid!

MARGUERITE: Biggest scroungers in the village. [*She grins.*] I only took her to show off.

PRUDENCE: Playing the lady? Well, why not? With those bones there isn't a door you couldn't kick open. I always had too much flesh. Flesh will take you so far, but after that it's bones – ooh, these are pretty! [*She swoops on the things* JANINE *has thrown down.*]

MARGUERITE [*without looking*]: Have them. [*She tries on a bonnet.*]

PRUDENCE [*prompt*]: That looks nice! Put it against what I owe you.

MARGUERITE: You don't think it makes me look pale?

PRUDENCE: All the better – class!

[SOPHIE *enters from bedroom, turns for* MARGUERITE *to hook her up, pulls a face at the hat,* MARGUERITE *pulls it off at once.* SOPHIE *tries on another bonnet, backwards, to tease* PRUDENCE.]

[*Nasty*] It makes your face look crooked . . . [*She grabs the hat crossly.*] . . . anyway, you couldn't afford it.

SOPHIE [*to* MARGUERITE]: Neither can you.

PRUDENCE: Unlike some I could mention, Marguerite is in funds. She's not a fool.

SOPHIE: Oh isn't she? Aren't you? [*But she relents, kisses* MARGUERITE *full on the lips, backs away dramatically from the hat-boxes.*] My life for a bonnet! [*She rolls her eyes, then, goosing* PRUDENCE, *goes, laughing.*]

PRUDENCE [*calls after* SOPHIE]: She's in for more than a bonnet! [*To* MARGUERITE] If you play your cards –

MARGUERITE: She's teasing!

PRUDENCE: You want to watch that girl. You shouldn't let her sleep with you for a start –

MARGUERITE [*surprised*]: Why not?

PRUDENCE: She coughs.

JEAN [*at the door*]: The woodman's here . . .

[MARGUERITE *gives him a note.*]

. . . there's last month's and all.

[*She gives him another, pulling a face.*]

JEAN-PAUL [*running on*]: Tan' Marie . . . Tan' Marie!

MARGUERITE: Jean-Paul! Ohh! [*She swings him round.*] . . . Yvette . . . I wasn't expecting you!

YVETTE [*enters*]: We got a ride on the potato cart.

MARGUERITE: Hoo, I bet your kidneys are red-hot. How's your mother . . . everything all right?

YVETTE: Yes thanks.

[MARGUERITE *waits*.]

Boots.

MARGUERITE: Ah! . . . he's growing – you're growing! [*She gives* YVETTE *money*.] Put it somewhere safe. [*To* JEAN-PAUL] What d'you fancy, what would you like – I know . . . cake!

JEAN-PAUL: Yes please!

YVETTE: Oh good, you said please.

MARGUERITE: Jean, fetch up a bottle of wine and some milk, and send out for an apple tart – oh, and bring up the chocolate cake.

JEAN: The one for tonight? Cook'll knife me –

MARGUERITE: Get on with you – here . . . [*She gives him a cigar. He goes.*]

PRUDENCE: No need to give him good cigars. You spoil them.

MARGUERITE [*to* YVETTE]: He's been well?

YVETTE: Ooh yes. Been climbing trees, 'aven't you?

JEAN-PAUL: Yes!

MARGUERITE: Here . . . littl'un . . .

[JEAN-PAUL, *who has been playing with the hats, turns to* MARGUERITE, *giving the hat to* YVETTE, *who smoothes it.*]

PRUDENCE: Ooh, be careful! [*making* YVETTE *jump*] You'll pull the threads! [*To* MARGUERITE] Her hands are rough, she'll pull the threads!

[MARGUERITE *gives* PRUDENCE *a venomous look, bends, finds a package and opens it, watched by the child.*]

MARGUERITE: I been keeping this for you.

[*It is a carousel.* JEAN-PAUL *lifts it reverently.*]

Look . . . [*She turns a handle and the carousel turns, playing a tune. He laughs. She watches his face. He takes the carousel, turns the handle.*]

JEAN-PAUL: Will it go backwards?

MARGUERITE: No, you'll break it.

YVETTE [*automatic*]: What do you say?

JEAN-PAUL: Thank you, *Tan'* Marie.

YVETTE: That's it.

MARGUERITE [*lifts him up*]: You still my little man?

JEAN-PAUL [*throws his arms about her neck*]: I'm your man!

JEAN: *Monsieur le Duc.*

MARGUERITE: Where?

JEAN: On the stairs.

MARGUERITE: God in heaven . . . [*She hugs* JEAN-PAUL *and runs, returns in anguish to kiss him again and flies out to bedroom, gesturing to* PRUDENCE *to see to things.*]

PRUDENCE [*to* JEAN]: Quick, down to the kitchen . . . goodbye, young man . . . that's right . . . [*as* JEAN-PAUL *takes his carousel firmly under his arm . . . She pushes* YVETTE *out firmly.*]

YVETTE: What? [*Confused, she is pushed out with the child.*]

PRUDENCE: Ah, *Monsieur le Duc* . . . !

DUC [*enters*]: M' lead horse went lame, so I walked!

JEAN: Glass of wine, Your Grace?

    [JANINE, *in full regalia, ribbons flying, swoops on with a silver tray.*]

DUC: Ah, Janine! And how is Janine this evening . . . sweet little thing!

PRUDENCE: Oh adorable.

JANINE: Wicked Jean, not making you comfortable –

JEAN: Hop it, you – clear off. [*to* UPHOLSTERER, *who sticks his head through the door*]

UPHOLSTERER: Three hundred francs or that sofa goes.

PRUDENCE: Glorious weather, Duke!

DUC: Is it, by God?

JEAN: Out.

UPHOLSTERER: Oh no, sonny, this foot remains.

JANINE [*stamping on it*]: No it don't.

    [*They push him out as* PRUDENCE *refills the* DUC's *glass.*]

DUC: Steady on, gal. Don't want to be *hors de combat.*

PRUDENCE: Early evening visits . . . so much more satisfactory.

UPHOLSTERER: Can I have my three hundred francs? [*as* MARGUERITE *enters.*

    MARGUERITE *shrugs and pulls a face. She has no more money.*]

JANINE: No you can't. Here . . . [*She gives him a big, juicy kiss.*]

UPHOLSTERER [*stumbling*]: Yes, well . . .

[*The* DUC, *seemingly unaware, puts his hand in his pocket, hands* MARGUERITE *a roll. She gives some to* JANINE, *who palms half, gives the rest to the* UPHOLSTERER *and pushes him out, following him.* MARGUERITE *puts the rest of the money away.* JEAN *disappears,* MARGUERITE *slips a note to* PRUDENCE *for keeping the old man happy.*]

MARGUERITE: *Mon cher!* No don't get up – that's an order.

DUC: Yours to command, she's so strict. I walked!

MARGUERITE: Good, you must be rewarded . . . however, if you haven't been behaving yourself I shall find out . . . let me say goodbye to Prudence . . .

DUC: Ah, Prudence . . . settling up, eh . . . active as ever?

PRUDENCE: *Plus ça change, cher Duc* . . . you old fool. [*To* MARGUERITE *at exit*] Shall I say yes to Armand?

MARGUERITE: Armand?

PRUDENCE: Duval. You said he might call.

MARGUERITE: No I didn't!

[*The* DUC *becomes restless, they giggle mechanically.*]

Prudence, I shall tell! Prudence is being very wicked about you, *Monsieur le Duc!* [*Sotto voce*] Why should I?

[*The* DUC *hems.*]

Oh very well, bring him with the others, damn you. [*She turns to the* DUC.] *Mon cher* Hercule, what are we going to do with you, hmm?

[PRUDENCE *slips away.*]

DUC: Something special?

MARGUERITE: Only if you're good.

DUC: I am, I am!

MARGUERITE: Are you? No, I don't think so. I think you're telling me a lie. You know what happens to little boys who tell lies, don't you?

DUC: I am a good boy, I am a good boy . . .

[*She helps him out.*]

Oh, my lovely Camille . . . oh . . .

Light change.
The same, evening.
JANINE *and* JEAN *come and go, preparing the room for a party.*
They move furniture and bring on flowers and glasses. JEAN *opens*
the piano. They bump into each other and she mutters and curses
irritably. He pulls a face at her. They finish and stand, surveying
their work. She tweaks a flower arrangement and is satisfied.

JEAN: Fancy a duck's wing?
JANINE: Asso to you.
JEAN: Yeah, that'll do.
  [*He gooses her, she yelps. Then they go, separately.*
  Pause.

  MARGUERITE *enters, a glass of water in her hand. She strolls,*
  sips, inspecting the room lazily. She touches a piece of
  furniture. And another.]
MARGUERITE: My things. My lovely things.
  [*She takes another turn, throws herself down in a chair. She*
  leans back, enjoying the rare moment of quiet.]
[*Puzzled*] I'm happy.
Why am I happy?
  [DE SANCERRE, *in the shadows, draws on his cigar so that we*
  see the glow. He walks up behind her.]
I'm expecting guests. [*But he stands, immovable.*
  She rises and crosses, he follows. Resigned]
You bastard.
  [*They exit.*
  Lights down.
  JEAN *enters with a candelabrum.* JANINE *enters separately*
  and idles, 'tidying'. She steps forward as DE SANCERRE
  enters, tying his stock.]
JANINE: Let me do it, sir. [*She ties his stock. He nods his thanks.*]
  Not at all, *Monsieur.* Anything you wish, *Monsieur.*
DE SANCERRE [*inspecting her coldly*]: Bones of a pigeon.
JANINE: Oh yes. I'd crack ever so easily . . . *Monsieur.*

[*She waits in his path, looking up at him with cool expectancy.*]

DE SANCERRE: You want to be careful.

JANINE: Oh I'm ever so careful, Monsieur de Sancerre.

[*He glares at her dangerously. But he puts his hand in his pocket and gives her money. And goes.*

JANINE *goes.*]

MARGUERITE [*off, furious*]: Janine!

JANINE [*off*]: I didn't know he was here, I never knew nothing!

MARGUERITE [*off*]: You devil, how much did he give you . . . I'll murder you –

[JANINE *runs on with an armful of crumpled sheets.*]

JANINE: How was I supposed to know! [*She stops short at the sight of a young man* (COUNT DRUFTHEIM) *who has entered with a large bunch of flowers and a package.* JANINE *changes key effortlessly.*] Monsieur le Comte . . . what a surprise. Mademoiselle will be pleased.

[*The young man, stiff and awkward, is the same young man who has been frightened off by* SOPHIE *in scene one. He is Swedish, with an accent.*]

COUNT: You think so? That is good.

JANINE: Take a seat. Wine?

[*He shakes his head, clutching his package and the flowers.*] How are you?

COUNT: I am very well. Apart, of course, from my heels.

JANINE: What? Oh . . . yes. I expect they'll get better soon. [*She gestures, offering to take the flowers, but he resists.*] You're in for a jolly time.

COUNT [*alarmed*]: Oh?

JANINE: We're having a party.

COUNT [*blanching*]: But I thought –

JANINE: No, you'll enjoy it – never mind, perhaps they won't stay long. Tell you what, I'll get rid of them for you.

[*She stands over him till he understands and gives her money. It is not enough.*]

Well, I'll try. Trouble is, they'll all very likely be giving me something to let the party run on. If you see what I mean.

COUNT [*gives her more money*]: This is enough?

JANINE: Oh, aren't you nice! I'm always telling Mam'selle what a sensitive man you are, *Monsieur le Comte*.

COUNT: Yes, that is true.

JANINE: I know, I just said so.

    [*Hiatus*]

    Oh . . . ah – the weather . . .

COUNT [*brightening*]: Ah! The weather! This morning was cold, I think one, maybe two degrees of frost, this is not unusual for time of year but damaging with these plants which are began their grow. I am thinking to wear ulster, you know what is this, an ulster? . . . for the possibility of rain because when I am looking outside window . . . hoop! [*He makes her jump.*] Black cloud! But when I have eaten my good breakfast and I am performed my exercises, hullo . . . black cloud is no more, so now perhaps it is possible no rain, but maybe later, so must I wear my good Swedish jacket for sure and – ow! [*as* JANINE *clouts him over the ear.*]

JANINE: Oh! No, it's all right, thought I saw a spider in your ear . . . there it is! [*Clips him another one*] Oh, it's only a bit of fluff . . .

COUNT: Oof!

JANINE: . . . still – don't want spiders in your ears, do we? [*She dusts him down.*]

COUNT [*his hand to his reeling head*]: Ooh . . . !

JANINE: All right?

    [*He nods, dodging warily.*]

    Uh . . . let's think – I know, how are the coins?

COUNT [*smiles happily*]: Ah, my good coins! I am –

JANINE: Haven't sold them then?

COUNT [*baffled*]: Sold? My coins? No, no, this I could never –

    [JANINE *is saved by* MARGUERITE *who enters, sees the* COUNT, *tries to withdraw, but it is too late.*]

MARGUERITE: Dear Canute! [*She pulls a face at* JANINE.]

COUNT [*loses his composure*]: Ah . . . ah . . . er . . . ah . . .

MARGUERITE: Still afflicted? And I thought we were making progress.

COUNT: Ah . . . oeer . . . er . . . ah . . . [*He thrusts the flowers at her.*]

MARGUERITE: How lovely! For me? Oh. Chrysanthemums.

COUNT: They are not fresh? . . . but I was assured —

JANINE: They're funeral flowers! For your grave.

COUNT: This is true? In Sweden not so.

JANINE: Well it is here. [*She sweeps them away and goes.*]

COUNT: Forgive me, please. [*He proffers a wrapped box.*]

MARGUERITE: It's nothing. [*She opens the box.*] Oh, what beautiful shoes!

COUNT: They are fitting? Please to try.

MARGUERITE: I'm sure they'll fit . . .

COUNT: Please to try. [*With an effort*] My dear.

MARGUERITE: There . . . that wasn't so difficult, was it?

> [*He kneels, puts the shoes on her feet with reverent excitement. In the second shoe is a diamond necklace.*]

Canute? Canute! Oh, they're lovely! [*She jumps to her feet.*] Like drops of rain!

> [*He does up the clasp.*]

Look . . . like tears!

COUNT: Yes, as in Sweden when the snow is melting . . .

MARGUERITE: Yes!

COUNT: First comes little drops, plink, plink, so . . . and then plink, plink, plink . . . and quickly now . . . plink, plink, plink, plink . . . and now running, plinkety pionk, plinkety plonk, plinkety plonk . . .

> [*The piano drowns him.*]

. . . yes, that is so . . . exactly this! [*He capers, still plinking, and dances, pulling her into the dance. And stopping abruptly as* JEAN *shows in* PRUDENCE, SOPHIE, CLÉMENCE *and* BELA.

> MARGUERITE *claps.*]

MARGUERITE: The Count was showing me an old Swedish dance — Clémence, Count Druftheim. From Sweden. Mademoiselle Clémence de Villeneuve.

CLÉMENCE: What's it called? [*She tries a hop.*]

COUNT: It is called the hopping dance.

> [*She hops, he hops, it turns into a galumph. She shrieks*

96

*happily as he hurls her round, then gives him a push which
. sends him flying. She pulls him up, laughing heartily.*]

CLÉMENCE: I enjoyed that!

COUNT: Yah!

[*They join hands to start again.*]

PRUDENCE: Enough! Dear Count, lovely to see you again . . . so
soon. [*She pulls a face at* MARGUERITE.] I thought Marguerite
was going to keep you all to herself. [*To* MARGUERITE, *as*
CLÉMENCE *talks to the* COUNT] My dear, you look enchanting.
Duval couldn't keep his eyes off you last night.

MARGUERITE: I hope he means to be more amiable this evening.

BELA [*approaching*]: Who?

PRUDENCE: Armand. He's joining us.

BELA: Here?

PRUDENCE: Why not?

BELA: I don't think so.

MARGUERITE: But can you assure me?

BELA: Absolutely. He's at the table enjoying the greatest pleasure
in the world . . . he's winning.

CLÉMENCE [*coy*]: And what's the second greatest pleasure in the
world, Prince?

BELA [*inspects her coldly*]: The second greatest pleasure in the
world is losing. [*He turns his back on her and walks away.*

CLÉMENCE *is furious at the snub.* SOPHIE *hands* CLÉMENCE
a glass of champagne.]

CLÉMENCE: Last time he set fire to the furniture! [*She crosses to
the* COUNT, *who is standing alone, awkward and shy.*] Not
bored, Count?

COUNT: Oh no . . .

CLÉMENCE: Only I know you foreigners – all that travel, you're
bound to be debonair.

COUNT: Yah.

CLÉMENCE: It must be nice coming from a long thin country like
Sweden. Cold though.

COUNT: Oh yah, yah! For example now in Sweden we are still in
the muff and the gaiter, and many degrees of frost . . . also fug.

[*stifled laughter from the others*]

BELA [*polite*]: Fug?

COUNT: Oh yah, very wide fug –

[*The others laugh aloud.*]

PRUDENCE: Marguerite, for God's sake play something!

MARGUERITE [*from over her shoulder as she moves apart with* SOPHIE]: Play? For my friends? Certainly not, I wouldn't be so cruel! [*To* SOPHIE, *apart*] What do you mean, leave Paris, if you need money I'll find it – I can get it for you tonight!

SOPHIE: No!

MARGUERITE: Why not?

[SOPHIE *doesn't reply. She inspects* MARGUERITE'S *new necklace.*]

Well?

SOPHIE: Exquisite.

MARGUERITE: Have them.

[SOPHIE *scoffs and walks off.* MARGUERITE *pursues her.*]

You want to be a laundress again?

[SOPHIE *smiles mockingly.*]

Suit yourself. [*Hisses, in a fury*] I've no such intention. Ever. [*She plays with the diamonds at her throat as* PRUDENCE *returns, with* BELA. PRUDENCE *inspects the necklace.*]

PRUDENCE: You must get them insured.

BELA: And keep an eye on your assets.

[*He gestures towards* CLÉMENCE *and the* COUNT, *who are laughing. They move away together.*]

CLÉMENCE [*intimately, to the* COUNT]: How many castles?

COUNT: Seven. My favourite is Druftenen . . .

CLÉMENCE: Ooh! Is that the biggest?

COUNT: It is very old and here is the bestest collection of my father and my grandfather and me –

CLÉMENCE: Collection? Jewels?

COUNT [*baffled*]: Please? Here are harness of horses of my family since many hundred years, also wheels and implements of many doings and makings, also specimen of mineral and fossil, carcase and small shell –

[*There is a general shriek of protest.*]

PRUDENCE: Play, play!

[*Music.*

BELA *hurls himself around the room in a wild Slavic dance, ending with a scarf around the* COUNT's *neck and the* COUNT *at his feet.*

Applause.]

SOPHIE [*clapping slowly after the applause has ended*]: Bravo. You dance like a peasant.

PRUDENCE [*calls*]: That's a compliment, *Monsieur le Prince*, believe me.

BELA [*snub*]: Indeed, Madame? [*He pursues* SOPHIE *as she moves apart.*] Shall I see you in the *Bois*?

SOPHIE: Undoubtedly, since I'm there every morning for my dogs to relieve themselves.

BELA: I'll join you.

SOPHIE: They bite.

BELA: Why do you never smile?

SOPHIE: A preference.

[*They regard each other steadily.*

MARGUERITE *sings.*]

MARGUERITE: Let me forever in tenderness lie,
Though doubt and darkness invade and enfold.
Here in your arms let me know no despair –

[*As the song begins* ARMAND *enters quietly. He stands by the door, watching* MARGUERITE. *She moves about, singing, unaware of him. On the third line of the song she turns and sees him. And breaks off at once and comes across the room to greet him with friendly formality.*]

Monsieur Duval?

ARMAND: Good evening, Mademoiselle Gautier.

[MARGUERITE *contemplates him for an instant. Then she breaks into a cheerful, vulgar song, dancing among her friends as she sings, and they join her in the choruses.*]

MARGUERITE [*sings, dancing*]:

The major's on the doorstep,
The colonel's on the stair,
The brigadier's in the chamber,
His corsets in the air . . .

But here's the cavalry captain,
A-galloping at full stride,
Bump de bump de bump de bump,
To take me for a ride.

[*The others join in.*]

Bump de bump de bump de bump!

The admiral's in the arbour
The subaltern's in the hall,
And two or three more outside the door,
And one perched on the wall . . .
But here's the cavalry captain,
A-galloping at full stride,
With a bump de bump de bump de bump,
To take me for a ride!

[*Laughter and applause.* ARMAND *stands, apart.*]
PRUDENCE: Bravo, bravo – I'm starving!
CLÉMENCE: Hungry, Count?
COUNT: Yah, most hungry!
CLÉMENCE: Come on, then, so am I! What's your favourite, mine's game pie . . . well, I like everything! There's nothing I don't like!
    [*They go.*]
PRUDENCE: She's such a good listener, Clémence.
BELA: Good. He can tell her all about the sewage systems of Stockholm. [*Raises his voice*] What's the matter?
MARGUERITE [*by the piano, suppressing a cough*]: Nothing, I caught my breath.
BELA: Is she ill?
PRUDENCE: Marguerite? Heavens, no . . . strong as a racehorse.
    [*She waits for his arm, but he stares across to* ARMAND.
    PRUDENCE *exits alone.*]
BELA [*to* ARMAND]: Are you coming?
    [*A slight pause.*
    Then BELA *exits.*]

MARGUERITE: Monsieur Duval? [*But she is taken with a prolonged fit of coughing.*

He fetches water. She drinks. The spasm subsides.]
Thank you. I must have swallowed a feather.

ARMAND [*takes the glass, sets it down*]: Why do you sing that song? It doesn't suit you.

MARGUERITE: You prefer something more sentimental? You surprise me, Monsieur Duval.

ARMAND: Why, have you been studying me?

MARGUERITE: No more than the door handle.

ARMAND: It's not your style.

MARGUERITE: What would you like me to sing? Something more elevated? Don't delude yourself, Monsieur – [*But she coughs again.*

He gives her his handkerchief as she waves away the water. She recovers, attempts a smile.]

ARMAND: Shall I send them away?

MARGUERITE: Of course not! [*She crosses, looks at herself in the glass.*] Heavens, how pale I look!

ARMAND: May I stay?

[*She shakes her head.*]
Why not?

MARGUERITE: It's impossible.

ARMAND: Why?

[*She lifts her hand with a smile of apology.*]
Is he coming back? De Sancerre?

MARGUERITE: Have you been spying on me?

ARMAND: Why can't I stay?

MARGUERITE: I'm not obliged to give you reasons.

ARMAND: Don't you like me?

MARGUERITE: No.

ARMAND: I think you do.

[MARGUERITE *walks about, inspecting him from time to time.*]

MARGUERITE [*pause*]: You lack grace, Monsieur Duval. It might do for some. Not for me.

ARMAND: Allow me to put myself in your hands.

MARGUERITE [*slight pause*]: Why do you seek to be less than you are?

ARMAND: You think I should aspire?

MARGUERITE: It might be more interesting.

ARMAND: Don't tell me you require virtue?

MARGUERITE: That would be provincial, would it not? [*She walks away from him again.*
  He watches her.]

ARMAND: Are you going to name your terms? And allow me to fill them?

MARGUERITE: What I should require from you is not, I think, yours to bestow.

ARMAND: And what is that?

MARGUERITE: Respect.
  [*He laughs aloud.*]
I mean, towards yourself.

ARMAND [*slight pause*]: Myself?

MARGUERITE: And a little honour.

ARMAND [*cold*]: You accuse me of lack of honour?

MARGUERITE: Oh, I daresay you keep faith with those of your sort. I'm talking of another kind of honour.

ARMAND: And what kind is that?

MARGUERITE: Between a man and a woman.

ARMAND: Ah, you want gallantry?

MARGUERITE: Just mutual courtesy. You find that bizarre?

ARMAND: I don't know what you're talking about.

MARGUERITE: No. Because you have a black heart. You're a monster.

ARMAND [*blocking her path urgently*]: Allow me to prove that I'm not.

MARGUERITE: Then begin by allowing me to pass. Which you are preventing.
  [*He bows, offers her his arm.*]
Thank you, Monsieur Armand. Why are you smiling?

ARMAND: You called me Armand.
  [*A game of hide and seek.* SOPHIE *and* CLÉMENCE *hide.* BELA
  hides under MARGUERITE's *skirt. The* COUNT *enters, finds*

102

the girls. The women range around MARGUERITE, *lift their skirts,* MARGUERITE *last.* BELA *emerges and the* COUNT *is shocked.* MARGUERITE *whispers to him, forcing a smile from him.*

A waltz. The COUNT *dances with* MARGUERITE, ARMAND *with* SOPHIE, BELA *with* CLÉMENCE. *The mood is languid.*

Light change.
ARMAND *dances with* BELA. *The others pass an opium pipe between them.*

MARGUERITE, *dreamy, dances alone.* ARMAND, *sitting apart with* BELA, *watches her. He gets up, and takes her in his arms. They dance.*

Light change.
ARMAND *and* MARGUERITE, *dancing together. The others are sleepy. Only* BELA *watches.*]

MARGUERITE [*as they dance*]: Why?

ARMAND: Because I must.

MARGUERITE: Is it so important?

ARMAND: Yes!

MARGUERITE: Oh, if it's so important . . .

ARMAND: Not if it isn't to you.

MARGUERITE: To me? You *are* sentimental! Such games come expensive in this house.

ARMAND: I don't want to play games.

MARGUERITE: Monsieur Armand, what do you want from me?

ARMAND: I want the truth.

MARGUERITE: The truth? Oh, I don't think you can afford that.

ARMAND: Nevertheless it's what I want.

MARGUERITE: Please go away. Your friend is waiting. Go away with him, please.

ARMAND: No.

MARGUERITE: You see? You are a monster.

ARMAND: If I am, you make me so. [*He stands before her, refusing to move.*]

BELA: Armand, are you coming?

MARGUERITE: Please go away.

ARMAND: No.

[*Pause*]

MARGUERITE: Very well. One night. If you insist. Then you can say that you know Marguerite Gautier. And that she is a disappointment.

ARMAND: Why should I say that?

MARGUERITE: I don't mind what you say, so long as you go!

ARMAND: Very well.

MARGUERITE: I have your word.

ARMAND: I promise to do whatever you want.

BELA: Armand –

ARMAND: I'm staying!

[*He lifts his head briefly in triumph, then follows* MARGUERITE *off.*

BELA *crosses. He pauses, and* PRUDENCE *puts a consoling hand on his arm. He thrusts her away angrily and goes.* CLÉMENCE *and the* COUNT *leave together.* PRUDENCE *wakes* SOPHIE, *and they go.*]

SCENE V

The bedroom. ARMAND *and* MARGUERITE *in bed. They are making love.* ARMAND *gasps.*

MARGUERITE *groans.*

ARMAND [*soft*]: What is it?

MARGUERITE: Nothing, nothing.

[*Pause.*
He whispers. She laughs very softly. They murmur. Then silence.

Lights to black.]

The bedroom. ARMAND *and* MARGUERITE.

MARGUERITE: How many?

ARMAND: None. Till now.

MARGUERITE: Liar. You must have been in love. Tell me.
[*Pause*]

ARMAND: I did love someone once.

MARGUERITE: Who? Who?

ARMAND: My father's riding master.

MARGUERITE [*slight pause*]: Was he handsome?

ARMAND: No. He was short and bandy, and had a foul tongue. [*He lies back, remembering.*] He lived with his mother and farted a lot.

MARGUERITE: Why did you love him?

ARMAND [*shrugs*]: I don't know. He turned my bowels.

MARGUERITE: No one else?

ARMAND [*slight pause*]: There was a girl –

MARGUERITE: Aha!
[*But he looks at her bleakly.*]
What was she like?

ARMAND: Ordinary. We were to have been married but it was postponed – her grandmother died. Meaner than a rat's ass.

MARGUERITE: Because she wouldn't? You might have refused to marry her because she wasn't a virgin – men do! No one since? I see. That's why you're unhappy.

ARMAND [*surprised*]: I'm not unhappy.

MARGUERITE: You're full of grief. [*She strokes his hair.*
He looks at her then leaps out of bed and prowls round the room, touching things.]

ARMAND: I love it here. Everything in this room. Everything you see . . . everything you touch . . . I love the mirror because it sees your face – I love these . . . [*He picks up a bottle.*]

MARGUERITE: Look at the crests, the initials. All different. Remember *that* when you start to feel sentimental.

ARMAND [*returns, leaps on to the bed, standing over her*]: Why did you let me stay?

MARGUERITE: Because you were a nuisance.

ARMAND: You could have had me thrown out.

MARGUERITE: Yes.

[*He embraces her passionately.*
Light change.
MARGUERITE *and* ARMAND, *in bed together.*
A pause. Then she lifts her head and regards him levelly.]

MARGUERITE: Very well. If you must. [*Slight pause*] My mother was a laundress. On a big estate.

ARMAND: Where?

MARGUERITE [*vague*]: Oh . . . in the country. My father died when I was nine. I have four younger brothers. [*Slight pause*] And I have a son.

ARMAND [*slight pause*]: You have a child?

MARGUERITE: Yes.

ARMAND: Where is he?

MARGUERITE: With a farmer's wife.

ARMAND: Is that why you . . . how you came to . . . to be . . . do you live this life because you love it . . . is that why you – ?

[MARGUERITE *throws back her head and laughs at him.*]

Go on . . . tell me everything – I want to know!

[MARGUERITE *leaps off the bed and walks about like a tiger.*]

MARGUERITE: You want to know? You want to know? What do you know? I know the way you live! Hot-house grapes, lofts full of apples, figs with the bloom on them . . . stables, libraries, a fire in your room. [*She lopes, fiery and restless.*] I used to clean the grates with my mother . . . five o'clock in the morning on tiptoe while you all snored. I saw them! The rugs, the pictures, the furniture . . . chandeliers . . . music rooms, ballrooms . . . all a hundred metres from where we lived on potatoes and turnips, and slept, the seven of us together, in a coach-house loft.

ARMAND [*slight pause*]: Are you accusing me?

MARGUERITE: Yes.

[*Pause*]

MARGUERITE: At thirteen, I became a housemaid. I slept in an attic

. . . my own bed, you can't believe the bliss! I couldn't wait to get up in the morning! To be in such a palace . . .

[*Pause.*

He shakes her gently to make her continue. She looks at him and away.]

After two years *Monsieur le Marquis* took me into his bed. It was his habit with the younger maids. It kept him young. A year later I had our son.

[*She plays with the quilt for a moment then speaks with musing objectivity.*]

You have no idea what difference a child makes. Your life is quite changed. For ever. Of course, with a man, this can never happen. Not in the same way.

ARMAND: How do you mean?

MARGUERITE: You're no longer alone. You're connected . . . with someone who is, and isn't you. Your own flesh. I love my brothers of course . . . but . . . you grow up . . . you go away, you're on your own. Until, if you're a woman, you have a child. Then you're never alone again. Whether you wish it or not . . . whether you see the child or not. It's there. Part of you. Of your body. You have reason . . . purpose – oh, no destiny too fine, for the child!

[*Pause*]

[*Light*]: I hardly ever see him. He thinks I'm his aunt.

[*She pauses . . . then, as* ARMAND *starts to speak*]

I was dismissed, of course. I went to my mother's sister and sat by the river wondering what to do. I had no money. The most sensible thing seemed to be to drown myself.

[*Pause*]

And then, one morning . . . my cousin came into my room. I was putting on my stockings – he started to shake. I didn't have the strength to push him away. Afterwards, he put his finger to his lips, and gave me a gold coin.

And there it was. I knew. All of a sudden. How to do it. How to go through the magic door. How to be warm, how to be comfortable . . . eat fine food, wear fine clothes, read fine books, listen to fine music. I had the key. A golden key. [*She laughs.*]

After all . . . what had I got to lose? Innocence? That had gone before I was five.

[*He leans on his elbow abruptly.*]

Look at me. I was a pretty child – do you know what that means? It means when your uncle sits you on his lap and gives you sweets he puts his thumb in you. It was worse after my father died. I had no protector – no one to break their jaws . . . and, there are the cakes . . . the apples . . . the money pressed into your hand, if you promise not to tell.

[*She pauses, dreamy.*]

My mother sent me for some vegetables one day. It was Sunday, the church bells were ringing. My uncle was in one of the hot-houses, pruning the peaches. He said I look flushed – I was hot, I'd been running. And then he said, 'Come over here' . . . and sat on some sacks. So I sat down. And he said, 'Well, my little maid, are you ready for me yet?' God, you should have seen the mess. I put up a terrible fight, had the whole tree down on him, but he took me anyway. He made me get a bucket of water after – to clean up the blood in case the dogs came sniffing.

ARMAND: I'm surprised you don't hate us.

MARGUERITE: Hate . . . love . . . [*She shrugs.*]

ARMAND: Yes. What about love?

MARGUERITE: Love? [*She laughs aloud.*] Love? Seven pregnancies in nine years? Arms swollen with soda from washing stains from other people's linen? Ask my mother. No. No love. Anyway, I had a child to support.

ARMAND: How did you come to Paris?

MARGUERITE: I took a chance. I went back to the house . . . the family were away . . . let myself in . . . and helped myself. I filled a valise and two basket trunks with what I needed – clothes, wraps, jewellery . . . even books. I took from that profusion what wasn't wanted, needed . . . or regarded. I equipped myself. Then I called up the butler. I said that *Monsieur le Marquis* had been kind enough to make provision for my change of address, and gave him the name of a hotel I'd found on the morning-room table. I fetched my son, took him where I knew he'd be well cared for . . . and I came to Paris! And sat in a hotel room for five days crying for my baby, and waiting for the police to arrive. I laid it all out . . . the ribbons, the shoes, the garnets that had never been worn, the turquoises that made Milady's skin look yellow. I sat, with my tortoise-shell brushes, the box with the violets from Parma on the lid, the bonnets, and the cape. You have no idea of the magic of things when you've never had any.

And nobody came.

And the first day I went out walking . . . he rode past me. *Monsieur le Marquis.*

ARMAND: What did he do?

MARGUERITE: Got out of his carriage, and hit me in the face. I still have the scar from his ring.

[*He inspects her face.*]

Now you know.

ARMAND: You're a lion. A tiger. A leopard. I honour your courage . . . and I respect your choice.

MARGUERITE: Choice?

ARMAND: To be a huntress, a marauder. [*But he looks away.*]

MARGUERITE: Nonetheless . . .

ARMAND: Nonetheless?

MARGUERITE: There is always a nonetheless. Nonetheless, how can I bear it? The life? It's what you all want to know. I bear it very well. At first you shut your eyes and dream of the handsome valet, the boy with the brown eyes. After that, if you're successful, who has time to think? And who's to say what goes on in our heads?

ARMAND: What do you think of when we make love?

MARGUERITE: Of you.

ARMAND: How can I be sure?

MARGUERITE: You can't.

[*They laugh.*]

ARMAND: What is it between us? From the moment I saw you, no gap . . . no distance. You accept my ugliness —

MARGUERITE: You're not ugly.

ARMAND: Oh I am. Believe me, I am. [*He studies her face.*] I don't have to open my mouth, you know what I'm thinking. You understand my disgust, my resentment. You don't condemn, but you're not indifferent – what is it? This . . . possibility between us – something . . . a possibility for something other. [*He slaps the pillow, then relaxes on his back.*] I'm at home with you. I never had a home before.

MARGUERITE: You? No home!?

ARMAND: No home. No family – except servants. I was sent away to school at four.

MARGUERITE: Your mother? Sent you away? Your mother?

ARMAND: Yes. My mother – the Duke's daughter. [*Slight pause*] Everything . . . the warmth of her smile, nuance of expression, inclination of her glance, every waking thought honed, tuned and fine-pleated to the smallest print of the hierarchy of class. Beyond excluding the rest of the world my mother felt, my mother said, my mother did nothing. Why should she? My mother was a lady.

MARGUERITE [*slight pause*]: And your father?

ARMAND: Like me. A cold devil.

> [*She kisses him.*]

When you kiss me, I come to life.

MARGUERITE [*bends over him, kisses him*]: Wake up, Armand.
> [*Crossfade.*
>
> MARGUERITE *sits on the side of the bed, begins to put on her stockings.*]

ARMAND [*lying on his stomach, sleepy*]: Where are you going?

MARGUERITE: I'm not. But you must.

ARMAND: Why?

MARGUERITE: Because I ask you.

ARMAND: Why? I'm never going . . . you know that – I tell you every minute of every day. Do you want to go out? Shall I drive you in the park? Tell me what you want, I'll get it for you.

MARGUERITE: Ssh. Please. You know you must go.

ARMAND: No one is to touch you. Ever again.

MARGUERITE: Please.

ARMAND: No. Never. I won't have it.

MARGUERITE: My dear, how am I to live?

ARMAND: I think I hate you.

MARGUERITE: No. No you don't.

ARMAND: You devil. All a lie, was it? Yes. Of course.

MARGUERITE [*goes off to change, calls*]: No, none of it. You know that. But what am I to do? How can I afford you if –

ARMAND: I can afford you!

[MARGUERITE *returns, towel in hand.*]

MARGUERITE: No. Never. The day that you pay for me I'm a dead woman.

ARMAND: Marguerite, please . . . oh my dear . . . my dearest love. You must understand . . . I can't allow you to . . . how can we be better – of course I must take care of you, it's my right and duty –

MARGUERITE: Please . . . don't. You know me for what I am – allow me to give what I'm able.

ARMAND: You mean, go on as before? With the old man? That fool of a Count? De Sancerre?

MARGUERITE: Why not?

ARMAND: I shall give orders that no one is to be admitted. No one is to enter.

MARGUERITE: If you do I shall never let you see me again. Can't you see . . . you mustn't pay! You must see that. How can you be jealous? I've known so many men, what difference does it make? Armand . . . you know, you knew that about me. Take what you can. What there is.

ARMAND: No. No more of it. That's over, for both of us. It's possible. A new life . . . a new way.

MARGUERITE: For how long? A month? Three? Six? [*She rises, resumes her restless prowl.*] Oh why should I justify my life to you? You'll betray me, like the rest of them. When desire fails . . . d'you think I'd lend you my heart for an instant – I'd be a fool! Give up my life? For what? [*She approaches him.*] Don't you know what I'm risking as it is? Prudence tells me to throw you out before you spend all my money. Sophie says I'm a fool, Bela refuses to speak to me . . . you're chasing my friends away – I need my friends! Even Clémence is moving in on my most reliable attachment . . . I don't know what to do – [*She starts to cry.*]

ARMAND [*abrupt*]: Don't do that.

MARGUERITE: The bank never leaves me alone – I have creditors at the door –

ARMAND: How much do they want, I'll pay it!

MARGUERITE: No. Nothing. Try to understand. If you pay, it's finished between us. I can afford you, for a little while at least. [*She coughs a little.*]

ARMAND: Have I not made myself clear? I mean to stay for ever.

MARGUERITE: For ever? Oh my dear, however short my life, it will last longer than your love.

ARMAND: You don't trust me. Come away with me. We'll find a house in the country, take your son –

MARGUERITE [*sharp*]: No. [*She covers quickly.*] It's not possible.

ARMAND: Why not?

MARGUERITE: I can't leave Paris.

ARMAND: Why not, you're free –

MARGUERITE: You think it's so simple? For Armand Duval, perhaps. A little adventure and arms await you. Armand Duval trips and there's a goosedown pillow to break his fall. The winds blow colder for me.

ARMAND: We won't be coming back.

MARGUERITE [*going off to dress*]: Oh? What guarantee can you give me? Your heart? Can I burn that to keep out the cold? You think I can leave everything . . . this is a house of business. It runs on credit. When my creditors hear I'm not seeing de Sancerre there'll be the devil to pay –

ARMAND [*calls*]: But you can't bear him!

MARGUERITE [*calls, off*]: His mother was a Rothschild, I can bear him very well.

ARMAND: Trust me. Come with me. Live with me. What do the rest of them matter . . . what does any of it matter?

MARGUERITE [*laughs, off*]: I've heard it all before! For you . . . for your eyes . . . for your breasts! [*She comes back, in her stays.*] You'd be back.

ARMAND [*lacing her stays*]: Why are you so sure?

MARGUERITE: Because, my dear, it's in your interest, as it's in mine to guard my freedom. God knows it's cost me enough. [*She kisses him lightly on the lips.*] We have what we have.

ARMAND: We have each other, what else do we need?

MARGUERITE: Are you asking me to be poor again . . . haul icy water, lift bales of straw for the price of a loaf? No. Not again. Ever.

ARMAND: Marguerite, I'm prepared to change my life for you –

MARGUERITE: And my life?

ARMAND: I'm asking you to marry me.

[Pause]

MARGUERITE: You're mad. You don't know what you're talking about!

[She bursts into abrupt and wild laughter.]

ARMAND: Very well. Since you find the idea ludicrous, we won't marry! It's all the same to me. It would undoubtedly bore you in a month and you'd misbehave . . . so, my beloved lion, don't you see . . . we're free! To do as we please! [He grasps and embraces her, rolling her on the bed, teasing her.] Too much love . . . that's what it is . . . too much love . . .

I'll arrange everything.

MARGUERITE: No.

ARMAND: Why not?

MARGUERITE: They won't let us.

ARMAND: They can't prevent it.

MARGUERITE: Can't they?

ARMAND: Trust me.

MARGUERITE [sad]: I do.

ARMAND: Then come away with me, live with me!

MARGUERITE: If everything were different – no! There is no world, no way that you and I can connect . . . except in the moment. Please – no, don't touch me. There's nothing for us. I could look over the wall at you all my life and never get to touch your coat-tails. Don't be a fool. Only a fool believes a lie. [She turns away from him and has a spasm. She tries to stifle it, but gives a loud, rasping sound.

He is at her side in a bound. She moves away from him, and is convulsed by a spasm of coughing which seems to go through her whole body. She grasps a chair and then doubles over the chamber pot, coughing and retching. As the spasm seems to *subside, he hands her a napkin. But as she rises she is overtaken again, and coughs and chokes. And there is blood on the napkin.*

She looks at the napkin, transfixed. He puts out his hand slowly, and takes it. He gazes at the blood, and slowly raises the napkin to his lips and kisses it. She gazes up at him.]

ARMAND: Now will you listen to me?

[*He goes to take her in his arms but she crawls away to the bed, and lies, turned away from him. He leans over her.*]

Has there been blood before? Marguerite?

MARGUERITE: It's from the throat, just from the throat, the doctor assures me. [*But she can hardly speak.*]

ARMAND: I know just where to go. There is a village – it's high, the air is good, there are pine woods. We'll find a house, and walk, and sit in the sun and you'll be well. My love, what is to prevent us? We'll go today – think of it . . . oak woods, bluebells . . .

MARGUERITE: You're mad . . . oh, if . . .

ARMAND: Find a coat this minute and come away. [*He takes her in his arms.*] We'll find a house with a barn and poplar trees, and we'll walk and ride, and you'll breathe, and be well . . . and I shall watch you from across the room . . . when you sleep . . . when you smile . . .

MARGUERITE [*murmurs*]: If I could believe it . . .

ARMAND: Believe it.

MARGUERITE: I don't. But if we can have six weeks . . . a month . . .

ARMAND: Believe it and I'll make you well.

MARGUERITE: My dear. [*She breathes, in and out, recovering.*] Oh, the air is so strong! [*She breathes deeply.*] I feel well! I'll live, won't I? Tell me I'll live!

ARMAND [*embracing her*]: Of course!

[*He kisses her, but, drawing back, his expression changes. He stumbles back from her, aghast.*]

MARGUERITE: What is it?

ARMAND: Your eyes . . . I can't see your eyes!

MARGUERITE [*opens her arms to him*]: My dear . . . a trick of the light . . . it's nothing . . .
   [*They embrace.*]
  Oh . . . is it possible?

ARMAND: Of course! I insist upon it!

MARGUERITE: A life together? [*She strokes his hair.*] A dream.

ARMAND: No. Real. [*He kisses her.*] Why not? [*He kisses her.*] What else is it all for?

MARGUERITE: Oh my love . . .

ARMAND [*murmurs*]: What else?
   [*They embrace.*
   Fade to black.]

ACT II

A graveyard, just before dawn. ARMAND *and* GASTON *enter, followed by an old* GRAVEDIGGER.

GRAVEDIGGER: Here we are, Monsieur, it's over here in the new plots. You'll see how nice and neat it is, not all higgledy-piggledy . . . now, where are we? There – you can see your party as easy as anything in the moonlight . . . it do look lovely. I wish they all took as much trouble with their dead as you do, Monsieur – begging your pardon, it was you left the orders for the camellias?
    [GASTON *gestures towards* ARMAND.]
Ah – you, m'sieu? As you see, fresh as the milk from the cow. Whenever a bloom fades, I picks him off. [*He whispers to* GASTON *as* ARMAND *moves away*.] Little friend of his, Monsieur? I hear she was one of that sort of lady . . . did you know her, Monsieur?

GASTON: No.

GRAVEDIGGER: Very civil of you to come, she do appreciate it . . . well, nobody else comes near her, you can't expect it. If I was to tell some of them who their late ones was lying by, ooh dear, they'd carry on . . . we should have to be moved about again, and 'tis all work. [*He calls to* ARMAND.] As you see, sir, it's a fine plot. Nothing wrong with this plot. Not like down there where the water lies. [*To* GASTON] Not that I minds the moving, sir . . . to tell the truth, this one's the dead body I do love the best – we're obliged to love the dead, you see sir, we're kept so busy we don't hardly have time for the living. My brother now, he had the job before me, but he took to melancholy and had to be moved to a

116

baker . . . the dough, you see, sir . . . reviving. [*Calls to* ARMAND] Why disturb the young lady, sir? Let her lie. She'm decently buried – not like some poor young things, throwed in without so much as a bit of pine, let alone oak around them. Still, if you've made your mind to shift, [GASTON *gives him money*] shift we shall. I better go and wait for the Inspector, make sure he don't lose his way. Course, with a bit of luck he might fall in one of the diggings.

GASTON: The man's right. I beg of you . . . abandon the endeavour.

ARMAND [*neutral*]: Why was it done?

GASTON: My dear Duval, what difference where she lies? There's a fine plane tree . . . the view is good –

ARMAND: It's unacceptable.

GASTON: Is it not more appropriate that she lies here, in this simple spot? Will she not be happier with those of her own kind . . . people she knew and understood and had affection for? You think she would prefer a grand vault . . . is that what you truly believe?

    [*Voices off.*]

They're coming.

    [*An* INSPECTOR *arrives, followed by the* GRAVEDIGGER *and a* COLLEAGUE.]

INSPECTOR [*to* GASTON]: Monsieur Duval?

ARMAND: I am Armand Duval.

INSPECTOR: Good morning, sir. Cold morning.

    You have the written permission?

    [ARMAND *gives him a paper. He scrutinizes it by the lantern.*]

And the certificate? [*He reads this too, hands it back.*] This you retain. The other we keep. Very well. Open the grave.

    [*The* GRAVEDIGGERS *move the flowers from the lid of the coffin.*]

GASTON [*draws* ARMAND *aside*]: It's still not too late. Tell them to stop, I beg of you. At least come away!

ARMAND: No.

    [*The men bring up the coffin.*]

INSPECTOR [*to* ARMAND]: You understand, sir, that it is my duty to have the coffin opened in cases of request for reburial of remains. The law demands that we identify the corpse.

[ARMAND *nods.*

The GRAVEDIGGERS *open the coffin. The men step back, put handkerchiefs to their faces, at the stench.* ARMAND *groans.*]

Get on with it, man!

[*The old* GRAVEDIGGER *unloops the shroud . . . revealing the body.*

ARMAND *backs away. He pushes his scarf into his mouth. He staggers and almost slips.* GASTON *supports him.*]

ARMAND [*whispers*]: Her eyes? I can't see her eyes!

INSPECTOR: Sir? You identify the remains?

ARMAND [*howls, breaks away from* GASTON]: No! No! [*He throws himself down beside the coffin.*] No – no . . . no . . . no . . . no! . . .

[GASTON *and the men drag him away.*

Lights to black. Music.]

SCENE II

Armand's rooms. A large open trunk. BELA, *in a blood-stained dressing gown, and with his wrists bandaged in stained, untidy bandages torn from sheets, is drinking brandy.*

PIERRE, *Armand's valet, pads quietly to and fro, filling the trunk with clothes. He pauses, looks at* BELA *and approaches.*

PIERRE: Breakfast, *Monsieur le Prince?*

[BELA *ignores him.*

ARMAND *enters with clothes which he gives to* PIERRE, *who packs them.*]

ARMAND [*to* BELA]: Where is the doctor?

BELA: I sent him away.

ARMAND: You'll die of septicaemia.

BELA: Poor Bela. And will you grow a rose on my grave?

ARMAND: Go to hell for all I care – what the hell d'you think you're doing?

BELA: I? What am I doing?

ARMAND [*trying to tie his stock, mutters*]: Mean and insidious blackmail . . .

BELA: Where were you?

ARMAND: You know where I was –

BELA: I waited –

ARMAND: No one asked you to make a nuisance of yourself –

BELA: My apologies. For the mess. I'll make a better job of it next time.

ARMAND: There won't be a next time.

BELA: Oh?

ARMAND: I'm leaving Paris. For good.

BELA: Ah. I see. You've made up your mind. [*He laughs.*
ARMAND *looks at him coldly.*]

The line of lunacy in my family seems not to be exclusive.

ARMAND: Be careful.

BELA: Ohh! He's in love! In love.

[ARMAND, *having ruined his stock, goes off quickly. Alone,*
BELA's *depression returns. He takes another drink.*

PIERRE *enters, followed by Armand's* FATHER.]

PIERRE: The Marquis de Saint-Brieuc. What will you take, Milord, the usual?

FATHER: Yes, yes. [*To* BELA, *cold.*] Good day.

BELA: An early call.

FATHER: Late more like, from the look of you.

[BELA *stares up at him insolently.*]

Is my son here?

[*But* BELA *turns away without reply. The Marquis* (FATHER)
walks about, taking in BELA's *appearance.*

PIERRE *enters with coffee and cognac. The Marquis drinks, standing.*]

FATHER: What have you done to your wrists? Riding accident?

BELA [*slight pause*]: You could say so.

FATHER [*to* PIERRE, *who hovers*]: Is my son in bed?

PIERRE: I'll get him, Milord. At once, Milord. [*He goes.*]

FATHER: I hear you distinguished yourselves at the tables last night.

BELA: I?

FATHER: Ruining himself —

BELA: I entirely agree.

FATHER: What?

BELA: He's gambling to win. Fatal.

FATHER: Then what do you —

BELA: There is nothing to be done. For the present.

FATHER: Run its course, you mean?

BELA: It won't last.

FATHER: Could you get him away — abroad?

BELA: For you? [*He looks at the Marquis with insolent dislike.*]

ARMAND [*at the door*]: What do you want?

FATHER: Good morning. I've been trying a new horse . . . a black devil. Bit of a rig, I believe I shan't take him. Thank you. [*To* PIERRE, *who refills his coffee.*
   ARMAND *takes coffee.* BELA *shakes his head, and sits picking at his bandages.*]

ARMAND: Why are you here?

FATHER: Matter of business.

ARMAND: Profitable?

FATHER: Remains to be seen.

ARMAND: Is there something you wish to discuss with me?
   [*The Marquis looks at* BELA. *Who rises indolently.*]

ARMAND [*to* BELA]: I'll see you before I leave? You'll be at the course?

BELA: Or in hell.

FATHER: Sorry about your wrists.

BELA: An *affaire du coeur.* [*He crosses, kisses* ARMAND *on the lips, waves his wrists at the Marquis, and goes.*]

FATHER: I note that you take trouble to find the most vicious company in Paris.

ARMAND: Surely his pedigree's good enough, even for you . . . finest quarterings in Europe.

FATHER: Degenerates, the lot of them. It amuses you to — dammit, be careful! You nearly scalded my hands! [ARMAND *has poured coffee as the Marquis waves a letter before him.*] What is this?

ARMAND: You find it unclear?

FATHER: I can't stop you realizing your capital –

ARMAND: It's mine. To dispose as I wish –

FATHER: Your mother was ill advised. How long do you think –

ARMAND: I'm living simply, and intend to –

FATHER: Simply? Simply? The money's flowing out like the Rhine! What are you both doing out there in your love nest . . . burning it to keep warm? You cannot continue to run through funds which rightfully belong to the estate – no – please . . . do me the courtesy to hear me out. I understand your position. We're alike, you and I. Women are necessary to us. The right woman, a woman of understanding, sympathy . . . experience . . . Nonetheless . . .

[ARMAND *looks at him*]

. . . nonetheless, watch out for the wire, eh? The ditch under the bramble? You can't afford a fall, you have responsibilities.

ARMAND: Any responsibilities I have are of my own choosing and I intend to assume them.

FATHER: Oh yes . . . the Bohemian life. Well, why not? Time enough for the halter.

[*Pause*]

ARMAND: There is something you must know. [*Slight pause*] I intend to marry Marguerite.

[*Silence*]

FATHER: That, as you know, is entirely out of the question.

ARMAND: She says the same. Nonetheless . . . that is what I intend to do.

[*Silence*]

FATHER: I forbid it.

ARMAND: You can't prevent me.

FATHER [*pause*]: Armand . . . none of us is here by choice. We are all random cards. If we're wise we play the hand dealt. You are my heir!

ARMAND: The land is not entailed. Let my brother have it.

FATHER: You're young, tradition means nothing to you. At your age it's necessary to break everything, start again. Listen to me. Trust me. Permanence, continuity, the preservation of the line – they're of the utmost value. What else is there? What else stands against chaos and dissolution? It's all that matters. Believe me.

ARMAND: To you. Not to me. I do not intend to live as you.

FATHER: Then have you no thought for your family?

[ARMAND *grimaces*.]

Do we mean so little to you? What about your sister, do you want to break her heart? Her engagement has just been announced . . . de Luneville will break it off at once . . . what's to happen to that poor girl? It's a love match. She's in love with him.

ARMAND: If it's a love match he'll marry her.

FATHER: And destroy himself? You know better than that.

ARMAND: You don't understand. [*Pause*] I have to marry her.

FATHER: Have to? Why? For God's sake, why?

ARMAND: It's my only chance.

FATHER: Only chance? For what?

ARMAND: Life.

FATHER: I see . . . you intend to create a new universe – above the aspirations of the rest of us, naturally. [*Savage*] What do you think marriage stands for? What do you think it is? Some sort of beatified love affair? Impervious to the winds that blow? You think that society runs on love? Hah! Talk to me of love in six months' time, when the money's run out.

ARMAND: Once our debts are settled we shall not be concerned with –

FATHER: She'll leave you.

ARMAND [*slight pause*]: Six months ago I should have agreed with you. With every word. Now, I'm the most fortunate man in the world because Marguerite Gautier loves me. Because Marguerite Gautier is prepared to spend her life with me. It is not a question of love even – though that goes without saying. It is a question of friendship. Of respect.

[His FATHER *turns on him in a towering and frightening rage*.]

FATHER: Respect? Respect?! For a whore?!! You dare to talk of love . . . you dare to talk of friendship – with a whore?

You dare to come to me, talk of marriage?

Introduce a harlot? Into my family? Are you seriously suggesting . . . that you want . . . as your life's companion . . . before God and the Church . . . as the mother of your children . . . as my heirs . . . a woman who has felt the private parts of every man in Paris?

[ARMAND *lunges at his* FATHER, *who stumbles and recovers.*] You become as depraved as the company you keep.

Good God, boy, what does it matter? One woman's slot or another?

ARMAND: I warn you. Don't speak of her.

FATHER: You won't silence Paris. [*He puts on his gloves. But he is no longer in a temper.*] Think it over. If necessary I shall be prepared to stop your allowance and disclaim all responsibility for your debts. If I post that publicly you may whistle for credit, there won't be one door open to you.

Come and see me tomorrow. At three.

[*He puts on his hat and goes.*

ARMAND *turns to the trunk at once.*]

ARMAND: Pierre? Pierre!

[PIERRE *runs on,* ARMAND *indicates the trunk, murmurs instructions. He picks up his coat and goes, eagerly.*]

SCENE III

The garden of the cottage. MARGUERITE *is on her stomach, with* JEAN-PAUL. *They are playing with a pair of doves in a cage.*

MARGUERITE: What are you going to call them?

JEAN-PAUL: Plume . . . and Hat.

MARGUERITE: Which is which – be careful, they'll peck you!

JEAN-PAUL: That one's Hat . . . after Madame Prudence.

MARGUERITE: You rogue!

[YVETTE *comes on with the boy's jacket, and she and* YVETTE *swing the boy round. They collapse, the three of them laughing. She tickles the boy, who shrieks.*]

Got you.

[YVETTE, *smiling, holds out the boy's jacket, and puts it on.* ARMAND, *in his shirtsleeves, strolls on, watches.*]

MARGUERITE: Will he need his coat?

YVETTE: Be on the safe side. [*She picks up her basket.*]

MARGUERITE: Go careful with the eggs.

YVETTE: Oh he's good, he finds them quicker than me, don't you? [JEAN-PAUL *dodges behind* MARGUERITE, *and* YVETTE *chases him. He runs off, followed by* YVETTE.]

MARGUERITE: Don't go in the water! [*She turns, and sees* ARMAND. *She crosses to him and they embrace.*] I should go in.

ARMAND: Why?

MARGUERITE: The bread's in the oven.
[*They embrace, a long embrace.*]

ARMAND [*sits up, heaves a heavy sigh*]: Ahh! [*He looks at her alertly.*]

MARGUERITE: What is it?
[*He shakes his head.*]
What's the matter?

ARMAND: Nothing.

MARGUERITE: No, tell me, what is it? What's wrong?

ARMAND: Nothing. I've been misled, that's all.

MARGUERITE: What do you mean, misled? I haven't misled you. How can you say I've misled you?
[*He kisses her.*]

ARMAND: Not you. Love.

MARGUERITE: Love?

ARMAND: I have been entirely misinformed. [*He sits, knees hunched, brooding.*]

MARGUERITE: You're upset? It's not what you hoped? Ah . . . you are disappointed.

ARMAND: No. No, not disappointed.

MARGUERITE: What then?

ARMAND: Surprised. [*He kisses her fingers.*]

MARGUERITE: Surprised? What did you expect?

ARMAND: Agony . . . sighs . . . letters in mauve ink . . . a mysterious need to walk the nights. And an alert and distinct involvement with poetry to the extremity of picking up a pen. Instead – [*He sighs.*]

MARGUERITE: Instead?

ARMAND: Instead, none of the old, rank paths . . . instead – [*He smiles at her.*] – a secret garden. Dark, mysterious, full of tall trees, oak and ash and cypress –

MARGUERITE: Not cypress, they're for cemeteries –

ARMAND: An olive grove then, and water – our own spring – very fierce – spray all over the rocks!

MARGUERITE: And flowers?

ARMAND: Everywhere. Roses . . . lilies –

MARGUERITE: And crocuses . . . celandines?

ARMAND: You won't be able to walk for them.

MARGUERITE: Is it possible? Can we . . . live there? You – me? The two of us?

ARMAND: Why not? Why not, if we choose. It's simple. We choose to live. No more dirt-eating corruption, anxiety . . . burning the vitals to win. We'll *use* our vitality . . . devote . . . employ! We're strong, Marguerite! Engines of possibility. [*He sits by her.*] You are here, and I am here, and it is decided between us. No more weapons, no more display. No more secrecy, we live openly, for all to see. Here we stand. To live, to have our children, to do what we can, what we must. I shall become your boring old lover, grinding my teeth when you flirt with the baker, the *curé* –

PRUDENCE [*off*]: So this is where you're hiding!

[*She sweeps on, followed by* SOPHIE *and* CLÉMENCE.]

MARGUERITE [*embraces them*]: What a surprise! Clémence, you look splendid, I never saw such pearls, they're as big as pigeons' eggs!

CLÉMENCE: I know. They catch in your brooches though.

MARGUERITE [*to* SOPHIE]: How are you?

SOPHIE [*kissing her*]: More to the point, how are you?

MARGUERITE: As you see . . . blooming!

[SOPHIE *looks at her, turns away and accosts* ARMAND.]

SOPHIE: Suit you, does it? Country life?

ARMAND: Yes. I shall be indistinguishable from the hayricks in six months.

[*The others laugh.*]

SOPHIE: Six months is a long time.

PRUDENCE [*calls*]: Wait till the winter and the mud – you'll be back!

SOPHIE [*to* ARMAND]: At least you're not out of temper.

ARMAND: Disappointing for you.

[ARMAND *grins at her, crosses to talk to* CLÉMENCE.]

ARMAND: How is the Count?

CLÉMENCE: We've been travelling.

MARGUERITE: Oh? Where?

CLÉMENCE: Lord knows. We keep having to be somewhere to get to somewhere else.

MARGUERITE: But you like him?

CLÉMENCE: Oh yes, he says such interesting things. He's not like any other Swede who likes coins and timetables I've ever met. If you see what I mean.

[*They laugh.*]

MARGUERITE: You must see the pond.

CLÉMENCE: Ooh! Is there a boat? [*She takes* SOPHIE *and* ARMAND *by the arm.*]

ARMAND: Afraid not.

CLÉMENCE: Never mind. People in boats are such hooligans. Can we fish?

[ARMAND *takes her off with* SOPHIE.]

MARGUERITE [*after a pause*]: How much?

PRUDENCE: Ten thousand.

MARGUERITE: What?

PRUDENCE: Marguerite, selling is not buying.

MARGUERITE: Did you see the Duke?

PRUDENCE: Nothing.

[YVETTE *comes out with drinks, bobs and goes.* PRUDENCE *looks at her speculatively.*]

MARGUERITE: Janine left me, she didn't take to country life again. I told her you might find her something.

PRUDENCE: I already have. [*Slight pause*] My dear, how long can this go on?

MARGUERITE: As long as the money lasts.

PRUDENCE: What then? The landlord's repossessed.

MARGUERITE: There was cash in hand!

PRUDENCE: All gone. I can't get credit in your name any more, even the little woman in the glove shop gave me her account. There are new stars rising. If you continue this nonsense I shall be forced to abandon you.

MARGUERITE: I thought we were friends.

PRUDENCE: Friendship is based on good sense. You can't expect the rest of us to follow you to ruin. For God's sakes, Marguerite, do you want to end up like me . . . everybody's catspaw? There's nothing so vacated as being a woman of my age – take my word for it, it won't last for ever!

MARGUERITE [after a pause]: He's asked me to marry him.

PRUDENCE: Has he, by God? So that's why his father is in Paris.

MARGUERITE: What?

PRUDENCE: He didn't tell you? There was a devil of a row. You'd be a *Marquise*, of course, if that's what you want, but there's no profit in it, the way things stand. No money! He'll go into drink – I've seen it all before.

MARGUERITE: I don't think so.

PRUDENCE: You love him, is that it?

MARGUERITE: Yes. Yes, that's it.

PRUDENCE: Good, then you won't want to ruin his life. He'll be ostracized, cut off from everything he knows. What about the boy, you want him schooled, don't you? Your brothers, just lifting their heads above water, thanks to you . . . your mother, she's not getting any younger. You're a beauty. Men desire you. You keep us all afloat . . . servants, seamstresses, shoemakers . . . not a bad achievement for a girl who couldn't write her name. My dear, don't throw it all away. [Slight pause] What are we all to do without you? [Slight pause] Listen. I've met this charming wine merchant. He saw you at the Opera and he's dying to meet you. Not young, but very soundly based. You could still see Armand – why not? He must learn to share! You'll afford him a lot longer if you give up these foolish notions of love in the attic. My dear, you can't trust it. I know these aristocrats. They're cold. Finished off in the cradle. He's like his father. Ruthless.

MARGUERITE: He's changed.

PRUDENCE: I doubt that. I doubt that very much. When the money's gone he'll revert. No man's constant, Marguerite. It isn't in their nature. I kept a rogue for twenty years, he couldn't wait to deceive me, not a week without it. Come back. I'll hire a carriage . . . once it's known that Marguerite Gautier is returning to Paris – new address . . . new wardrobe . . . my dear, you should see the silks this year . . . colours like light, you won't be able to resist! There's a beautiful *coupé* with a couple of bays I could get at a price –

MARGUERITE: Prudence . . . I appreciate your coming to see me. Honestly . . . truly . . .

PRUDENCE: But you're not coming back?

MARGUERITE: No.

PRUDENCE: We'll give it another month.

MARGUERITE: No.

PRUDENCE: Very well, my dear. If you change your mind, let me know. *Au revoir*, I don't want to drive back in the middle of the day, the horses will get hot.

    [*She goes.* SOPHIE *enters.*]

SOPHIE: What's the matter?

MARGUERITE: Can't you guess?

SOPHIE: You're a fool.

MARGUERITE: How's Paris?

SOPHIE: Amusing.

MARGUERITE: Where are you living?

SOPHIE: Montmartre.

MARGUERITE: You always liked that sort of life.

SOPHIE: It's not going to last, you know. Why ruin yourself, for a man?

MARGUERITE [*smiles*]: Particularly Armand Duval.

SOPHIE: For any man. You're free!

MARGUERITE: Am I?

SOPHIE: You *like* him?

MARGUERITE: There seems to be some sort of necessity. I am, almost, persuaded. Some of the time.

SOPHIE: I'm thinking of going abroad.

MARGUERITE [*dismayed*]: Oh! Where?

SOPHIE: Africa. Will you miss me?

MARGUERITE: Very much. Who with?

SOPHIE: A man.

MARGUERITE: Can he afford it?

SOPHIE: Oh yes.

[ARMAND *returns with* JEAN-PAUL *on his shoulders and* CLÉMENCE *and* YVETTE, *who goes inside.* CLÉMENCE *has her skirts tucked up and is carrying her shoes.*]

CLÉMENCE: Marguerite, I fell in!

JEAN-PAUL: Right in the pond! In the water!

CLÉMENCE: I wasn't looking, I was drinking it all in!

[*They laugh.*]

MARGUERITE: Come and eat burnt bread.

CLÉMENCE: It smells lovely. Roast lamb? [*Sniffing the air*]

ARMAND: Slaughtered in your honour.

[*She squeals in protest and runs off, followed by* JEAN-PAUL *and* ARMAND.]

MARGUERITE [*to* SOPHIE]: You're looking well.

SOPHIE: Yes. I'm not coughing any more.

[*Pause.*
The party re-enters, replete after the meal. They sit.
MARGUERITE *sits between* SOPHIE's *legs.* ARMAND *tickles*
JEAN-PAUL.
Pause. Music. Pause.]

MARGUERITE [*lazily*]: Azure.

SOPHIE: Black.

ARMAND: Chrome yellow.

CLÉMENCE: That's two words. Oh, all right. Damson.

JEAN-PAUL: Damson? That's not a colour.

CLÉMENCE: Yes it is.

JEAN-PAUL: What colour's damson?

CLÉMENCE: Everybody knows what damson looks like, silly . . . how old are you?

JEAN-PAUL: Seven.

CLÉMENCE [*scornful*]: Is that all?

SOPHIE: He's right. Do you mean the skin, or the flesh –

MARGUERITE: Or stewed damsons –

CLÉMENCE: I mean damson and cream, like when people say something's raspberry coloured they mean raspberry fool –

SOPHIE: Oh come on, whose turn is it? Jean-Paul –

JEAN-PAUL: But are we having fruit –

MARGUERITE: We ought to have a policy –

CLÉMENCE: Oh let's not have policies, we don't want policies –

SOPHIE: All right, we accept damson. [*She whispers to* JEAN-PAUL, *who cannot think of a colour beginning with* E.] Evergreen . . .

JEAN-PAUL: Evergreen!

ARMAND: Rejected.

>   [JEAN-PAUL *wails.* MARGUERITE *throws a cushion at* ARMAND.]
>   What about eiderdown . . . [*As* JEAN-PAUL *attacks him with a cushion*] Eggy? Ellow?
>   [*They shout him down.*]
>   Very well . . . [*He whispers to* JEAN-PAUL.]

JEAN-PAUL: Emerald.

>   [*They clap.*]   ·

MARGUERITE: Flame.

SOPHIE: Garnet.

CLÉMENCE: Garnets come in lots of colours.

ARMAND: Reject.

SOPHIE: Grey then.

CLÉMENCE: H. Oh I thought of one just now . . . now I've forgotten it.

SOPHIE: Double marks to me if I give you one.

CLÉMENCE: Oh we're not having marks, are we?

ARMAND: H. House . . . home . . . happy . . .

>   [*Light change.*
>   JEAN-PAUL *runs off.* ARMAND, *hat in hand, waits as* MARGUERITE *kisses* CLÉMENCE *goodbye. She turns to* SOPHIE.]

MARGUERITE: Write to me!

>   [*They kiss passionately.* CLÉMENCE *and* SOPHIE *go.* MARGUERITE *turns to* ARMAND.]
>   Must you go?

ARMAND: A few things to settle.

MARGUERITE: I've spoken to Prudence. We shall survive.

ARMAND: You may depend on that.

MARGUERITE: You'll see him again? Your father?

ARMAND: Yes. It's of no consequence. None of it matters. They can't hurt us. They can't touch us. There is no argument they can use to dissuade us. They cannot pull us apart, Marguerite. I shall do as we planned. Become a printer – perhaps, write, if I've the talent . . . if not, print the works of those who have. We'll work together, side by side. Without ambition, except to excel, without greed, except to offer the best of ourselves. To find work, that must be our aim. To live . . . to support our children . . . to read . . . to think – and to be as clear as we can.

MARGUERITE: Yes! Oh . . . yes . . .

> [*They embrace. She draws back.*]

Must you see him again?

ARMAND: My father? I said I would.

MARGUERITE: Be careful.

> [*He looks at her in query, and she takes his arm and speaks quickly, changing the subject.*]

Is it true? About Bela? That he cut his wrists?

ARMAND: You know what he's like. [*Kisses her.*] Don't wait up.

MARGUERITE: You know I shall.

> [*They embrace and he goes.* MARGUERITE *walks back and forth, troubled.*
>
> JEAN-PAUL *runs on, followed by* YVETTE.]

JEAN-PAUL: Tan' Marie, Tan' Marie, we're going to catch frogs!

MARGUERITE [*as he runs past*]: You . . . didn't finish your lunch!

JEAN-PAUL: It was only the cabbage!

YVETTE: Only the cabbage!

> [MARGUERITE *laughs, watching them go. But she resumes her walk, anxious and reflective.*
>
> ARMAND'S FATHER *enters behind her.*]

FATHER: There was no one to announce me so I took the liberty of walking round. [*He bows.*

> MARGUERITE *turns, and he recognizes her.*]

MARGUERITE: *Monsieur le Marquis?*

131

FATHER: Oh, it's you. [*He recovers himself at once and regards her with an unhurried stare.*] You look well.

[MARGUERITE *moves, rings a bell.* PIERRE *appears.*]

FATHER: Ah, Pierre!

PIERRE: *Monsieur le Marquis?*

FATHER: Yes. Fetch me an Armagnac and water.

[PIERRE *goes.*]

Pretty spot. [*He gazes out at the view.*] Fine view of the river. Damned hot dusty drive though.

[PIERRE *returns. The Marquis* (FATHER) *waves him away, and mixes his own drink.* PIERRE *goes.* MARGUERITE *watches in silence as he measures the drink without haste.*]

Fine old Armagnac . . . can you afford it?

MARGUERITE: We keep it for creditors.

FATHER [*inspecting the bottle*]: Not a lot left.

MARGUERITE: As you see.

FATHER: I hear you're being sold up.

MARGUERITE: And what are you going to do about it?

FATHER: I? Not my affair. If my son chooses to ruin himself, that's his concern.

MARGUERITE: How do you expect him to live?

FATHER: How indeed, since he's cashing up, it seems, on your behalf.

MARGUERITE: I've not asked him to do so. I've tried to prevent it.

FATHER: So much so that he's gone through his mother's inheritance in a month. A pity, since I propose to withdraw financial support, including my name to all bills.

MARGUERITE: You can't!

FATHER: Can't I? The disclaimers are in my pocket.

MARGUERITE: He has as much right to the money as you have. You didn't earn it!

FATHER: Come, no need to lose your temper. Wearing thin already, is it?

MARGUERITE: You'd like to believe so.

FATHER: No pleasure for me, watching my heir make a fool of himself before the whole of Paris . . . let alone upsetting his family.

MARGUERITE: So you've come to offer me money.

FATHER: Of course.

MARGUERITE: How much?

FATHER: Fifty thousand.

MARGUERITE: You have a sense of humour.

FATHER: I'll go to seventy-five.

MARGUERITE: You're wasting your time.

FATHER: A hundred then. That's the top.

MARGUERITE: Have you got it with you?

FATHER: Don't play the fool with me, girl. There's a closed carriage outside, to take you back to Paris. Come with me now and I'll pay the rest of your debts. I *could* have your name placed on the list of undesirables, you wouldn't see much of Paris then. Come, be honest, Marie, aren't you bored? After Paris? It won't be so pretty in the winter. [*Pause*] He'll understand – if not now, later . . . he'll respect you for the rest of his life. You can't stand by and see him ruined if you truly and genuinely love him. Come, take my arm . . . [*And he touches her.*

  She springs away from him, as if burnt.]

MARGUERITE: No! Get away from me! Go away! I don't want to see you, ever . . . don't you ever come here again! I don't want to see your face, I don't want to hear your voice – I don't want you near me! You get your stinking smell out of my house. You've no right to come here threatening me under my own roof, do you think I can't take care of myself –

FATHER: Don't get hysterical.

MARGUERITE: You think because I'm a woman you can come here and bully and threaten? You think I'm nothing? Something to be pulled out of the way, like a piece of wood on the road? We don't need you. You pollute the air you breathe, the ground you walk on. You have no control, no influence over us. So take your foul breath and your rotting teeth and your stinking ass out of my house! Get out!

FATHER: Stop it –

MARGUERITE: Get out! Get out . . . get out! [*She picks up a knife.*]

FATHER: I'll have you put away as a madwoman!

MARGUERITE: Get out!

FATHER: Very well. If you choose to be unreasonable, I shall take appropriate action.

[YVETTE *returns with* JEAN-PAUL. *He carries a jar.*]

JEAN-PAUL [*Running on*]: Tan' Marie, look . . . [*He stops at the stranger.*

MARGUERITE *freezes. She waves* YVETTE *to take the boy away but the* MARQUIS *approaches.*]

MARGUERITE: Don't touch him!

FATHER: That's a fine frog, my boy. A fine frog like that deserves a *louis*. [*He takes it from his pocket, gives it to the boy, who, nudged by* YVETTE, *bows.*]

JEAN-PAUL: Thank you, sir. Oh, a gold one! [*He shows* YVETTE.]

FATHER [*to* YVETTE]: Boy's a credit to you.

YVETTE: Thank you, sir. [*She curtseys and smiles.*]

MARGUERITE [*harsh*]: Take him in, Yvette.

[*They go. Silence.*]

FATHER: A fine child. Good-looking boy.

MARGUERITE: Leave him out of it.

FATHER: I had no idea. A little rough in his speech, perhaps, but that's soon amended.

MARGUERITE: That's not your concern.

FATHER: Is he not? What plans do you have for him?

MARGUERITE: My plans are none of your affair.

FATHER: He'll need decent schooling . . . That's not cheap.

MARGUERITE: Will you go?

FATHER: A fine boy, I'm taken with him. He has an air of Armand at the same age. [*Slight pause*] I see you still have the scar on your face.

MARGUERITE [*she seems exhausted*]: Go . . . just go.

FATHER: The idea takes me. I'll strike a bargain with you, Marie. Come back to Paris in the coach with me, here and now, and I'll give the boy an education.

MARGUERITE: No.

FATHER: What's his future to be? Hawked about with you and my son, not a *sou* between you? A couple of years' schooling if he's lucky . . . to become a labourer in the fields . . . an ostler . . . with an ageing mother to support?

MARGUERITE: I tell you no.

FATHER: I might even be prepared to take him . . . accept him publicly as my natural son. Give him my name – after all, in a way it's his birthright. We'll hire a tutor, start him on his declensions.

MARGUERITE: You devil. You're a devil.

FATHER: He'll be reared as a gentleman.

MARGUERITE: You think I want him to be like you?

FATHER: Do you want him able to read, think for himself, carry on a profession? Able to keep a decent household . . . live a civilized life? It's in your hands, Marie. It's for you to choose. You're his mother. What shall it be? Will you choose for yourself? Or for the child?

MARGUERITE: No . . . no . . .

FATHER: After all, I am the boy's father.

MARGUERITE: No! No!!

FATHER: Very well, then I shall get a magistrate's order that you are an unfit mother. What do you think you're playing at? Have you forgotten your place?

MARGUERITE: Don't – oh don't! Don't . . . no . . . don't . . . no . . . no! [*She becomes hysterical.*
  The boy runs on, followed by YVETTE. MARGUERITE *clasps* JEAN-PAUL *feverishly.*]
No! No!
  [*The Marquis takes the boy from her, gives him to* YVETTE.]

FATHER: Take the boy away.
  [YVETTE, *frightened, goes out with* JEAN-PAUL.]

MARGUERITE: No . . . no . . . [*She weeps.*]

FATHER: Be reasonable, Marie. Take what you can get.
  [*She weeps.*]
You were always a realistic girl. Courageous, too . . . I admired your spirit.
  [*A long pause*]

MARGUERITE [*low*]: I want him educated.

FATHER: As I've said.

135

MARGUERITE: And you'll adopt him? Give him your name?
[*He nods.*]
I don't want him left to servants!

FATHER: I am about to marry again. An Italian. I believe they like children.

MARGUERITE: Please . . .

FATHER: He will be well treated.

MARGUERITE: Shall I . . . shall I see him again?

FATHER: Perhaps . . . when he is a man. Let time create him for us. Then we'll see. A fine child. I congratulate you. [*He gives her his arm.*] Come . . . we'll go into the house and you can write the note.

MARGUERITE: The note?

FATHER: To Armand. Saying that you have returned to Paris. That you are bored with the country, with your present life. That you prefer your former existence. There must be no confusion. No doubt as to your intentions. After that we'll drive into Paris together and the boy can come home with me.

[*He helps her inside.*

The light goes. Pause.
PIERRE, *the valet, comes out and lights the lantern. He looks off, but there is no sign of* ARMAND. *He goes.*

Lights to black.

The slow light of the moon.
ARMAND *enters, wearing a cloak.*]

ARMAND: Marguerite?
[PIERRE *enters, hands him a letter and retires.* ARMAND *opens the letter, reads.*]

ARMAND [*muttering*]: . . . 'it is over. Try to forget you ever knew . . . a few moments' happiness . . .' ahhhh!
[*He falls to his knees, crushing the letter, and uttering a loud, prolonged and eerie howl of anguish.*]
Marguerite . . . !!!

The foyer of the Opera. The two WAITERS *prepare for the Entr'acte. The sound of a woman singing as the doors open and* CLÉMENCE *enters, fuming, followed by* COUNT DRUFTHEIM.

CLÉMENCE: I'm just not standing for it!

COUNT: My snowdrop . . . you are not enjoying the opera?

CLÉMENCE: Letting him pester her like that, it really riles me!

COUNT: But it is the making ups, not the true . . . and the singing – oh, so full and round! . . .

CLÉMENCE: Well it makes me go outraged.

COUNT: Beloved –

CLÉMENCE: She should punch him in the head.

COUNT: You have the soft, warm heart. [*He kisses her hand.*]

CLÉMENCE: We'll go again tomorrow, see the rest.

COUNT: No. We will not. You shall choose.

[*He bows as the old* DUC *enters, squiring the young* GIRL, *but the* DUC, *busy, does not see him. The* GIRL *and* CLÉMENCE *exchange a laconic nod.*]

CLÉMENCE [*sitting*]: I would have enjoyed it more, only one of my stays went and I lost the drift a bit.

COUNT: Ping, ping! [*Heads together, they giggle and whisper as the* DUC *and his* GIRL *promenade.*

PRUDENCE *enters with* JANINE, *her new protégée, now dressed to kill.*]

JANINE: We'll miss the ending!

PRUDENCE: Nonsense, what do you care, anyway I've seen it before, she kills herself. Where's Armand, what's happened to Armand? [*She turns, retracing her steps.*]

JANINE [*surly*]: He's at the bar.

PRUDENCE: Now why did you allow that – [*She sees* CLÉMENCE *and the* COUNT *and screeches*] – Count! Clémence! What a wonderful surprise! [*She embraces* CLÉMENCE.] Wicked! When did you arrive?

CLÉMENCE: Yesterday . . .

PRUDENCE: You should have left a note for me! How well you look . . . both of you . . . don't they look well, Olympe!

JANINE: Yes. Like a couple of Parma hams. What? [*As* PRUDENCE *digs her in the ribs to mind her manners.*]

COUNT: Madame Prudence. [*He kisses her hand.*] You are from the opera? So fine, is it not?

PRUDENCE: Oh yes.

JANINE: Miserable though.

CLÉMENCE: Yes, why can't they leave her alone! If she could just think of some way out! She should escape!

JANINE: Yeah!

COUNT: *Jah, jah.* First we see the young girl, so happy and innocent. Then comes the father, and we –

PRUDENCE [*quick*]: How was your voyage?

CLÉMENCE: Lovely. Every minute.

[*She and the* COUNT *exchange a doting smile.*]

PRUDENCE: You enjoyed yourselves then?

COUNT: Oh yah. The first day was warm, but not so warm that we are without the jackets, then on the second day is coming little shower –

[PRUDENCE *flees, pursued by the* COUNT.]

JANINE: How are you getting on with him?

CLÉMENCE: Like a couple of roosting hens, you should see us!

JANINE: I told you, didn't I? Who put you up to it, remember?

CLÉMENCE: He's ever such good company – and clever? Mind you, he eats a lot. I expect that's to feed his mind.

JANINE: Yes. Build it up.

CLÉMENCE: Tonight he ate half a side of venison. [*She belches, eases her stays delicately.*] I ate the other half.

[*The* COUNT, *having lost* PRUDENCE *and his way, wanders on again.*]

JANINE: Count – over here!

COUNT [*bows*]: How do you –

JANINE: It's Janine! Don't you remember? Only I'm called Olympe now. [*Aside, to* CLÉMENCE] You'll never guess who I've got as a patron. [*To the* COUNT] How did you find Italy?

CLÉMENCE: It took a week or two.

COUNT: Florence is a most beautiful city with many statues and paintings and art works which, of course, we have seen all.

JANINE: I hear you've been eating well.

COUNT: The food is good, yes, but it is not so agreeable to look up and see swimming before you in the river, rats . . . also cats, sometimes swimming and sometimes dead. I have been sending to the Mayor documents and diagram of my new, improved system for the disposal of –

[PRUDENCE *reappears. The* COUNT *greets her joyously.*]

Aha! Madame Prudence! And as I was saying, Madame . . . ninthly . . .

[PRUDENCE *is saved by the appearance of* SOPHIE *and* BELA.]

PRUDENCE: Sophie!

SOPHIE: Prudence! [*She swings* PRUDENCE *round, then does a cartwheel.*]

PRUDENCE: Now the season can begin. Where have you been?

[SOPHIE *and* CLÉMENCE *embrace.*]

SOPHIE: To Africa!

PRUDENCE: You look like a pair of Zouaves. [*As the* COUNT *kisses* SOPHIE's *hand*] Very unfashionable. Pale is in.

BELA: Oh? [*Kissing her hand*]

PRUDENCE: My dear Prince, pale is the thing.

BELA: It will suit La Gautier, I hear.

SOPHIE: Is Marguerite ill?

PRUDENCE: Never more sparkling. [*She moves away.* SOPHIE *pursues her.*]

SOPHIE: She's ill.

PRUDENCE: I haven't said so. You should see the Russian bear she has in tow!

SOPHIE: How ill?

PRUDENCE: Skin like watered milk.

SOPHIE: What is it . . . opium? The lungs? [*She shakes* PRUDENCE.] Tell me!

PRUDENCE: Don't!

[SOPHIE *grabs her by the arm and they walk apart, whispering urgently.*

ARMAND *enters. He and* BELA *meet.*]

ARMAND: Well.

BELA: Well.

ARMAND: A blackened face from the past. I began to think you were dead.

BELA: As you see, very much alive.

[JANINE *runs to* ARMAND, *takes his arm.*]

JANINE: Armand! We missed you!

BELA: What's this?

[ARMAND *whispers in* JANINE's *ear. She giggles. He looks at* BELA.]

BELA: I see.

ARMAND [*to* JANINE]: Get out. [*He throws her off.*

She crosses to PRUDENCE *and the others.*]

BELA: Why?

ARMAND: Because she is disgusting.

PRUDENCE: Armand . . . over here!

[BELA *and* ARMAND *join the group.* ARMAND *bows to* SOPHIE. JANINE *takes his arm again.*]

JANINE: Surprise, eh?

SOPHIE [*to* ARMAND]: Not in the least. [*She looks at* JANINE.] God help us all.

JANINE: Do you like my dress?

SOPHIE: You look like a firework.

[ARMAND *grins and pulls* JANINE *away.* BELA *laughs as* ARMAND *makes a public display of affection.*]

What have you been up to?

[PRUDENCE *shrugs.*]

That bitch? Are you desperate . . . [*She watches* ARMAND *and* JANINE] . . . those two mean devils will get nothing from each other –

PRUDENCE: Do you think I don't know that? Why do you think he does it? To spite her, that's why.

SOPHIE: You mean Marguerite?

[*But, turning, her attention is diverted by the entrance of* MARGUERITE. *She is in black, and is accompanied by a heavily built, older Russian* PRINCE.]

[*Shocked by* MARGUERITE's *appearance*] God in heaven . . .

PRUDENCE: Quick . . . he mustn't see her – [*She moves to* ARMAND.]

SOPHIE: Too late.

[ARMAND *and* MARGUERITE *meet.*]

ARMAND [*bows low*]: Good evening, good evening. Up for a breath of fresh air, Mademoiselle Gautier?

MARGUERITE [*tries to pass*]: Monsieur Duval.

ARMAND: How are you, Prince? Ah, out of action, I see. [*The* PRINCE *is paralytic.*]

MARGUERITE: Please.

ARMAND: Your servant. I compliment you on your choice of . . . transaction. The perverse . . . the elderly . . . the *hors de combat* – a convenient *galère*, Mademoiselle.

JANINE: Well, if it isn't Marie – you look old. Armand, come and dance! I could dance all night . . . you won't tire me out!

[ARMAND *and* JANINE *dance.* MARGUERITE, *trapped on the* PRINCE'*s lap, is forced to watch.*]

ARMAND [*calls, to the* PRINCE *en passant*]: You'll find the lady wanting, *Monsieur le Prince* . . . failing in contractual commitment –

PRINCE [*in Russian*]: Fuck off before I kill you.

[SOPHIE *dances with* BELA, CLÉMENCE *with the* COUNT. *The old* DUC *hobbles on, waves his stick happily at* PRUDENCE, *and hops round the floor with her. The* PRINCE *rises majestically, takes* MARGUERITE *in his arms, spins her to the centre of the room, and crashes to the ground with her.*

Laughter and applause.]

ARMAND: Throw them some buns! Come on, Mademoiselle, up on your haunches, let's see the next trick.

JANINE: Don't waste your time, Armand . . . who wants yesterday's mackerel?

[*The music stops as she speaks and her voice rings out.* SOPHIE *steps forward. She approaches* JANINE *like a tiger stalking its prey.* JANINE *withdraws. But* SOPHIE *strikes, and boxes* JANINE'*s ears. The two girls fight, rolling over and over, screaming and clawing and going for each other's hair.*

JANINE *begins to gets the worst of it.* SOPHIE *is cheered on as* JANINE *begins to dodge about, evading.*

MARGUERITE *manages to extricate herself from the* PRINCE. *She makes unobtrusively for the exit. But* ARMAND, *who seems absorbed and delighted in the fight, moves swiftly to cut her off, as* PRUDENCE *and* CLÉMENCE *pick up the snivelling* JANINE.]

ARMAND: You're leaving us, Mademoiselle Gautier?

MARGUERITE: Don't.

ARMAND: Honoré de Sancerre waiting with his whips and his costume trunk?

MARGUERITE: Armand, there's no point. Let go.

ARMAND: The monster obliges.

[*He bows and, somewhat drunk, slips and almost falls over. She is obliged to help him up. In each other's arms, they cannot move.*]

MARGUERITE: No. Armand, please . . .

[*She looks up at him. It looks as though they will embrace. Then he cracks her across the face.*

BELA *and the* COUNT *run to her assistance.*]

COUNT: No . . . please!

BELA: For God's sake, Armand!

COUNT: Please, this is not possible!

JANINE [*bursting into tears*]: Armand . . . Armand!

PRUDENCE: Shut up, you.

[*She gives* JANINE *a clout and runs after* SOPHIE, *who goes to* MARGUERITE'*s assistance.*]

BELA: For God's sake . . . [*pulling* ARMAND *away*]

SOPHIE [*bending over* MARGUERITE]: Are you all right?

[MARGUERITE, *in pain, holding the side of her face with both hands, nods.* PRUDENCE *and* SOPHIE *help her to her feet.*]

CLÉMENCE: Armand!

[MARGUERITE *takes* SOPHIE'*s arm and they leave as the old* DUC *hobbles across. He pauses and peruses* MARGUERITE, *shakes his head.*]

DUC: Too thin, too thin!

[*Assisted by a* WAITER, *he walks away as* MARGUERITE *goes.*]

BELA [*to* ARMAND]: A public scene, for that?

PRUDENCE [*crosses and confronts* ARMAND]: That was ill done.

ARMAND [*bows*]: I beg your pardon. Deepest apologies.

PRUDENCE: She is ill.

ARMAND: So am I. So am I. [*He goes, pushing* JANINE *aside.*]

PRUDENCE: Why did he do that? There was no need . . . he shouldn't have done that.

[*They leave.*
Music.]

SCENE V

Marguerite's bedroom. MARGUERITE *being helped into a dressing gown by* YVETTE, *who then gives her water to sip.* SOPHIE *walks about, angry.* YVETTE *goes quietly.*

MARGUERITE: My dear – [*she crosses, takes* SOPHIE *by the arm.*] There's no need!

SOPHIE: I'll kill him. With cyanide.

MARGUERITE: No, you won't.

SOPHIE: He hit you!

MARGUERITE: Yes! As you see, I'm all right! I feel . . . full of life!

SOPHIE [*looks at her shrewdly*]: Don't dare.

MARGUERITE: Of course not. Of course not. It's over.

SOPHIE: Is it?

MARGUERITE [*laughs*]: He was drunk. Shall we go shopping tomorrow?

SOPHIE: We could drive out to Malmaison. The air will be good for you.

MARGUERITE: I'm perfectly well.

SOPHIE: Are you? Have you thought of going south?

MARGUERITE [*quick*]: I can't leave Paris.

SOPHIE: Why not? Go to Italy. Take the Russian – it's all the same to him where he drinks.

MARGUERITE: No.

SOPHIE: Why not?

MARGUERITE: I need to be in Paris.

SOPHIE: You should think of your health. If not for yourself, for the boy.

MARGUERITE [*slight pause*]: I . . . I've had him adopted.

SOPHIE: What?!

MARGUERITE: So . . . as you see . . . I don't see him any more.

SOPHIE: Why did you do that? [*a protest*]

MARGUERITE: He'll be educated – [*As* SOPHIE *makes to reply*] – it's more than we are!

SOPHIE: Is it? Well, I wouldn't let him go. I'd rather he was a pimp than let him go if he was mine.

MARGUERITE: Well he isn't so that's an end of it.

SOPHIE [*a whine*]: I liked playing with him!

MARGUERITE: Have one of your own then.

SOPHIE: Hardly likely, after all the knitting needles.

[*They laugh.* SOPHIE *makes to go, bends over* MARGUERITE *to kiss her good night.*]

MARGUERITE [*quick*]: No, don't kiss me. [*Covers*] Is it serious, with Bela?

SOPHIE: The fact that he owns half Moldavia's serious. We understand each other. [*Shrugs*] He loves Duval. Get over it, Marguerite.

MARGUERITE: How?

SOPHIE: I knew!

MARGUERITE: Well don't stand there looking at me like a cross Pekinese.

SOPHIE: More like a cowpat the water cart's run over – mind you, I left my mark on the bitch . . . those were your seed pearls she was wearing. Forget him.

MARGUERITE: I already have.

[SOPHIE *goes.*
Voices, off.
MARGUERITE, *who seems suddenly exhausted, rallies, checks her hair in the glass. She coughs.*
YVETTE *enters.*]

PRUDENCE [*off*]: I'm not intending to stop, girl! [*Enters.*] My
dear, what a fracas . . . unforgivable, the whole of Paris is talking
about it, are you recovered, you're looking very pale!

MARGUERITE: Nonsense – Yvette, a glass of cognac for Madame
Prudence!

PRUDENCE: Clémence sends her love, I've left them below.

MARGUERITE: She's a duck.

PRUDENCE: A goose, you mean. But more sense than I gave her
credit for . . . she's going off to Sweden as his Countess . . . yes!
I daresay he's been turned down by all the Swedes, well, half a
minute and you're gasping but she thinks he's a wit, they're
studying wasps now.

[*Shouts of laughter off. She lifts her eyes.*]
You're all right?

MARGUERITE: Of course!

PRUDENCE: Good, because the Prince is on his way. I've told him it
was his fault, he thinks he's the one who slapped you – well, does
no harm. He's bringing them round.

MARGUERITE: Who?

PRUDENCE: The emeralds, you fool!

MARGUERITE: No! You haven't!

PRUDENCE: Necklace, ear-rings, bracelets . . . the whole *parure*! I
told you it could be done. *Niet, niet*, was all I got from the
drunken wretch – so – what did I do? I told him they were out of
fashion! I said you'd never wear them! Well, you know the
Russians . . . can't bear to be thought provincial – he's had them
all reset! Specially for you!

[*Noise and laughter, off.*]
I'd better go before they turn your place upside down. I'll be in
tomorrow, we'll settle up. [*At the door*] Get out the brandy
bottle. Tomorrow you can tell him what a stallion he was and get
another night off and the next quarter's rent paid into the
bargain.

MARGUERITE: Yes, why not? Thank you!

[PRUDENCE *embraces her, makes to kiss her, but draws
back.*]

PRUDENCE: Good. Well, I mustn't keep the horses. We're all off to the *Variétés. Au 'voir*, my dear – heavens, what a noise they're making!

[*She goes, to the sound of laughter and banging. The crash of an outer door.*

Silence.

YVETTE *enters.* MARGUERITE *looks up with a smile.*]

MARGUERITE: They've gone?

YVETTE: Yes, Madame.

[MARGUERITE *leans back, exhausted.*]

Is there anything I can get you, Madame?

MARGUERITE: Oh, a shawl, Yvette, I'm so cold!

YVETTE [*surprised*]: But – [*She finds a shawl, puts it about* MARGUERITE'*s shoulders.*]

MARGUERITE: Thank you. [*She touches* YVETTE *on the cheek.*] You're so good to me.

YVETTE: Shall I go for the doctor?

MARGUERITE: Whatever for?

YVETTE: We wouldn't have to pay him. He'd come for you.

MARGUERITE: But I don't need him! [*She laughs at* YVETTE *happily.*] You see? I'm perfectly well!

YVETTE: Good, I'll bring supper!

MARGUERITE: No!

YVETTE: A little soup . . . just a little?

MARGUERITE: No, no. [*But* YVETTE *stands over her.*] Well, if you must.

[YVETTE, *triumphant, rushes out.*

A door clangs below. The sound of voices. ARMAND *bursts into the room.*]

ARMAND: What's the matter, she ran down the stairs like a weasel!

MARGUERITE: Nothing's the matter. The silly girl's got a soft heart.

ARMAND: You look pale. I didn't hurt you – did I hurt you?

MARGUERITE: No, I'm just cold.

ARMAND: Cold? The room's stifling . . . have you a fever? [*He puts a hand on her cheek.*] You're icy!

MARGUERITE: It's nothing.

ARMAND: I hit you.

[*He looks at her, then takes off round the room, prowling restlessly, looking at everything, touching things.*]

The room! [*He spins round, taking it in.*] It's exactly the same as before! I thought everything had been sold?

MARGUERITE: I managed to buy some of the furniture. The rest I had copied.

ARMAND: Why? [*He inspects the room, checking.*]

MARGUERITE: I wanted everything to be the same.

[*Pause*]

ARMAND [*low*]: I should like to burn this room. And you with it.

MARGUERITE: Do it, then.

[*Pause*]

ARMAND: Why?

MARGUERITE [*slight pause*]: You know why.

ARMAND: I don't believe it.

MARGUERITE: It's the truth.

ARMAND: All a lie. All those days, all those nights. Coming up for air, not just from love but from the ecstasy of talk. All nothing?

Do you know what I've been through? I'm a dead man. Look at me. I'm uglier than before. At least then there was no possibility.

MARGUERITE: Forget . . . survive me. I'm useless to you! If I loved you the best thing I ever did for you was to let you go.

ARMAND: Is that why? You thought you'd ruin me –?

MARGUERITE [*harsh*]: No. It's as I said in my letter. I was bored. I'd had enough.

ARMAND: I don't believe you. Look at me. Do you know what it's cost me to come to this house? What am I doing in this room . . . ?

MARGUERITE: Don't . . . [*She weeps.*] . . . don't . . .

ARMAND [*desperate that she shouldn't cry*]: Don't – oh don't . . .

[*He sweeps her into his arms. They hold each other in a desperate embrace.*]

My love . . . my own love! I've been dead . . . everything dry, everything smelling of metal in my head . . . I see, I hear people's voices, but I'm cut off, I'm not part of it any more . . . Please . . . oh please . . . please, please, please, please . . .

MARGUERITE: No. You mustn't. You don't understand, Armand – oh, your dear, beautiful face –

ARMAND: Nothing . . . all I . . . just to . . . never, never let me go . . .

MARGUERITE: No, never! No! I don't care! Armand . . . !

ARMAND: You won't go away again? You won't go . . . ?

MARGUERITE: No, of course not. Never. It was . . . I won't leave you . . . I'll never leave you, how could I –
[*They kiss.*]
We'll be together, what does it matter, all the rest – unimportant. I'll fetch my son, I'll get him back. We'll go away, the three of us. Just us. Our life. On our own.

ARMAND: Yes! We'll go to Italy! [*He kisses her hands.*] . . . we'll see the hill towns – Siena, Perugia . . . and along the valley . . . Verona, Vicenza . . . all the way to Venice . . . ah, Venice – my love, you're so cold!

MARGUERITE: No, I'm warm!

ARMAND: We'll sail the Bosphorus. Then Greece . . . the Parthenon . . . Egypt – what is it? [*To* YVETTE, *who stands at the door.*
YVETTE *looks from* ARMAND *to* MARGUERITE.]

YVETTE [*soft*]: It's the Prince, Madame.

MARGUERITE: Tell him to go away! Tell him I'm not here . . . I shall not . . .
[*She turns, smiles at* YVETTE. *Then she pauses, looks from one to the other.*]
Wait. Yvette . . .

YVETTE: Madame . . . ?

MARGUERITE: Wait . . . why not? Why not? Oh! [*She laughs, full of life and energy, and waves to* YVETTE *to bring up the* PRINCE.
YVETTE *nods and goes.*]

ARMAND: What are you doing?

MARGUERITE: My love! A gift!
I shall not come to you empty-handed! [*She kisses him feverishly.*] We can buy a string of camels . . . a fleet of gondolas . . . a palazzo!

ARMAND: You'd have him? Here? Now?

MARGUERITE: Armand – emeralds! Rivers of them! They'll buy us a lifetime of freedom! You see? I bring you a dowry!

[*He breaks away from her.*]

Oh Armand! He'll fall asleep on the carpet!

ARMAND: Why?

MARGUERITE: It has nothing to do with us! It's not important! Don't!

No, don't . . . you can't . . . not now . . .

[*He throws money in her face and goes.*]

MARGUERITE, *on the floor, becomes hysterical.*

YVETTE *enters.*

MARGUERITE *looks up.*]

Is he still there? The Prince?

YVETTE: Yes.

MARGUERITE [*feverish and imperious*]: Then show him up!

[YVETTE *goes.*

MARGUERITE *crosses to her dressing table. With an effort, she makes herself beautiful.*

She turns from the dressing table, smiling, alight and alive as YVETTE *opens the door and the Russian* PRINCE *lurches into the room.*]

PRINCE [*in Russian*]: My beautiful shining, bright-eyed herring . . .

MARGUERITE: Sergei . . . [*She takes his arm.*] My dear . . . [*She manhandles him across to the elbow chair.*] You look tired . . . Yvette, what are you thinking of . . . brandy, for His Highness . . .

PRINCE [*in Russian*]: Don't talk shit, where's the brandy?

MARGUERITE [*helping him off with his coat, coos over him*]: You've been in a skirmish again . . .

[*The lights begin to go.*]

PRINCE [*in Russian*]: What have you got your clothes on for?

MARGUERITE: My bear . . . [*She begins to fondle him.*] . . . You'll feel better . . . So much better . . .

[*The Russian grunts. He falls asleep, half trapping* MARGUERITE. *A pause, he breathes heavily. Then* MARGUERITE *begins to struggle, trying to free herself. She half rises from the bed. And has a massive haemorrhage.*]

SCENE VI

MARGUERITE *is in bed.* YVETTE *moves about the room quietly. A* MAN *comes to the door. She goes to him, speaks to him quietly, indicating* MARGUERITE. *But he insists, and she stands back, to allow him in. He begins to take an inventory of the room. Eventually he approaches the bed.*

MAN: Begging your pardon, Miss. [*He makes an inventory of the bed and its hangings.*]
MARGUERITE [*a whisper*]: How much for me?
MAN: Beg pardon?
MARGUERITE [*sighs*]: Not a lot.
    [*The* MAN *goes.*
    A PRIEST *arrives and begins to murmur.*
    The rest of the company arrive severally and sit about at a distance. The PRIEST *finishes his prayers and rises quietly.*

    A long silence. Only MARGUERITE'*s breathing can be heard.*]
    [*half rises*] Jean-Paul?
    [*The others half rise, but* MARGUERITE *subsides.* YVETTE *tidies the bedsheet swiftly.*

    MARGUERITE'*s breathing rasps. It strengthens and falters, becomes irregular.*

    MARGUERITE *dies.*]

SCENE VII

The Tuilerie Gardens, very early morning. The birds sing. The sun becomes stronger, slanting through the trees. A clock strikes six.

Pause. Then GASTON *and* ARMAND *appear. They stroll, side by side, without speaking.* ARMAND *pauses, looks up.*

ARMAND: What time is it?

GASTON [*consults his watch*]: Just after six.

ARMAND: You're not tired?

GASTON: Not in the least.

ARMAND: Nevertheless I have exploited your good will.

GASTON: On the contrary, if it has been of the least assistance for you to tell me your story I am more than delighted to have missed a few nights' sleep. I only wish, now that the lady lies in peace, that you were . . . that you were able to –

ARMAND: To what?

GASTON: To forgive yourself. There is no doubt that Mademoiselle Gautier was a sick woman. And . . . forgive me . . . her way of life – I beg you not to misunderstand me, I imply no criticism. But . . . alas . . . we are the sum of our circumstances and our past. Your pardon if I seem harsh.

ARMAND: I wish you had known her.

GASTON: Yes. I daresay.

[*Pause*]

It's a fine day. Spring. Summer soon.

[*He turns at the sound of voices.*

PRUDENCE *enters, followed by* BELA, SOPHIE, CLÉMENCE *and the* COUNT. *They are all in evening clothes.*]

PRUDENCE: My dear Armand! What a surprise! We all thought you were abroad! [*Politely*] Monsieur . . . [*She inclines her head to* GASTON.] We've been celebrating an engagement! Clémence and Canute, Armand! What a coup!

[*A* WAITER *serves brioches to* CLÉMENCE *and the* COUNT *and they eat stolidly.*]

BELA [*to* ARMAND]: Where have you been hiding?

PRUDENCE [*enjoying the sunshine*]: How splendid! Glorious weather!

CLÉMENCE: Yes, makes you glad to be alive!

SOPHIE: Why don't you shut up?

[CLÉMENCE *remembers* ARMAND, *claps her hand over her mouth.*]

PRUDENCE: We've been making plans for the summer. We're all off to Sweden for the wedding. Come with us, Armand.

CLÉMENCE: I can't wait to hear them call me Milady!

BELA: Come to England, for the racing. We'll buy stock, go north after for the hunting.

GASTON: I think Monsieur Duval wishes to remain in Paris.

PRUDENCE: Nonsense.

CLÉMENCE: He can't stay in Paris.

BELA [*sits by* ARMAND]: Stop it.

SOPHIE: Leave him. Well, he finished her, didn't he?

BELA [*to* ARMAND]: Such . . . enjoyment.

GASTON [*clears his throat*]: Your friends are right. Travel, I beg of you. Go to Italy . . . the hill towns – Siena, Perugia . . . go to Venice . . . Venice, my dear fellow!

> [ARMAND *weeps.*]

BELA: Goddamn it, what have you said to him!

PRUDENCE: No. Leave him.

> [*The others draw off.* PRUDENCE *allows* ARMAND *to cry.*]

Ah, my friend, no more rapture? No more grand passion? Well, can it last? At least you lived it. For a while. At least now you understand. That it's all we have. Even I know that. Armand, don't betray what you had by destroying yourself. Do you know what she would have done if you had died? She would have gone away for a season – wasted a year of her looks. And then she would have remade her life. From necessity.

ARMAND: I have no life.

PRUDENCE: Poor Armand. You thought to rescue Marguerite Gautier and you lost her.

> [*He does not reply.*]

Perhaps, after all, she preferred her freedom.

> [*He looks up.*]

Has it never occurred to you that some of us might prefer the life – given the alternatives?

ARMAND: No. No. [*He rises.*] You killed her.

Were we so threatening? One man? One woman? It was the wrong transaction.

There was a chance. A chance for something real. Something mutual. There for the taking like an apple on a tree. Something ordinary. Unnoticeable.

PRUDENCE: A dream.

ARMAND: There was respect. Honour. Possibility. But you don't want that. What do you want?

[*Pause.*

PRUDENCE *looks at him, and then across to* GASTON.]

PRUDENCE [*lightly*]: Who's your friend?

ARMAND: You make me ugly.

Unpleasant.

Very well. If that's what you want . . .

[*He goes.* PRUDENCE *looks after him, frowning in the sunlight. Then, dismissing the thought of him, she rises, putting up her sunshade.*]

PRUDENCE: *Eh bien, mes braves* . . . a little beauty sleep! Monsieur Gaston, my card. Call on me – no, I insist! I am at home every afternoon at five. You need enjoyment – you see, I can tell. Trust Prudence. Bela . . . Sophie? Where's the Countess?

[CLÉMENCE *and the* COUNT, *eating steadily, look up.* PRUDENCE *descends on them and ushers them away.* SOPHIE *laughs and walks off.* BELA *turns, bows ironically to* GASTON *and follows* SOPHIE *off.*

GASTON, *alone, looks after them. He puts on his hat and goes, separately.*]

LOVING WOMEN

CHARACTERS

FRANK
SUSANNAH
CRYSTAL

Loving Women was presented at the Arts Theatre on 1 February 1984 by David Jones and Jonathan Gems. Jonathan Gems was the designer, Stephen Rolfe designed the lighting and the production manager was Tony Harpur. The play was directed by Philip Davis.

The cast was as follows:

SUSANNAH	Marion Bailey
FRANK	David Beames
CRYSTAL	Gwyneth Strong

SYNOPSIS OF SCENES

ACT I

SCENE I: Bed-sitting room of a flat in Notting Hill Gate, London. The time is 1973.

SCENE II: The same, a year later

ACT II

The same room, ten years later

THE SETTING

The furnishings and style of the room reveal the inhabitants. As they change, so the room changes, and from the physical alterations we deduce their social, political and psychological history.

ACT I

*The interior of a flat, 1973. The bed is on the floor, a mattress with
an old eiderdown over. Furniture is sparse, but there is a hi-fi with
large twin speakers. Political or ethnic posters, including Ché and
Mao.*

*A man sits up in bed, propped up with cushions. There is something
worrying about him . . . something sharp, intense, melancholy,
even dangerous. He looks ill – his face is pale under the beard. This
is* FRANK.

*The young woman sitting on the floor and leaning over him is thin
and angular in tight, faded jeans. She is not particularly good-
looking or noticeable until her face becomes alive with humour or
feeling. She wears a battered old anorak, has an enormous cloth
shoulder-bag weighed down with books and papers. This is*
SUSANNAH. *She leans over* FRANK, *groping in her bag with a smile,
then presents him with a record, looking at his face to record his
pleasure. He takes it and looks at it neutrally.*

FRANK: Oh . . . thanks.
SUSANNAH: I knew you'd want it.
FRANK: Yuh.
SUSANNAH: Quite a job to get it – sold out!
　　　[*He nods, inspecting the sleeve.*]
　　Well. So – how's it going?
CRYSTAL [*enters*]: Hey you're not gonna talk about work, are you?
　　　[*She is dazzling, young and fresh with long limbs and shining
　　　hair, her clothes bang on fashion.*]

159

SUSANNAH: No, no.

CRYSTAL: Only he's not supposed to.

SUSANNAH: Sure.

CRYSTAL: The doctor said no worry.

SUSANNAH: Sure – great. No . . . everything's O K. The department's coping all right . . . well enough for you not to worry . . . not so well that you aren't missed, of course. [*She puts her hand on her heart.*] 'It ain't the same, mate!'

FRANK: What are you doing?

SUSANNAH: Oh a fantastic new scheme . . . we're involving *all* the kids – music, design, dance . . . everybody involved, we're after total interdependence. [*Hugs him.*] Natural follow-on from you, love.

FRANK: Sounds quite a big thing.

CRYSTAL: Come O N! He's not supposed to talk about it!

SUSANNAH: Oh . . . sorry! No . . . great . . . sorry, Crystal! How's she been as a nurse?

FRANK: Fine. Beautiful pair of knockers bending over me, I have to feel good.

> [*He reaches for a cigarette, and* CRYSTAL *quickly gets up and lights it for him.* SUSANNAH *notices that he is smoking, and shakes her head, frowning slightly.* FRANK *draws gratefully on the cigarette and picks up the disc, examining the sleeve.*]

SUSANNAH: Do you want to hear it?

FRANK: Yeah.

> [*She hands him the earphones, crosses, puts on the record.* FRANK, *wearing the earphones, nods and smiles briefly.* SUSANNAH *and* CRYSTAL *move apart for a chat.*]

SUSANNAH: How is he?

CRYSTAL: Not too grand.

SUSANNAH: He looks terrible. Thanks a bundle, Crystal, it's really great of you, I'd no idea it was going to be such a chore.

CRYSTAL: Don't worry about it.

SUSANNAH: I feel awful –

CRYSTAL: No I enjoy it, honest. Gives me something to do at nights . . . least I don't go out spending money. Anyway, for

God's sake, you done me a favour! Couldn't wait to get out of that squat.

SUSANNAH: Squitty?

CRYSTAL: I had to clean the whole place out so's me Mum could come and visit. Hey, she said . . . our Crystal . . . you're never living in here with all these fellers! Give her the thrill of her life.
  [*They laugh.*]
  She needn't have worried.

SUSANNAH: What do you mean?

CRYSTAL: We-ell . . .
  [SUSANNAH *continues to look puzzled.*]
  . . . they're all your sort of lot, ain't they?

SUSANNAH: What do you mean?

CRYSTAL: They're all – liberated. Puts you off.

SUSANNAH: Oh . . . why?

CRYSTAL: You know Harry, the one with the beard?

SUSANNAH: Tall?

CRYSTAL: No, that's Pete, his is all scratchy, no, the silky one . . .
  [SUSANNAH *lifts her head in a nod.*]
  – you don't know what you're getting, mate of mine didn't half get a shock when her old man shaved off, he had a hare lip . . . they were married and all. Anyway . . . this Harry . . . asks me out for a burger . . . nips in for a six-pack on the way home, I think iyiy . . . back to the squat, he sits me down on one of them big cushions you keep rolling off . . . starts pulling on his boots and I think we-ell, he smells all right . . . you know, clean – anyway, I get a bit of a cuddle, I'm just relaxing, fishing round for it when all of a sudden he puts his mush in me ear and whispers, 'What would you like me to do, Crystal?'
  [*They both burst out laughing.*]

SUSANNAH [*laughing*]: What did you say?

CRYSTAL: I thought of a thing or two, I can tell you. 'Look,' he says, 'I'm not one of those geezers that jumps a gal . . . I'm not the bam-bam, thank-you ma'am type.' I said, 'What?' Got out the bloody cigarettes.

SUSANNAH: It put you off?
  [*There is an objective curiosity in* SUSANNAH's *glance.*]

CRYSTAL: I thought he was going to bring out the manual – Christ, what are they after, good marks or something?

SUSANNAH: You like the man to take the lead?

CRYSTAL: Sure . . . within reason. Tell you one thing, your lot's never gonna be up for rape.

[SUSANNAH *gives her another mild look, as at a specimen.*]

SUSANNAH: How long had you been there . . . at the squat?

CRYSTAL: I was only filling in, till I got somewhere. I couldn't find anything. It's ridiculous.

I really love the room here, I'm ever so grateful . . . I mean, what with it being near the salon –

SUSANNAH: Sure . . . well, it's OK for now. I mean, when I get back, we'll have to –

CRYSTAL: Sssh. [*As* FRANK *stirs, listening to the music*] Did you say something, Frank?

[FRANK *lifts the bins inquiringly.*]

Need anything?

[*He smiles, shakes his head, puts back the earphones.*]

[*lowering her voice*] He's been ever so rough.

SUSANNAH: Oh? Why didn't you let me know?

CRYSTAL: He didn't want to.

SUSANNAH: You should have told me.

CRYSTAL: He said not to worry you, what with the new job and everything. It was all in his eyes.

SUSANNAH: His eyes?

CRYSTAL: This rash . . . all up the side of his head! The ulcers got in his eyes, it was terrible! [*Her eyes glisten at the horror of it.*]

SUSANNAH: My God!

CRYSTAL: Oh, it's OK now.

SUSANNAH: You're sure? I must talk to the doctor –

CRYSTAL: Nah, honest. He says just to build him up . . . you know.

SUSANNAH: You should have told me. It's so bloody unfair! He's worked so hard!

CRYSTAL: Will he get his job back?

SUSANNAH: Oh yes, he's established – but he's missing this marvellous new project. It's a follow-on from what we were doing here at the Centre – d'you remember, we were telling you about it.

CRYSTAL: Oh. Yeah.

SUSANNAH: I wish you'd go down there, Crystal. The girls would love to hear about hairdressing . . . you know, just to tell them what it's like . . . nothing formal, just a gossip. I could give them a ring if you like – what nights are you free?

CRYSTAL: I work late quite a bit.

SUSANNAH: What about next Thursday . . . they all come for the disco.

CRYSTAL: No, not really.

SUSANNAH: 'It's for the community' . . .

CRYSTAL: No, well . . .

SUSANNAH: I don't want to force you.

CRYSTAL: You know how it is.

SUSANNAH: Sure.

CRYSTAL: Only I'm on my feet all day.

SUSANNAH: No, I understand, really. It was just that –

CRYSTAL: Oh, sure. I'll get his dinner.

[*She exits.*

SUSANNAH *crosses to* FRANK, *takes off his earphones.*]

SUSANNAH: OK, love?

FRANK: Come here.

[*They embrace.*]

FRANK: I've missed you.

SUSANNAH: How's it been?

FRANK: OK.

SUSANNAH: No, really –

[*He gives a funny little mirthless smile that doesn't convince her.*]

– God, I should be here!

FRANK: You're keeping things going.

SUSANNAH: Yes. Birmingham needs you! How long do you think it will be before –

FRANK [*quick*]: Hard to say.

SUSANNAH: But you're feeling better?

FRANK: Yuh. Well . . . more real.

SUSANNAH: Great. Wait till you see the new schedules . . . we have not been idle! [*She delves into her bag.*] I brought you some of that ginseng . . . Vitamin E . . . Clare made some sesame cakes but the dog with the complicated psyche ate them. God, my mother turned up. She's into haute classe gardening now . . . peonies – are you feeling all right?

FRANK: Mmm.

SUSANNAH: No more panics?

FRANK: A bit. Coping. [*He gives her a darting, accusing look.*] I was bloody glad to get out, I can tell you that.

SUSANNAH: But I thought – I thought you liked it.

> [*He looks up at the ceiling with a grimace of distaste.*
> *Slight pause*]

Yes. Not funny. Still, we were lucky . . . getting you into Ian's group.

> [*He nods briefly.*]

Look I know you hated jumping the queue. [*Slight pause*] What could I do – you were going up the wall! The only alternative was to –

FRANK: I couldn't have stood –

SUSANNAH: I know, we've seen it. [*With a little shudder*] Knowing too much makes it tough. Anyway, Ian's a marvellous guy.

FRANK: Yeah. [*Another darting look, unobserved by* SUSANNAH.]

SUSANNAH: Human.

FRANK: Mmm.

SUSANNAH: There should be thousands of small units like that, places where you can work things out without hassle instead of awful great wards full of –

FRANK: Yup.

> [*A silence*]

SUSANNAH: How goes it with Crystal?

FRANK: Crystal? Oh, fine.

SUSANNAH: Not too – she doesn't bug you?

FRANK: No, no . . . she really looks after me, she's great.

SUSANNAH: Good! Of course it works on a bilateral level –

FRANK: What?

SUSANNAH: It's not a patronizing situation . . . she's able to contribute. There's no question of tenure . . . I mean, when I get back –

FRANK: When are you coming?

SUSANNAH: Tomorrow! [*She hugs him fiercely.*] I wish it was tomorrow! Don't worry. I'm not about to abandon the fort. I know the last thing you need is some soppy, individualistic gesture . . . hang on, Snoopy! We'll sort Crystal out – for God's sake she can afford an economic rent, fair rent anyway, she pulls a fortune crimping. I asked her to go down to the Centre, talk to the kids.

FRANK: What did she say?

SUSANNAH: Nothing in it for her. She's pretty single-minded really. After some upmarket guy in a sports car. You can understand it, her background's pretty deprived . . . still . . . I mean, they are her own sort.

FRANK: She's OK.

SUSANNAH: Oh, great. I was afraid she might be getting on your nerves, she comes on a bit. Still, fine for now. We're lucky really, it bridges the gap –

[CRYSTAL *enters with a tray of food.*]

CRYSTAL [*to* FRANK]: I done you some supper and you got to eat it. [*To* SUSANNAH] You didn't want nothing, did you, love?

SUSANNAH [*with a swift appraisal of* FRANK'*s tray*]: No thanks. [*To* FRANK, *in surprise*] Are you eating meat?

CRYSTAL: Oh I got him off that vegetarian – it's useless! You can get deficiencies, I read it. You have to eat pounds of chickpeas to get the protein, unless you're doing heavy labour you can't work off the starch, it's a load of rubbish. D'you want some sauce, Frank?

FRANK: Thanks!

[*He sloshes on the sauce and begins to eat heartily, to* SUSANNAH'*s astonishment.*]

CRYSTAL: I'll get the crumble. Sure you don't want none, Susannah?

[SUSANNAH *smiles, shakes her head.*
CRYSTAL *goes.*]

SUSANNAH: Darling, I can shove it all in my *Evening Standard*, she'll never know.

FRANK [*mouth full*]: It's fine, thanks.

SUSANNAH: You should be on a decent diet – that's dried potato!

FRANK: She puts butter and pepper in, it's good.

[*He offers her a forkful. She shakes her head, smiling.*]

SUSANNAH: Oh I don't care what it is, it's great to see you eating again.

[*She grasps his hand. He is busy eating.*

CRYSTAL *enters. She puts down the pudding, sets* FRANK's *napkin straight.* FRANK *looks up at her and grins.*]

Are you still on antibiotics?

CRYSTAL: His bum's like a pincushion.

[*She gets a look from* FRANK. *He bends to the plate, eating.*]

SUSANNAH: He ought to be on goat's milk yoghurt. It puts the flora back in the stomach.

CRYSTAL: I'll get him some cream. [*She goes out.*]

SUSANNAH [*embraces him*]: Have you missed me?

FRANK: Mmm.

SUSANNAH: If it weren't for this bloody project! Oh! Your hands!

FRANK: What's the matter?

SUSANNAH: They're so thin!

[*She takes his dinner plate, fondles his hands. He lies back among the cushions.*]

You're getting better. I can feel it. There's so much to do. If you could see the kids! I was in tears the other day . . . tears of rage – I had to talk to this pisser of a headmaster about this kid . . . he wants to be a doctor – he's bright, for God's sake, but a West Indian . . . not even a Paki, well, I mean, Christ, no wonder we fragment! Oh, my love. But we grow! It's painful . . . the mould cracks all the time, it makes us invalids – but we do reshape, we do grow! Did I tell you, we've got twenty-five per cent coloureds in the group now!

[CRYSTAL *enters, bearing the cream. She is wearing the most beautiful, semi-see-through kimono in fragile silk, with floating wisps and panels, making her look like a creature from another world.*]

166

CRYSTAL: Here, Susannah, what d'you think of this?

SUSANNAH: Wow . . . 'great, man'!

CRYSTAL: Got it off a client.

SUSANNAH: Fantastic. Is it . . . um . . . is it for anyone special?

CRYSTAL: Nah, I'm breaking it in on Frank . . . bit of skin therapy.
[*She laughs loudly, and begins to walk about, showing off the kimono, doing a turn.*]

SUSANNAH [*to* FRANK]: You're not tired?

FRANK: I'm fine.

CRYSTAL: Guess who this is?

SUSANNAH: Oh . . . ah . . . Racquel Welch?

CRYSTAL: Nah.

SUSANNAH: Marlene?

CRYSTAL: No! Come on, Frank . . .

FRANK: Marilyn Monroe.

CRYSTAL: Right! Your favourite!

SUSANNAH: Marilyn Monroe?

CRYSTAL: Right. He's been holding out on you, Susannah.
[*She puts on some music and begins to move to the music.*]

SUSANNAH [*to* FRANK]: Do you really go for her?

FRANK: What, love?

SUSANNAH: Marilyn Monroe.
[*He nods, watching* CRYSTAL.]

FRANK [*watching* CRYSTAL]: Why not?

SUSANNAH: No reason. You and a few million other guys.
[*Slight pause, they watch* CRYSTAL.]
She was such a sad woman.

FRANK: Oh, I don't know.
[*Slight pause, they watch* CRYSTAL.]

SUSANNAH: What do you mean?

FRANK: What?

SUSANNAH: Nothing.
[CRYSTAL *dances. She is beautiful.* FRANK *watches, a dazed expression on his face.* SUSANNAH *watches with a smile, wagging her head to the music.*
The music ends.]

CRYSTAL *throws herself down, legs in the air.* FRANK *does a slow clap, then applauds.*]

CRYSTAL: Phew . . . wow! Rrrah! Hey! I nearly forgot . . . Frank – the surprise . . . we forgot! [*She trips off in her mod shoes to the kitchen . . . calls back*] . . . Susannah's present!

SUSANNAH: For me?

CRYSTAL: Hang on, won't be a sec!

SUSANNAH: She's great, isn't she?

FRANK: Yeah.

CRYSTAL [*off*]: Oh sod it.

SUSANNAH: Never mind, Crystal, next time will do if you can't find it.

CRYSTAL [*as she enters*]: I'm getting it all over me. Here. For you.

SUSANNAH: What is it?

CRYSTAL: Lemon curd. We made it. Frank said you liked it.

SUSANNAH: Oh – lovely! Oh . . . [*She smiles, happy, at* FRANK.]

CRYSTAL: Here, have a taste. [*She takes back the jar, unscrews the lid, dips a finger in and tastes.*] Ooh it's great, here – no, go on . . .

[*They all dip in . . .*

To FRANK]

you twot, you've got it all over the bed . . . oh, fantastic, now he's got it in his hair . . . honest! You should of seen him in the kitchen, Susannah, Jesus! [*She laughs, leans over the bed, cleaning him off.*] Here, Susannah, want to lick it off?

SUSANNAH: Do you need a tissue?

[CRYSTAL *takes the tissue from her, dabs at* FRANK. *The tissue sticks to his hair.*]

CRYSTAL [*giggling*]: Now he looks really pretty! Don't he look a pretty boy – you got to stay like that, eh Susannah?

SUSANNAH: It's very good, Crystal. Is it your own recipe?

CRYSTAL: Me Mum's. It would have been even better only someone was demanding onion soup at the time, so it tastes a bit of onions.

SUSANNAH: No, it's lovely.

CRYSTAL: All the real thing –

FRANK: Sugar, lemons –

CRYSTAL: Butter and eggs – see, we'll get him doing it yet!

[SUSANNAH *tightens the lid carefully, wraps the jar in a scarf and puts it carefully into a shoulder bag.*]

SUSANNAH: Shit, I must go. [*She looks at* FRANK *poignantly.*]

CRYSTAL: Oh. Right. I'll just go and . . . [*She makes herself scarce. Slight pause*]

SUSANNAH: I hate leaving you . . . I hate it, it doesn't feel right. Are you really OK?

[*He nods briefly.*]

You're sure? [*She bends and kisses him, and then hugs him urgently.*] This thing is really fantastic, love. If it works and it's bloody going to after all our struggle we'll stream the pilot and introduce a play-integrated growth scheme for every school-leaver in the UK – urban, rural, the lot. Believe it, love . . . just hang in there, hmm? [*She bends, kisses him on the mouth, squeezes his hand in a last affectionate gesture and rises, giving a clenched-fist salute in farewell.*] Up the revolution!

[FRANK *looks up at her, nods.*]

CRYSTAL [*off*]: Oh, you off?

SUSANNAH [*going*]: I must go. Keep an eye on him for me, Crystal.

CRYSTAL [*off*]: Sure.

SUSANNAH [*off*]: Look, you will give me a call if . . . you know . . . if anything –

CRYSTAL [*off*]: Yeah, course I will.

SUSANNAH [*off*]: He's lost so much weight!

CRYSTAL [*off*]: Don't worry, soon build him up.

[*Their voices become distant. The sound of a door, sonorous.* CRYSTAL *returns. She crosses to the window, parts the curtains slightly to watch* SUSANNAH *recede across the street. She turns, as* FRANK *looks up. He looks away.*]

Feeling bad?

FRANK: No, I feel fine.

CRYSTAL: Good! [*She sits on the bed.*
He stares ahead, his mind elsewhere. She slips a look at him, jumps up.]

Ahh! I'm a nurd!

[*She runs over to the table, picks up a large envelope, returns, and showers travel brochures over the bed.*]

Right, what do you fancy? Club Mediterranée? It's a new idea, you get to meet people . . . nah, maybe not this time . . . [*She forages*] . . . what about Costa del Sol – warm there. Friend of mine works in a bar near Estepona, in the winter she goes skiing – yeah, in Spain, she's says it's only a two-hour drive, they're really going to open it up, bring in facilities.

[*He laughs briefly.*]

Good for yuh! Muscles! [*She looks at other brochures.*] What about the Canary Islands?

[*He looks at her. She smooths his hair back.*]

Think about nice things.

[*He nods.*]

Why not? You might as well. [*She sings, and rises and does a march to the song.*] 'What's the use of worrying, It never was worth while, So, pack up your troubles in your old kitbag, And smile, smile, smile!' [*She salutes at the end of the song.*] My Uncle Ted used to sing that to me when I was little. Course he really went for the Dorsey brothers and Glenn Miller . . . you know, swing.

Come on.

My trouble is I talk too much.

[*She sits on the bed again, nestling close.*

whispers in his ear] Fancy a tongue sandwich?

[FRANK *grabs her with a sudden, urgent savagery, and they embrace so fiercely that they roll on to the floor. She hooks her knees round him in a fierce, prolonged embrace. They break apart.*]

FRANK: What's the matter?

CRYSTAL: Nothing.

FRANK: What are you thinking?

CRYSTAL: Nothing. You got a bit of colour in your face, that's all.

[*The lights begin to go.*

They stay on the floor, arms about each other.]

Course there's always Jersey, that's nice in the summer. Or Capri – what about Capri?

The same. A few changes. The bed has gone. There is a sofa, some cane furniture, a mobile, bright cushions and a carrycot. The pictures have been changed. Mao and Ché have gone and are replaced by the Aristide Bruant and a Mucha poster of a girl.

SUSANNAH *is onstage. She wears a coat, her bag over her shoulder. She prowls, inspecting the room, sees a wedding photograph on a bookcase, crosses, picks it up and looks at it intently.*

CRYSTAL [*off*]: Won't be a minute . . . I'll just turn the oven down. [*She enters, bright in a Laura Ashley dress and a Twiggy bandeau.*] Oh, don't look at that, we was all pissed out of our heads.
    [SUSANNAH *replaces the photograph carefully.*]
SUSANNAH: You look wonderful.
CRYSTAL: Yeah, not too bad. Cost a fortune that. I was thinking of having it dyed, so I could wear it round the clubs.
SUSANNAH: It's beautiful.
CRYSTAL: So . . . how've you been?
    [SUSANNAH *shrugs.*]
  Sit yourself down, take your coat off – here, I'll hang it up for you.
SUSANNAH: Don't bother.
CRYSTAL: No, it's no trouble.
SUSANNAH: Thank you.
CRYSTAL: You look ever so well.
SUSANNAH: Thanks. [*She sits.*]
CRYSTAL: Frank's not back. Any minute. Would you like a drink? I don't know what we've got . . . [*It is all sitting there ready, on a tray.*] Whisky? Gin, vodka? Bacardi?
SUSANNAH: Oh . . . ah, I'll . . .
CRYSTAL: How about a sherry?
SUSANNAH: Fine.
CRYSTAL: Light or dark?
SUSANNAH: What? Oh, light.
CRYSTAL: It's more dry. The light.

SUSANNAH: Yes.

> [*She watches as* CRYSTAL *pours the sherry carefully into the correct glass, then pours herself a very generous whisky.*]

CRYSTAL: It's been ages. You didn't mind me ringing –

SUSANNAH: Of course not.

CRYSTAL: Only we met some of his friends and they said, like, you was back. It seemed silly not to . . . well, you know . . . you're all friends and we often have little do's – anyway, I said, listen, I'm going to ring Susannah –

SUSANNAH: What did he say?

CRYSTAL: Huh, don't listen to him, no, it's really nice. Cheers.

> [*They drink. Slight pause*]

I'm glad you could come.

SUSANNAH: You're looking very well.

CRYSTAL: Put on a bit of weight.

SUSANNAH: It doesn't show.

CRYSTAL: I still have to suck in. [*She draws herself in.*] Come and see Nicole.

> [*They go. We hear their voices.*]

[*off*] There! What do you think of her . . . ah . . . she's asleep . . . ah! Who do you think she looks like? Look, a little bubble, did you see? Mum made the jacket, it's wool, most of the stuff I got's acrylic, it's better for washing, but wool's warmer really. Look at her little fist she always does that, d'you like the blue elephant? My sister-in-law give it me, I said it should have been pink – ooh now don't wake up, there's a good girl . . . perhaps we better . . .

> [*They return.*]

SUSANNAH: Are you feeding her yourself?

CRYSTAL: I did at first – hey, it makes you ever so tired. Anyway, I'm back at work now so she's on the bottle. It's better really. You're more free.

SUSANNAH: You manage all right?

CRYSTAL: Oh yes. I drop her in at the nursery, I'm dead lucky, it's only down the road. Then, pick her up at four, do the shopping, get back in time for Frank's tea. It works very well really.

> [*Silence*]

SUSANNAH: She's lovely.

CRYSTAL: Ah, she's no trouble. I like babies, well, they're cuddly, ain't they . . . even if you do have to clean up the shit! So . . . how have you been? Still working with the – what was it you were doing . . . with the kids?

SUSANNAH: Oh – no, that finished. There was a change of authority.

CRYSTAL: What a shame.

SUSANNAH: Yes.

CRYSTAL: Didn't you do that panto thing, that show you was into?

SUSANNAH: No – well, actually we did a smaller piece – sort of goodbye thing.

CRYSTAL: Nice. What was it about?

SUSANNAH: We tried to improvise on things the kids brought themselves . . . we were anxious not to impose.

[CRYSTAL *nods wisely*.]

Obviously the idea was to celebrate *their* feelings, *their* values.

CRYSTAL: Sort of do your own thing sort of thing?

SUSANNAH [*delighted*]: Yes!

CRYSTAL: What did they choose, horror comics? [*With a laugh*.]

SUSANNAH: I know! Actually we did a thing on canals.

CRYSTAL: Canals?

SUSANNAH: We got them going round the libraries, researching the records . . . you know, old maps, books, songs . . . the singing was great . . . [*She sings*]

> If thou'll plod me,
> Then I'll plod thee,
> And the horse'll plod, the three o' we.
> The towpath's long,
> But my man is strong,
> And to Pluckett's Lock,
> We'll surely be.

[*She ends dashingly, looks to* CRYSTAL *for response*.]

With a rock backing, of course.

CRYSTAL: Oh. Yeah. Sure.

SUSANNAH: I brought some pictures. I thought Frank might like to see them.

    [*Silence*]

CRYSTAL: I'm sorry you couldn't come to the wedding. We missed you.

SUSANNAH: Yes.

CRYSTAL: If it wasn't for you, we wouldn't have met. I mean, it's not as if you and Frank was serious.

SUSANNAH: We weren't married, if that's what you mean.

CRYSTAL: He said you didn't want to.

SUSANNAH: Oh. Well, he certainly never asked.

CRYSTAL: But you're not into it, your lot. You've jacked all that in. [*Pause*] It was his idea, you know, getting married.

SUSANNAH: You didn't think about an abortion?

CRYSTAL: No! I hate it, I wouldn't . . . anyway, I'd be too scared – you can get yourself knocked up for good doing that, happened to a friend of mine. Anyway . . .

    [SUSANNAH *looks at her.* CRYSTAL *shrugs.*]

Look, he'd already asked me by then. We was going to get married . . . that's why I never bothered. We was well away when you came down to see us that time. It was a bit awkward really.

SUSANNAH: I didn't know that.

CRYSTAL: No, well, he should of said. Still, he was ill. I think he didn't want to upset you.

SUSANNAH: Upset me!

CRYSTAL: He was feeling bad about leaving all the work to you.

SUSANNAH: Why didn't he tell me? He could have said something! For God's sake! We'd been together for five years!

CRYSTAL: But you were never serious.

SUSANNAH: Serious? What's that supposed to mean? I'm sorry but – look, this *was* my home! I *found* it!.. . . God knows it took long enough. I even plastered the walls. When I found this flat – when I found this flat there was one cold tap sticking out of the wall over there . . . that was it! I can't believe it's the same place. I'm sorry, Crystal, I don't want to be rude. It's just that everything looks so different.

174

CRYSTAL [*small*]: Well it's bound to, isn't it? [*Slight pause*] Frank's changed.

SUSANNAH: Changed? What do you mean – he's all right?

CRYSTAL: Oh yes. But he's given up all that – well, you know.

SUSANNAH: All what?

CRYSTAL: All that stuff.

SUSANNAH: What do you mean? What stuff?

CRYSTAL: You know – projects. What you were doing together. He's settling down, Susannah.

SUSANNAH: Frank? Settling down? [*She gives a brief yok.*] He's vulnerable, he always has been . . . used to faint when we visited loony bins, it gets the men . . . no, not Frank. He's a fighter. Look . . . Crystal . . . I'm not trying to . . . look, believe me . . . it's just that Frank's very special – not just to me – well, to me as well . . . after all, we were together for a . . . [*She falters*] . . . for a long time. Naturally it was a blow . . . it was a shock, you must have realized that, both of you. How could I have come down, I'm surprised you even thought of asking, couldn't believe it . . . to be honest I still can't. Then when I heard about the baby there wasn't much point . . . [*She sighs*] . . . was he hurt? That I didn't come . . . to the wedding?

CRYSTAL: I think he was relieved, really. You know what they're like.

SUSANNAH: Anyway, there it is. And after all, five years of me and he ends up in the bin.

CRYSTAL: Nah it wasn't that, it was overwork!

SUSANNAH: Yes. Yes, he did risk himself. We all did. A lot of it . . . OK, a bit half-assed but at least . . . some of it will stick! You have to try. It's not going to work any more, running for the same old burrows . . . we're rafting off into space – God! Frank sees it. He said to me one day, 'Suse . . . you know what's going to do for us all? Not the failure of intellect, moral, muscle – but the failure of imagination! They're all too busy with their snouts in the trough to smell the fire.'

CRYSTAL: Yeah, he says some really daft things.

SUSANNAH: He'll never give up. I know that. That is one thing I know. For certain. You're obviously what he needs. If it's working for him – just so long as he's on his base again, got his head back. I couldn't – but there's no danger of that. Not Frank. How is he, in himself?

CRYSTAL: He's fine. I mean, he's different – my mother says he's a changed man.

SUSANNAH: How?

CRYSTAL: Drop more?

[SUSANNAH *shakes her head.*]

Sure? We've got plenty.

SUSANNAH: No thanks.

CRYSTAL: I'll just freshen mine up.

[*She crosses, helps herself liberally to more whisky.*]

He's settled down . . . [*She helps herself to ice.*] . . . well, you're bound to, I mean, with the kiddie and all.

SUSANNAH: Yes.

CRYSTAL: He's getting on ever so well at the school. He likes teaching – I mean, we don't go out much, we're saving up, I can't wait to get a place of me own – a proper house, you know, with a garden.

SUSANNAH: Does he see any of his friends?

CRYSTAL: Oh yes, now and then. We've joined the Labour Party . . . well, it was to please my Dad, really.

SUSANNAH [*shocked*]: You what?

CRYSTAL: The Labour Party. We go down there for a drink every Friday.

SUSANNAH: Oh God.

CRYSTAL: What's the matter? Don't you approve?

SUSANNAH: Of Social Democracy? My God. Well, that's it.

[*She gets up, picks up her bag.*]

CRYSTAL: You off?

SUSANNAH: Yes, I'm sorry, there's no –

CRYSTAL: But I've got a steak and kidney in the oven . . . what's the matter? Susannah . . . [*A wail, as she bursts into tears.*]

SUSANNAH: Oh love . . . oh . . . tch! Sit down . . .

[*She cuddles* CRYSTAL, *who weeps.*]

Don't cry . . . oh my dear . . . all right, you cry – have a good cry.

CRYSTAL: I've been a bit tired lately, what with working and the baby . . . he's late!

SUSANNAH: Bastard was always late – hang on, I've got a hankie somewhere.

CRYSTAL: He promised he'd be back in time.

SUSANNAH: Would you like another drink?

[*There is a sound at the door. They both turn.* FRANK *is standing there.*]

CRYSTAL [*voice quivering*]: You're late!

FRANK: What's the matter?

[CRYSTAL *runs out of the room, weeping.*]
What's up?

SUSANNAH: I seem to have upset her.

[*He turns away, takes off his coat, puts down his stuff.*]
I hear you've joined the Labour Party.

[*As he exits to see to* CRYSTAL. *He returns almost at once.*]
Is she all right?

FRANK: Yes.

SUSANNAH: I shouldn't have come, of course.

FRANK: Why not?

SUSANNAH: Yes, it's probably more organic . . . or isn't that the in word any more?

FRANK: I don't know.

SUSANNAH: Well, since I am here, you might as well fill me in. Like, why you did it.

[*He doesn't answer.*]
Was it the breakdown?

[*He looks, nervous that* CRYSTAL *might hear.*]
Well what? Some sort of gesture . . . direct-action consciousness raising? Or did you just fall for nursey?

FRANK: Susannah . . . [*He gestures her to keep her voice down.*]

SUSANNAH: I want to know!

FRANK: Look, will you –

SUSANNAH: I want to know, dammit! [*She walks about, angry.*]
You didn't even get in touch! When I tried to ring, all I got was her on the line rabbiting on about a white wedding – she even asked me to be a bloody bridesmaid – did you know that?

FRANK: No, of course not.

SUSANNAH: I'm not talking about her, I'm talking about *you*. Why? Why didn't you ring . . . I mean, you must have . . . what did you think . . . didn't you think about me? You must have thought *something* . . . unless you were round the bloody twist. I'm sorry. But why? Just tell me why. You owe me. I want to know why.

[*Pause*]

FRANK: I had to.

SUSANNAH: What do you mean?

FRANK: I had to, that's all.

SUSANNAH: Because she was pregnant?

FRANK [*after a pause*]: Ye-es.

SUSANNAH: You bloody liar. She told me you asked her to marry you before that. You hateful sodding liar. [*Slight pause*] Christ.

[*Pause*]

FRANK: I don't know. [*Pause*] She was there when I needed someone.

SUSANNAH: You had me.

FRANK: That was different. [*Slight pause*] Different world.

SUSANNAH: Our world.

FRANK [*frowns*]: Yes. [*Pause*] It wasn't real. It was all out there. Unreal.

SUSANNAH: And she *was* . . . real?

FRANK: Something like that.

SUSANNAH: Oh come on! Look . . . I know it cracked for you, God knows you – but . . . Frank. [*She takes a turn.*] What do you mean? Aren't high-rises real? Aren't the kids we work with real? For God's sake . . . weren't WE real?

FRANK: No. Not really. I don't think so.

SUSANNAH: Not real? All that work? All that fucking we did – not real?

FRANK: It was different.

SUSANNAH [*after a pause*]: What you mean is, you've given up. Caved in.

FRANK: I don't know. Perhaps.

SUSANNAH: Well I do. I felt it coming, long before the breakdown. Manic! Social guilt! Idiotic! The rest of us couldn't even see a movie! Remember the night you found me reading Maigret? Your face! I thought you were going to knife me. [*Slight pause*] Ian told me it would end in suicide or a crack-up –

FRANK: He said that?

[CRYSTAL *appears in the doorway, in an apron.*]

SUSANNAH: He said it to you!

CRYSTAL: Chicken soup?

SUSANNAH: You wouldn't listen!

CRYSTAL: It's ready.

[*They wave at her vaguely.*]

SUSANNAH: We trusted you. Stuck our necks out –

CRYSTAL: Where shall we –

SUSANNAH: Serves us right. Nothing but bloody, bourgeois, individualist adventurism. [*to* CRYSTAL]

CRYSTAL: Eh?

SUSANNAH: The guru! [*waving a hand at him.*

CRYSTAL *gives him a blanched look and disappears.*]

You should have gone for a Jesus cult, you'd be king of the ashram by now.

FRANK: Oh stop it.

SUSANNAH: Well what do you know? What have you ever known? You're privileged.

FRANK: Me?

SUSANNAH: Yes, you! You've never been off the tit. Eleven-plus, scholarship, research fellowship, project grant. You're free . . . white – and male. And you've caved in.

[*Pause*]

FRANK: I'm sorry. I wish I could – [*He sighs deeply, rubs his head.*] – the fact is, I'm tired. I've been teaching all week . . . my brain's a mash.

[*Slight pause*]

SUSANNAH: And the rest of us don't work, I suppose.

[*Another slight pause*]

FRANK: What are you doing now?

SUSANNAH: I'm with Brian Mason. New set-up, kids in care. Not more than eight kids to a house . . . at least the numbers are possible.

FRANK: Sounds good.

SUSANNAH: Except that I've just been promoted. At the moment it's eight little pairs of accusing eyes – God, just when they were beginning to trust me! [*Slight pause*] Where are you teaching?

FRANK: Compton Beck.

SUSANNAH: What? My God. Middle class! My – God. Three years we worked to get that project off the ground . . . fighting the bloody government, the GLC, Nuffield, Arts Council, Rowntree . . . keep going till they crumble, remember? And then you cop out. And bring the rest of us down with you.

A breakdown, yes. But you never came back!

[*Silence. He moves about the room. He pauses by the table, picks up a book and turns the pages idly.*]

FRANK: I read to her. In the evenings. [*He puts the book down. Pause*] It died on me. All of it. All the collaborative, collective crap of it. And the polemic – yes, the polemic we were peddling –

SUSANNAH: What's wrong with that? Group decision! Raise consciousness among the cases – fight submissiveness –

FRANK: So we indoctrinated . . . oh, we weren't into fascism, there weren't any slogans or uniforms, no giveaways – 'Hi kids, I'm Frank, this is Susie, what say we all sit in a circle?' And straight into the knocking copy.

SUSANNAH: I don't recall you with a better suggestion. On the contrary –

FRANK: Banging away at the pit props with fraternal smiles . . . oh, we were going to clear the lot away – revolution . . . fresh start –

SUSANNAH: You believed it.

FRANK [*smiles at her*]: The humanist dream.

SUSANNAH: Yes!

FRANK: Only without blood, of course. Messy stuff, that.

SUSANNAH: Right. Damn right. Our way. The possible way. Words . . . media . . . subversion.

FRANK: Subversion? Subversion . . . us? Susannah – we're the bloody props!

SUSANNAH: What!?

FRANK: Destroy the system . . . our sort? We cultivate it. 'Inter-Related Structures of Third World Matrix Performances . . . foreword by Professor Schumberg, Cal. Tech.' Whatever it is we nourish, it isn't the oppressed. When we arrive, when we knock on all those doors, the tension goes UP!

SUSANNAH: Balls. Who brought every resident on the Churchill estate out on the street –

FRANK: Was anything done? [Slight pause] We're social workers. It's us and Valium instead of a housing policy. We got rid of the nuclear family all right – for you and bloody Brian Mason to go and play mothers and fathers with the debris. Till it's time to make the right career choice and move on.

SUSANNAH: I can't believe this. Industrialized society got rid of the extended family. We, the robot consumers, exist to man the machines. I quote you.

FRANK: Oh? So . . . leave us not impose ourselves – Gahd, we're not into hierarchy. Boss figures? Us? As though we aren't imposing ourselves by just being there? What the hell are we doing, crashing into people's lives?

SUSANNAH: I'm not listening to this, it's sick –

FRANK [shouting]: We add to the pain! We're one more threat!

[CRYSTAL erupts into the room, indignant.]

CRYSTAL: Look, d'you mind? You'll wake the baby!

SUSANNAH: Oh . . . God – sorry, love. No, don't go.

FRANK: Stay, Crystal – don't go.

[CRYSTAL sits on the edge of the sofa. Silence.]

SUSANNAH [mutters]: I refuse to accept them and us, I never have. It's your problem. [Direct] I do not detach myself from the human race as you so consistently and fatally do – and please don't correct my grammar. Nobody's pretending it's easy. God knows there's little enough on offer for most people –

CRYSTAL: Yeah.

SUSANNAH: What? – but if we can break out a few choices . . . give them a chance to choose, make some sort of celebration –

FRANK: Choose?

CRYSTAL [warning]: Frank . . .

FRANK: Choose what? Celebrate what? Fly-overs? No, stay! [*to* CRYSTAL]

SUSANNAH [*to* CRYSTAL]: Don't go –

FRANK: What was it? Yeah, sure . . . community theatre – the great civic venting operation . . . steel bands, your actual black faces . . . way out, man. Only, when they got themselves a carnival together last year, you were all shitting yourselves. It was getting out of hand, right? Or was it that you felt that your delicate white faces weren't all that gratefully welcome. After all . . . [*He directs this at* CRYSTAL, *who happens to be in front of him.*] . . . it is our backyard, right? Robert Ardrey on territory, right?

[CRYSTAL *grimaces at him for hush, goes quickly.*]

SUSANNAH: Frank, that's so unfair. OK . . . OK.

FRANK: There's no need to humour me. I'm perfectly all right.

SUSANNAH: I didn't suggest that you weren't. I think you're being unfair, that's all. But if that's what you believe – I'm not claiming to lay down lines. On anything.

FRANK: Sure. I know. The atom is random . . . we make ourselves up. The old order smasheth, decadence rules. So what do we have? Here we are, kids . . . come and get it – a great big, steaming basinful of fucking nothing at all. Not even a fart.

SUSANNAH: Frank, I don't know what you're talking about.

FRANK: No? No, of course you don't. You're bolted up the bloody middle like Frankenstein's monster, same as the rest of them. Listen . . . listen! Aren't *we* people, too? We've turned ourselves into fucking computerized case histories, along with the rest of them. My God! I'm telling you! The more we stepped backwards into that sour-faced vacuum, the more I – oh Christ, run for your life! Find it, quick . . . a world of green forest and wet pools – lakes of white water . . . leaves and violet skies . . . blue electric toads, hopping . . .

SUSANNAH [*alarmed, she speaks in a careful, level voice*]: Frank . . . what are you talking about?

FRANK: The more 'real' we became, the more I . . .

[*Words fail him and he plays with a lamp fitting, unable for a moment to continue.*]

We're parasites.

SUSANNAH: Don't.

FRANK: We suck the life out. It makes us feel good. The pay's shitty, we say, who can afford a car? Never mind, it's the work that counts. That's what features.

SUSANNAH: Yes. It is. And what is more, some of us see it as more than bandages. A vehicle for change.

FRANK: Change? – oh, we change things. We're the Changemakers all right. We take the magic out of life, and what do we give them? Who needs books on cows and rabbits, are they real life? Let's celebrate reality, for fuck's sake, pop-up sex manuals, Jenny and Kevin at the supermarket – who needs Hans Andersen, anyway wasn't he a pederast or was that Lewis Carroll? Dante . . . Titian – are they the revolution? Rembrandt . . . Tolstoy – elitist garbage, man, culture's for the pooves! Remember your beauty contest? Eight-year-old girls in stuffed bras?

SUSANNAH: Yes, you did make your feelings known, may I remind you that as far as the kids were –

FRANK: 'Kids' –

SUSANNAH: Yes, kids – what do you want me to call them, juveniles? They enjoyed themselves. What's wrong with tits, for God's sake . . . anyway, look, we agreed! Some diminution in quality – yes! If we were challenged – yes. For as long as it takes.

FRANK: We kill people.

SUSANNAH: You're mad.

FRANK: We suck the life out.

SUSANNAH [*in a singing tone*]: I think I hear the cracked bell of revisionism.

FRANK: Remember going to Austria last year?

SUSANNAH: I asked you to come, you wouldn't take the time off.

FRANK: Once to ski, and again in the spring . . . to renew yourself. For the fight. You didn't even bring back pressed flowers. You took pictures, but you didn't show them to the kids – why not?

SUSANNAH: I don't know!

FRANK: Because it was nothing to do with them. That was *your* life . . . anyway, ours not to point up the gap. Bridge-building? Common ground? Skiing, for the likes of black kids in North

Kensington . . . not on. And don't remind me that your father once worked for the Water Board. Not one act of imaginative love. Not one.

SUSANNAH: You seem, at least, to have your energy back.

FRANK: I've been trying to get it right. [*He sighs deeply.*] I don't even know what 'it' is any more.

SUSANNAH: Oh for God's –

FRANK: I don't know anything. Except her. [*Pause*] I read to her. In the evenings. We're reading *Lord Jim* at the moment. Remember the opening, where he goes on about Jim's job as a tout for a ships' chandler?

SUSANNAH: What?

FRANK: After a couple of pages describing the tattiness of a tout's life he ends up . . . 'a beautiful and humane occupation'. Irony. She liked that. She got it.

[*Pause*]

SUSANNAH: You pompous renegade. You bloody social-democrat do-gooder.

FRANK: It's real. I feel real.

SUSANNAH: Well good luck to you. [*She picks up her bag.*] What's she like in bed?

FRANK: A goer. I have trouble keeping up.

SUSANNAH: I notice she does all the cooking and shopping, all the work. What's in it for her?

FRANK: She wants a husband, children. She's not after the world.

SUSANNAH: She'd better be, or she'll end up like your Mum and mine . . . vicious. You bloody exploitative shit. I hope it rots off.

[*She leaves.*

A short pause. CRYSTAL *enters in a dressing gown.*]

CRYSTAL: She gone?

[*He nods.*]

Jesus. [*He doesn't reply. She contemplates him.*] I had a shower.

FRANK: Oh?

CRYSTAL: Smell me.

FRANK [*grabbing her and burying his face*]: Mmmmm . . .

CRYSTAL: Guess what it is . . . no, you got to guess . . .

FRANK: It's called 'Expensive'.

CRYSTAL [*laughing*]: You ain't seen nothing.
[*She drops the dressing gown. She is wearing very little, but it is sensational.*]

FRANK: Christ!

CRYSTAL: Thought I better do something.

FRANK: No need.

CRYSTAL: Really?

FRANK: Look, it's old history.

CRYSTAL: I started to feel like, you know, a fucking gooseberry in me own place.

FRANK: Finished. Over.

CRYSTAL: Right. Well . . . in that case . . . [*She sits on his lap, legs astride.*]

FRANK: Here, what about my dinner?

CRYSTAL: It'll keep. [*She kisses him.*]

FRANK: I'm a hungry man.

CRYSTAL: I know. [*Kisses him.*] I've made allowances. [*Kisses him.*] Last course first tonight . . .
[*They embrace as lights to black.*]

ACT II

The flat, ten years later. The decor is now a simple retro, with Thirties' lamps, and some pictures of old movie stars in plastic frames. There are signs of children . . . a child's bicycle, toys brimming from a traditional washerwoman's basket. Apart, there is a large old trestle table with a typewriter, and piles of papers and books. Near the table is a bookcase brimming with books which have spread to nearby furniture. There is a large board, with leaflets tacked up . . . these, too, have spread to the wall. This is FRANK's *working area. It is in sharp contrast to the smart sofa, lamps, and the retro side table with the music centre.*

FRANK *sits at the table, working. He is absorbed in what he is doing, writing an article straight on to the typewriter. He makes errors and curses under his breath. He reaches behind him, grabs a bottle of beer, has a drink and continues to work.*

The telephone rings. He grabs it absently.

FRANK: Yup? Oh, hullo Ann – good . . . yeah, I brought them here, we managed to get some transport. Yeah. Right, look, don't bother, I'll drop you in a thousand copies in the morning, the sooner we move them – yeah. See you.
  [*He puts down the telephone, and resumes working.*
  CRYSTAL *enters. She is now a successful West End hair-dresser. She looks slender in highly fashionable clothes, with beautifully washed, simple hair and a model's modulated make-up. Her shoes and bag are expensive. She carries two bags, one an expensive-looking carrier, the other with food. During the next scene she takes the food to the kitchen . . . comes and goes, taking a shower, eating a slice of quiche,*

looking for a pair of shoes, changing her clothes. At one point she comes to the living room to do her eyes, where the light is best.

From time to time FRANK *watches her, in casual appreciation. Obviously a familiar ritual. She smiles and gives him a genial wink and wag of the head once in acknowledgment.*]
That you?

CRYSTAL: Nah, Brooke Shields . . . your lucky night. [*She unpacks the food, takes it out to the kitchen.*] What's the time?

FRANK: Half-past seven.
[*She returns, takes an expensive-looking dress from the glossy carrier bag, holds it up against herself briefly, for his inspection, and goes, with the dress.*]
You going out again?

CRYSTAL [*enters, throwing off her clothes rapidly but without fuss*]: What's it look like – aw, I'm bushed. [*She goes again. He gets up, picks up her clothes, takes them out.*]

FRANK [*returning*]: Anything special for the kids? [*He picks up the food carrier, reads the label.*] Christ.

CRYSTAL [*off*]: At least I know they're getting some decent nosh, tell them it's in the fridge. Where are they?

FRANK: Next door, watching the film with Inez.

CRYSTAL [*re-enters, drying herself and throwing on clothes*]: That bloody water's not hot again. Did you ring the plumber?
[FRANK *claps his hand to his head, he has forgotten.*]
Oh no! I need a bloody shower when I come in . . . I'm sweating like a navvy! [*She grabs the telephone and dials.*]

FRANK: What're you doing?

CRYSTAL: Ringing up for an emergency –

FRANK: Don't do that! It's thirty quid before they come through the door – I've told you, I've got somebody –

CRYSTAL [*dials*]: Hullo? All-Night Plumbers? Yeah, me again. Yeah, same problem. Could you –? Good. Right. Hey . . . hullo? Could you ring both bells? Yeah. [*She puts down the telephone.*] They'll be here in half an hour.

FRANK: I'm going out. I thought *you* were going to be in tonight.

CRYSTAL: It's all right, I've told them to ring Inez's bell.

[*She finishes getting ready. He watches her.*]

FRANK: You look good.

[*She blows him a kiss.*]

Where are you off to, anywhere special?

CRYSTAL [*spitting into her eye make-up*]: Now, now.

FRANK: What?

CRYSTAL [*turns*]: Listen, love. I don't ask about your things.

FRANK: Sure.

CRYSTAL [*doing her mouth*]: Just a couple of beers with the mates. You doing a movie?

FRANK: Yeah, thought I might.

CRYSTAL: Which one? [*She gives him a swift, speculative look behind his back.*]

FRANK: Alan Arkin.

CRYSTAL: Good, you like him. Tell you what, why don't you look in on Jean and Freddy after?

FRANK: I'll see how I feel.

CRYSTAL [*en passant, as she finishes her toilette with rapid precision, gives him a hug*]: Yeah, go on . . .

FRANK: Why not?

CRYSTAL: You could eat at that Greek place.

FRANK: OK.

CRYSTAL: Be nice, that.

FRANK: Right. That's me sorted out.

CRYSTAL: Ah, you know what I'm like.

[*She turns for him to do up the back of her dress, throws her coat over her shoulders, remembers something, totters in her heels to the bag she has just emptied when changing her bag, finds an envelope, thrusts it under his nose.*]

FRANK: What's this?

CRYSTAL: Can't you read, it's the phone bill.

FRANK [*reading the amount, whistles*]: Christ!

CRYSTAL [*checking herself in the glass*]: Yeah. Down to you and your lot.

FRANK: Come on, you're never off the bloody thing.

CRYSTAL: Rubbish, you're here more than me, why don't you pass the hat round those mates of yours, ripping you off for free calls, I wouldn't stand for it – ahhh! [*Making him jump.*]

FRANK: Now what's wrong?

CRYSTAL: They keep sitting on it!

FRANK: Who?

CRYSTAL: All those limp dicks of yours –

FRANK: Why not, it's a sofa –

CRYSTAL: There you are! Cigarette burn. Ah . . . what a shame.

FRANK: Come off –

CRYSTAL: *And* this end's all squashed. Tch. [*She plumps up the sofa, muttering*] Bloody meetings . . . how can you ask anybody back, it's all crummy. [*She tidies swiftly.*] It's no wonder I want to get out of it.

FRANK: Do you?

CRYSTAL: What?

FRANK: Want to get out of it?

CRYSTAL: Oh don't be so daft.

FRANK: You brought it up.

CRYSTAL: I need some fun at the end of the day, that's all.

FRANK: So do the kids.

CRYSTAL: What's that supposed to mean?

FRANK: Crystal, we never see you.

CRYSTAL: Don't tell such lies.

FRANK: This last few weeks –

CRYSTAL: I've told you, we're under-staffed!

FRANK: They miss you.

CRYSTAL: Oh yes, go on, I'm a rotten mother now.

FRANK: I didn't say that.

CRYSTAL: You can't expect me to stick in every night. *I* want a bit of fun out of life, I won't have it for ever –

FRANK: I'm not trying to stop you . . .

CRYSTAL: I earn it, I gotta right to spend it . . . I'm the one that pays the bills –

FRANK: That's not true.

CRYSTAL: Most of them . . . more than half. Everything in this place is what I've bought –

FRANK: Rubbish.

CRYSTAL: I have!

FRANK: Balls.

CRYSTAL: Thank you. Lovely. Super language coming from a schoolteacher, no wonder they're all hooligans.

FRANK: Oh Christ, your tongue.

CRYSTAL [*she flares, then changes her mind*]: Frank . . . don't be like that.

> [*She cuddles him . . . he kisses her.*
> *The telephone rings.*]

Go on . . . it'll be for you.

FRANK [*picks up telephone*]: Hang on, please . . .

> [*He divests himself from* CRYSTAL, *who picks up her things, ready to go out.*]

CRYSTAL: Which one is it . . . [*in an upper-class accent*] Lady Jane . . . or the little fat one? You know why she sits and reads all that stuff of yours, it's pathetic really. I'm off.

> [*She crosses, for a perfunctory kiss.*]

Listen, that quiche and toffee pudding's for the kids so keep your thieving mitts off it. [*But it is said jokily.*

> *She kisses him again.*]

Ciao, lover.

> [*She is about to go, changes her mind, crosses, takes most of his cigarettes from the packet.* FRANK *looks after her, then remembers the phone in his hand.*]

FRANK: Hullo . . . hullo . . . sorry to keep you . . . hullo, yes . . . speaking . . . why? No! I don't believe it! Where are you, where are you speaking from . . . haha . . . no, no, I'm just knocked out, that's all.

> [*Pause. He listens, nodding.*]

Oh fine . . . fine . . . good – you mean you – no . . . where are you now . . . no, sure, why not? Great! I thought you were in Bolivia . . . yeah, OK . . . no, just come straight up . . . hey, Susannah . . . hullo . . .

> [*But she has gone.*

He puts down the telephone, and throws himself down momentarily on the sofa, legs up . . . he is very affected. He

*looks around the room, galvanized . . . scrapes his papers
together, takes the dirty coffee cups from his table, pushes odd
books under the sofa. He looks around, moves the furniture
slightly . . . takes a look at himself in the mirror . . . goes off.
He returns, putting on another shirt . . . goes out at once after
a quick glimpse in the mirror, comes in with another shirt,
goes out, returns putting on his original shirt. Puts a record on
the record player, low, finds glasses, and opens a bottle of
wine.*

To the bottle] Chambrez, you devil.

[*He puts it on the radiator. He stands back, spins round for a
look . . . has his back to* SUSANNAH *when she appears . . .
spins back to find her standing there.*]

SUSANNAH: The door was open.

FRANK: You were quick.

SUSANNAH: I was just round the corner.

[*For a second they regard each other across the room. Then
they leap into each other's arms, he swings her round, and
they hang on to each other as for dear life. She gives a
little, sad, animal moan. Eventually they pull apart,
and both become matter-of-fact in manner, bridging the
moment.*]

You look older.

FRANK: I am older. You look just the same.

SUSANNAH: I don't, my skin's a terrible mess.

FRANK: You look fine to me.

SUSANNAH: How is everyone? Crystal?

FRANK: You've just missed her.

SUSANNAH: And the family?

FRANK: Fine. They're with the people next door, watching Alan
Ladd.

SUSANNAH: Alan Ladd?

[*They laugh.*]

Have you had any more . . . children?

FRANK: No, just the two . . . Nicky and Pete.

SUSANNAH: How old are they now?

FRANK: Ten and nine . . . nearly.

SUSANNAH: My God, is it really that long? The last time we met was in Leeds . . . that awful symposium.

FRANK [*together*]: The symposium! And once in the Fulham Road.

SUSANNAH: Coming out of the pictures.

FRANK: You were with some Chileans.

SUSANNAH: That's right.

[*A pause*]

FRANK: So you're back.

SUSANNAH: I'm back.

FRANK: Back in the oo-ld country.

SUSANNAH: As they say.

FRANK: Good. Good. How does it feel?

SUSANNAH: Pretty weird. I'm a bit disorientated.

[*She prowls, inspecting the room, calm, unsmiling, dignified in black.*

Bending to look at a picture, murmurs] I'd no idea I was so chauvinistic.

FRANK: Land of hope and glory, eh? Bit of a change from the dark sub-continent.

SUSANNAH: Yes. So small! How on earth did we ever do it?

FRANK: Conquer the world, you mean? You're right. Distinctly puzzling.

SUSANNAH [*sits*]: I got an aeroplane to Paris, then the boat train. Amazing. It was like coming back to a tiny old ghost-town . . . everything looks grey, even the people! Nothing seems to work any more . . . holes in the roads, the clocks tell the wrong time. I went to the Post Office. Four booths shut, two long queues, one not moving. When it was my turn I asked for the postal rate to Bolivia. He said he didn't know. I said, you must know. He went away and he didn't come back. What's happened?

FRANK: Oh, c'est la guerre.

SUSANNAH: When I left there was confrontation, colour –

FRANK: Hah.

SUSANNAH: What happened? Where did it go?

FRANK: Very simple. The money ran out. It *was* happening. We were getting somewhere. Mrs down-the-road from the shop got on the Council. Real change. Movement. And then the Arabs upped the oil –

SUSANNAH: And down fell Jack.

FRANK: Oh yes. And out of the thickets they came. The carrot-and-stick boys, the law-and-order analysts. The up-you bastards. [*Upper-class voice*] 'There you are, you see? Doesn't do, chaps. Back in the old cage.'

SUSANNAH: I'm so out of touch – you mean –?

FRANK: Yeah. Cold climate. When there's no wage packet or hope of employment – [*He shrugs.*] Fear works. Put your hand in the flame, you won't do it twice . . . ask any circus trainer.

SUSANNAH: What about North Sea Oil? I thought we were all going to float away on it.

FRANK: Sold off. Good capitalism – talk national, deal international. Sound Tory dogma.

SUSANNAH: Depressing.

FRANK: Mmm. So much for the right to work.

SUSANNAH: Yes. I've been reading the figures. It's – [*She shakes her head, overcome with shock and indignation.*]

FRANK [*slight pause*]: They fished a man out of the canal last week with his toolbox tied to his leg.

[SUSANNAH *gasps.*]

They call it shake-out. [*Pause*] Same old story. Who are you governing FOR? [*Slight pause*] So . . . it's Jingo-shit movie time and Space Invaders.

SUSANNAH: Space Invaders? [*She smiles, shaking her head, baffled.*]

FRANK: Yup. Who knows? Perhaps we'll go to sleep for four hundred years, like Spain. Could happen.

SUSANNAH: Oh I doubt that! Not here . . . not without a fixed system.

FRANK [*from the kitchen, getting glasses*]: We've always had that!

SUSANNAH: What?

FRANK [*enters*]: We've always had that . . . the fucking shires.

SUSANNAH [*groans*]: Oh no, not all over again!

FRANK: Sure thing. Flat 'at, gun under the arm. They're all

peddling heating systems during the week, but it's up the M1 and let's play squire at the weekends.

SUSANNAH: The old class nastiness? You mean it?

FRANK: And the new Puritanism.

SUSANNAH: Puritanism?

FRANK: 'Victorian values' is the phrase. If you're poor, jobless, it's your own fault so – [*He makes a punching gesture.*]

SUSANNAH: A touch of the Puritans may see us through. A bit of sharing, inconspicuous consumption – [*She smiles.*]

FRANK [*hugs her fondly*]: It's good to see you! [*He gives her a drink.*] Welcome home!

SUSANNAH: To your very best health.

FRANK: To you.
   [*They drink.*]

SUSANNAH: How's the job?

FRANK: I'm supply teaching at the moment.

SUSANNAH: Are you? I had you all dug in as senior history master. You look pretty busy. [*She picks up a pamphlet.*]

FRANK: Socialist Combination. I've thrown my lot in, now that it's highly unfashionable.
   [*They laugh.*]

SUSANNAH: And what about freedom from party dogma?

FRANK: Ah. Freedom. Plenty of that about. Freedom to sink. To go to hell. Opportunities for boys to train as butlers – I'm not kidding, there was a programme on television.

SUSANNAH: Jesus.

SUSANNAH: What about women?

FRANK: Unemployment hasn't helped. The scene's changed since you left.

SUSANNAH: Oh, how?

FRANK: More polarized, I think. I'll run you down to Greenham.

SUSANNAH: Already been. So, you're active?

FRANK: Full-time from next month.

SUSANNAH [*surprised*]: You're giving up teaching? Completely?

FRANK [*nods*]: I'll miss it.

SUSANNAH: Can you afford to?

FRANK: Just about. [*He shrugs.*] Crystal pulls a fortune.

SUSANNAH: I see. [*Pause*] Is it OK . . . you and Crystal?

FRANK: No. But there are the children.

SUSANNAH: Wouldn't they be better off?

FRANK: Possibly. I doubt it. They're still a bit young. Can I fill you up?

SUSANNAH: Mm, please. It's good . . . luxury – I'm used to something much rougher.

FRANK: Yes! What about you? What have you been doing?

SUSANNAH: Working in a mining town.

FRANK: Same place.

SUSANNAH: Most of the time. [*She drinks.*]

FRANK: Well? What's it like? [*He leans forward, eager.*]

SUSANNAH: Oh . . . very high up . . . very wet . . . very cold – not a bit picturesque.

FRANK: What were you doing there? Martin Raven said he'd heard from you but that was ages ago.

SUSANNAH: Not much point in writing. I was too tired most of the time. Nothing really, Frank. [*She looks at him bleakly.*] No quaint costumes worth a television team . . . [*shrugs*] just people, trying to stay alive.

FRANK: Sounds rough. What were you doing there?

SUSANNAH: Documentation. I was a field officer.

FRANK: Vital.

SUSANNAH: I had to change in '81 . . . there was a coup. I've been doing union work.

FRANK: Great!

[*She turns to look at him, seemingly puzzled. She looks about the room, seemingly absorbed in the decorations.*]

SUSANNAH [*absently*]: They chew coca leaves. Stops the hunger pangs.

FRANK: You sound bitter.

SUSANNAH [*lightly*]: Oh I am, I am. No one in their right mind would stay there for an hour if there were anywhere else on God's earth. For the last year I've been counting the days – and it rained for most of them.

FRANK: That bad?

SUSANNAH [*short laugh*]: Goes for most people on this globe. I sat next to this shit of an American woman on the plane. She was telling me about her villa, near Malaga. All built in the traditional style – guitar-shaped swimming pool.

[*He laughs.*]

Only one 'prahblem' . . . the Spanish people . . . so 'dirdy' – [*She falters.*]

FRANK: Suse?

SUSANNAH [*recovers*]: I was talking to one of the miners' wives just before I left. She'd lost another baby. I tried to console her. No, she said, you don't understand. I said I thought I did but she said no, I couldn't. I was rich. I tried to tell her that I wasn't, that I didn't own a thing. And she looked me in the eyes, it's a thing they never do but she was a bit mad from losing the child, and she said, 'You're white. You're rich.'

[*A pause*]

FRANK: You're not going back?

SUSANNAH: I should. I'm experienced. I can just about balance my worth against what I eat. No. I'm not going back. Ever.

[*Pause*]

FRANK: What are you going to do?

SUSANNAH [*lightly*]: Have a baby, I hope.

FRANK: What? [*Pointing to her stomach in smiling inquiry.*]

SUSANNAH [*shaking her head*]: No, no. It's just that the only thing I really want to do right now is have a baby. The need to [*exaggerated drawl*] 'give birth' has been rather overwhelming lately. I seem to be somewhat . . . seething with it. [*She drops the number.*] I want a child before I start getting infertile.

FRANK: Is there anyone in mind? I mean –

SUSANNAH: No.

[*They look at each other. He laughs.*]

FRANK: It's fantastically good to see you. Well! Right. So. How are you going to go about it? You going solo?

SUSANNAH: Possibly. I shall have to find somewhere to live, acquire an income somehow – I thought teaching . . . could you help me with that?

FRANK: Sure.

SUSANNAH: Then there's the father. Have to find myself a feller.

FRANK: What kind of feller?

SUSANNAH: Oh, either a healthy and intelligent one-night stand with intent on my part and innocence on his . . . or I could try to set up a more permanent arrangement with a fatherly citizen, preferably with a roof over his head. God, I'd love my own patch . . . a few rooms, an apple tree to sit under with my children. You'd be amazed at the things I can do with a few spuds and an onion. Delicioso.

FRANK: You want to settle down?

SUSANNAH: Probably. It sounds like it.

FRANK: You mean marriage?

SUSANNAH: Possibly.

FRANK: You've changed!

SUSANNAH: Ye-es. No longer the heroine of the revolution.

FRANK: I'm sorry to hear that.

>   [*She turns, surprised.*]

They're all on the run now. Following the action. I didn't think you would.

SUSANNAH: It's funny, isn't it? The last time we were here – hah, I remember it –

FRANK: So do I!

SUSANNAH: You seemed to be – I thought you'd . . . I mean, I really did think you'd –

FRANK: Sold out?

SUSANNAH: I've gone over and over it in my mind. I should have been there. When you were ill. I realize that now.

FRANK: I wasn't myself.

SUSANNAH: I should have been there. That bloody project – God, we were so intense! We were going to change the world. Hah.

FRANK: I know.

SUSANNAH: I thought we were indissoluble. Mistake number one. We were so in step . . . at least, that's what I thought. That fucking Pill.

FRANK: What?

SUSANNAH: If it weren't for the Pill I'd have been pregnant three times over, the way we went at it. Remember the woman downstairs coming up with half the ceiling in her hair? And you offering to show her how it was done? We thought we were so clever. Beating nature. I've been done out of it.

FRANK: Still time.

SUSANNAH: God, the agony of choice! [*She groans.*] I mean! There's never a good time to have a baby, if you can afford it you're too old, and who needs Marmite sandwiches and little morons for ten years when you're just getting your head together – God, how I envy Crystal!

FRANK: Is that why you've come back? A touch of the domestics?

SUSANNAH: There was a bad mine accident. We lost half the men in the village. Makes you think. About going it alone.

FRANK: Very fashionable now, single parenting.

SUSANNAH: Is that what they call it? Orphaning children? No.

FRANK [*shrugs*]: The right to choose.

SUSANNAH: Oh, rights! They need their father – there's a right if you like. I saw the loss, in the tribe. Imbalance. I've begun to have a silly respect for that rare constant in human psychology – the blood relation.

FRANK: Hah! [*Laughs*] We spent half our time together fending off our bloody parents!

SUSANNAH: Yer . . . well . . . they were squares . . . straights . . . 'don't show me up, man'!

[*He laughs and hugs her.*]

Still do anything in the world for us. Who else can you say that of? You couldn't say it of me. I pissed off when you were ill. Your mother didn't. They cashed in their life insurance to send you and Crystal on holiday.

[*She moves apart, walks about.*]

I want them. My family. Sisters, aunts, cousins . . . great-uncles once removed. Someone to go to . . . argue with . . . grumble about – at least they're there! I watched television last night. God, I couldn't believe it. Programme after programme . . . the Twenties . . . the Thirties . . . bath after bath of nostalgia, all created with such love, affection. What the hell have we done?

[*She walks, restless.*]

I'm tired of being on my own. It's an over-rated privilege.

FRANK: You have changed.

  [*She laughs.*]

SUSANNAH: I still talk too much. What about you? What about you, Frank?

FRANK: Here and now? I don't know. Yes. Excited. Pretty excited.

SUSANNAH [*turns to him, her face alight, just as he turns away*]: You mean . . . ?

  [*She sees that he does not mean because she is back, and covers quickly.*]

  Why? What about? About changing your work?

FRANK: Don't know. Can't say. Yes, I suppose it is that. Taking the risk. Only this time it's sane. No more shrieking about revolution, man the fucking barriers. Kids' talk. Murderers' talk. Our aims are as clear as we can make them. Precise. Practical. And modest.

SUSANNAH: Gradualist?

FRANK: Remember what you used to say? Not one hair of one baby's head?

SUSANNAH: You gave me shit for it.

FRANK: We have to be realistic. Select . . . win where possible, influence, subvert, create models, communicate – God knows the channels are open now. Anything's possible, d'you see? Because everything's collapsed. Politics . . . religion . . . imperialism. At least it makes for clarity.

SUSANNAH: Dangerous.

FRANK: Do you think so? I wonder.

  At least there's less shit. People won't stand for it . . . no, not any more. They're a lot more criminal, sure . . . or rather, they know where criminality lies, they see the con. I think we could be in with a chance. We're misty bloody Islanders, with a head full of words. Which is a problem.

SUSANNAH: How, how d'you mean? [*She leans forward, loving the talk, not able to get enough of it.*]

FRANK: Romantics, the lot of us. Shakespeare spawn. We could double the gross national product if we put turrets on the factories. I've even thought that maybe we should stick with titles . . . only not be so farting mean with it . . . spread them around the way they did in Russia before the Rev. Everyone in with a chance for a fur-collared overcoat.

SUSANNAH: Don't tell me *you've* become a royalist?

FRANK: Stranger things have happened.

I'm kidding. Under this string vest there beats a pure republican heart.

SUSANNAH: I'm not convinced. You're an Englishman. Quite capable of being corrupted by a piece of twopenny ribbon.

[*Laughing, she prowls among his papers.*]

What's the party line?

FRANK: Anarcho-syndicalist.

SUSANNAH: De-centralization?

FRANK: Community politics, fifty-fifty ownership, management and labour, government and people. Internationalist. Some ecology. We're eclectic. And pragmatic.

SUSANNAH: Sounds like the new . . . what is it . . . the SDP.

FRANK [*throwing a cushion at her*]: Marxist hack!

SUSANNAH: And you're happy?

FRANK: Nothing's perfect. I have regular moments of pure fascism . . .

SUSANNAH: Plus ça change . . .

FRANK: . . . and I wish I could make some money, like my brother.

SUSANNAH: How is he?

FRANK: Weighs fifteen stone and has five children, boxer dog, and a villa in Majorca, mit pool.

SUSANNAH: Nice?

FRANK: Very comfy.

SUSANNAH: Ye-es. Yes . . . I want a baby. How about it?

FRANK: You looking at me, squire?

SUSANNAH: You'd do. You'd do very well. In fact . . . in fact it's going to be difficult to find a substitute for you.

FRANK: Suse . . .

[*They kiss gently. He takes her hand again.*]

SUSANNAH: I saw your daughter. Just after she was born. When I came to see you and we had that flaming row. I remember it very clearly. I wasn't into babies at all and Crystal had her tricked out in pink with obscene rabbits in spats camping about all over the cot.

FRANK: I remember.

SUSANNAH: I really hated being forced in there, and I was deter-
mined not to make the usual noises. What I wasn't prepared for
was this . . . person. She was fast asleep and frowning, as though
she was concentrating on something as hard as she could, it was
as though she was . . . growing. She had your long skull . . . I've
never forgotten. Are you faithful, you and Crystal?

FRANK: I am. She isn't. She's very good with the children . . .
natural mother. As they say. We-ell, at the moment it's not so
hot, she's stopped feeding us.

SUSANNAH [drily]: Oh dear. Poor old you.

FRANK: Figure of speech.

SUSANNAH: What's gone wrong?

FRANK: She's fed up.

SUSANNAH: With you?

FRANK: Mostly.

SUSANNAH: Why?

FRANK: I don't stand up to her. Not in the way that she wants.

SUSANNAH: Why not? If that's what she needs.

FRANK: Come on. You can't play a part in your own home. Home's
where you leave off.

She's restless. She doeṣn't know it but what she really wants is
a child every other year. That's what her body wants. They're all
breeders, the women in her family. Insatiable. She has such a
body . . . breasts . . . contours . . . valleys . . . all – alive! It's a
crime to clothe her . . . she should be decked with flowers and
worshipped. I'm a mere mortal. I deprive her. So she takes it out
of me.

SUSANNAH: It sounds disastrous.

FRANK: Yeah. But it's poetry. And the children. I live in a perma-
nent daze of wonder at the beauty of them. The things they say!
New! Fresh . . . another coinage. They don't see with our eyes.
They come after us. They judge us. Of course at the moment I'm
Dad . . . I can do no wrong. They'll find me out soon enough.
Realize I'm not Superman.

SUSANNAH [slight pause]: Frank . . . it's bad, isn't it?

FRANK: Yes.

SUSANNAH: Let go.

FRANK: I can't.

SUSANNAH: But surely –

FRANK: 'My Kingdom'.

SUSANNAH: But if it's no good? I could put up a fight this time. I'm much tougher now.

FRANK: No. Not yet, anyway.

SUSANNAH: Oh for Christ's sake! If you think I'm going to stand back and watch you – have you any idea what I've – [*She catches herself up with difficulty.*] I'm sorry. It's your life. But oh, Frank, if you knew. How lucky we are. To waste any of it . . . !

   [*Pause*]

It's self-indulgent to talk of bringing even one more mouth into the world. We're cannibals, the lot of us. Living off cash crops when we could . . . [*She pauses, then turns, speaks mildly.*] We should stop. Here. Right now. This minute. All of us. Most of the volume of pain in the world could be easily prevented. We have the means. [*She sighs.*]

   I escaped. Because I could. Every night I'd crawl into my damp, sagging hammock and dream about clean dry clothes, about red meat . . . beef, chops, liver . . . about lights that switched on . . . warmth . . . about cars, buses, smooth roads . . . shops, theatres, libraries . . . all the things I could have again, and that they would never, ever have.

FRANK: Love . . . [*He puts an arm about her.*]

SUSANNAH: The woman on the plane showed me her new handbag. Crocodile. A thousand dollars – and she was proud of it. Enough to feed a village for a year.

FRANK: Yes. Yes, a bit of a joke.

SUSANNAH: Most of all our sort. The do-gooders.

FRANK: We're not arms dealers.

SUSANNAH: Sure. [*Pause*] I don't know what to do. Except, as I say . . .

   [*Slight pause*]

FRANK: Join us. [*He indicates the poster on the wall.*]

SUSANNAH: Save the baby seals?

FRANK: That amongst other things. That as well. For all these kids you're about to have. The Greens aren't wrong . . . we are the custodians . . . of the planet.

SUSANNAH: Hah! [*She laughs.*] When were you any good at maintenance?

[*They both laugh.*]

FRANK: You'll need something.

SUSANNAH: Perhaps. I don't know. [*She ruffles his papers.*] So much . . . paper.

FRANK: Recycled though.

[*She laughs.*]

You must belong to something. I mean, you have to. Otherwise it's just –

[*She nods.*]

FRANK: Give us a try. There is a space – we can't pay much, you'd need something as well. Think about it.

SUSANNAH: Perhaps.

FRANK: Have a look round, of course.

SUSANNAH: Yes. Perhaps. [*Pause*] Frank. I need a child. You could give me a child. You could give me a child here and now. If you like I'll go away and never see you again. If you love her.

[FRANK *gets up, walks away. He plays with things on the table. Silence*]

FRANK: It was fine at first. I was educated, a college boy, she thought she'd got a real bargain. She liked showing me off, doing her friends in the eye.

SUSANNAH: What about you?

FRANK: Oh, fantastic, just to be with her. It's a big aphrodisiac being with a woman other men want. And I'd done it . . . married a straight-down-the-line working-class girl. You'd have loved some of the confrontations with our more bourgeois acquaintance . . .

[*She looks at him objectively.*]

It wasn't the reason I'd married her, but it was damned exhilarating. We were both on a real high. And then the pregnancies. She was magnificent. Brave. Like a lion. God, bloody painful – [*He catches* SUSANNAH's *eye.*] – she was fine. Eating steak and chips the minute Pete was out.

   [*Pause*]

And then . . . I don't know. She went back to work . . . we needed the bread. The hours are dodgy, it's a strain . . . it's not just that you're on your feet all day, you're giving out to people. You've no idea what people tell their hairdressers, Christ, she's heard the lot . . . little old ladies getting a last hairdo before a major cancer operation . . . cheering up a woman who's just had her nose broken by her old man and wants something to make him fancy her on her birthday. The end of the day, we were both knackered and with two young kids – one's all right, you can cope, but with two it's a family . . . they need . . . [*He shrugs, pauses.*] And then . . .

   I don't know. I began to relax. Stopped playing games. I let her get right in – she has that contemptuous familiarity of people bred at close quarters with no privacy, no respite for the mind. She's used to quarrelling, picking fights . . . she gets off that way. I can't do that. I couldn't rise. God, she can be vicious!

   [*He walks about. Pause.*]

She got bored. Began to take me for granted. And there are all those randy hairdressers, they're not all gay, believe me. She'd tell me about it . . . getting a quick one between floors on the way down to the tinting . . . parties . . . pick-ups . . . musicians after a gig . . . discos . . . receptions . . . you make big money doing hair privately. There'd be dances, weddings – she'd get it from the waiters . . . the best man . . . the bridegroom . . . even the bloody bride . . .

SUSANNAH: She tells you?

FRANK: She's a blabbermouth. She doesn't like to feel uneasy.

SUSANNAH: Phew!

FRANK: She's settled down a bit. She has . . . boyfriends. There was a big Irishman, then an actor, then some electronics wizard with a pocketful of money. This one, the one she's got now, is really loaded . . . Formula One racing driver, man about town, knows the score. And tough. She likes a man who's tough. I talk soft. I don't come on all the time. I look for tenderness and she wants invention. What I ought to do is take a strap to her. She'd like that.

SUSANNAH: You're obsessed.

FRANK: Yes. She escapes me.

SUSANNAH: Oh my dear.

[*He sits beside her, smiles, caresses her face.*]

You've been in my thoughts for years.

[*He makes to kiss her.*]

CRYSTAL [*from the door*]: Ahhh!

[*She enters, genial, puts down a bottle.*

To SUSANNAH] God, where the hell have you been? What's happened to your skin?

SUSANNAH [*standing awkwardly*]: I've been working in Bolivia.

CRYSTAL: You didn't leave a day too soon.

SUSANNAH: You look wonderful.

CRYSTAL: Drink?

[SUSANNAH *shakes her head.*]

Well, carry on. Don't mind me. [*She sits, crossing her legs flamboyantly.*]

FRANK: Carry on what?

[*But* CRYSTAL *jumps up with a clatter, making them both jump.*]

CRYSTAL: I know! Stereo! Whatcha fancy? [*Peering at* SUSANNAH'*s face en passant*] Christ. [*She fumbles with the records.*]

SUSANNAH: How are the children?

CRYSTAL: Oh, I expect he's been filling you in. With the details.

SUSANNAH: No . . . as a matter of fact I've only just –

CRYSTAL [*puts on a disc . . . To* FRANK]: I thought you was going to the pictures?

FRANK: Changed my mind. So?

CRYSTAL: Well, it's a bit awkward.

FRANK: Why?

CRYSTAL [*moves about, restless*]: Look . . . why don't we get sensible? I thought you was going to be out a couple of hours, I got a friend coming in. I mean, I don't mind . . . you've kept it very dark –

FRANK: What do you mean? There's nothing going on –
   [*He looks to* SUSANNAH *for support but she sits like a totem pole.*]
   – who's coming?
CRYSTAL: Nobody. Friend of mine.
FRANK: A girl?
CRYSTAL: No.
FRANK: Have you been making a habit of this?
CRYSTAL: Hark at him, you can tell he's a schoolmaster, can't you . . . that's how he goes on. Look, cock, this is my place.
FRANK: No it isn't.
CRYSTAL: It bloody is –
SUSANNAH [*rising*]: I'd better go.
FRANK [*irritable*]: No.
CRYSTAL: All I'm saying is, why don't we –
FRANK: No!
CRYSTAL [*a whine*]: Frank . . . he'll be here in a minute!
FRANK: I've told you – no!
CRYSTAL: Come on! You might as well –
FRANK: What? Might as well what?
CRYSTAL [*sullen*]: It's not as though you don't know about it. Look –
FRANK: Shut up!!
   [*There is a long silence.* SUSANNAH *makes to speak, thinks better of it.*]
CRYSTAL: Right. That's it, then. We know where we are.
SUSANNAH: Frank –
CRYSTAL: All right for some.
FRANK: What are you talking about?
CRYSTAL: I'm not having it.
FRANK: Having what?
CRYSTAL: You can make your mind up. What do you want to do . . . do you want to finish?
   [*He looks at her, aghast.*]
SUSANNAH [*seeing his face*]: Crystal, I've only just come back. Frank and I haven't seen each other for –

[*But, at the sound of a loud knock,* FRANK *and* CRYSTAL *make for the door.*]

CRYSTAL: Shit! [*As she makes for the door.*]

FRANK [*pushing her out of the way*]: Get out of it –

SUSANNAH: Frank, don't! [*She moves to the door, trying to hear.*]

FRANK [*off*]: You, push off.

MAN [*upper class*]: What's the matter, what's going on?

CRYSTAL: Look love, it's off, Frank's got his girlfriend in –

MAN: Has he, now?

CRYSTAL: You better go.

MAN: I'm coming in –

FRANK: Go on, get out – out! [*The sound of a fight*]

SUSANNAH [*runs off*]: Frank, don't!

CRYSTAL: Leave it off, you bloody fool – leave him alone, get out of it, you big prick –

[*Sounds of a further scuffle.*

SUSANNAH *and* CRYSTAL *enter, supporting* FRANK. *He is bleeding.*

CRYSTAL *exits. We hear her whispering urgently to the man.*]

CRYSTAL [*off*]: Naow . . . don't! No, you done enough already! How can I . . . I can't, can I?

MAN: Listen, ducky, make your fucking mind up –

CRYSTAL [*off*]: Oh shove off. [*Comes in.*] Now he's on the fucking turn.

SUSANNAH [*mopping* FRANK's *face*]: Was he hurt?

CRYSTAL: You kidding? [*She fetches water and Listerine.*] Keep still.

SUSANNAH: Is it deep?

[*They inspect the cut.*]

CRYSTAL: I don't know, what do you think . . . is it hurting, Frank?

[*He mumbles.*]

God, he's really out of it.

FRANK: Ow! [*As she puts on the antiseptic and a Bandaid*]

CRYSTAL: Sorry, love.

[SUSANNAH *lights up, offers* FRANK *a cigarette, he shakes his head.*

CRYSTAL *takes the bowl out.*]

SUSANNAH: You all right?

CRYSTAL [*returning*]: He'll be OK.

FRANK [*to* CRYSTAL]: So you were bringing him back here?

CRYSTAL: Yeah.

FRANK: Here, to our bed?

CRYSTAL: Yeah, why not?

FRANK: Sure, why not invite the kids in, make it a show.

CRYSTAL: There's no need to be filthy.

SUSANNAH: I think I'd better go.

FRANK: No, don't.

CRYSTAL: No, stay.

FRANK: It's not the first time, is it?

CRYSTAL: Forget it, you're upset.

SUSANNAH: I'd better go.

FRANK: No.

CRYSTAL: Sit down. Have a drink – I know, cup of tea.

> [*She exits to kitchen, but he follows her off. We hear their voices, prolonged.* SUSANNAH *is uncertain whether to go or stay. The voices are raised, she picks up her bag to go. There is a screech from* CRYSTAL, *she decides to stay. Silence. Now she is really non-plussed. What are they doing? Could they be –? She goes to the kitchen door, to listen. Just manages to step back as* CRYSTAL *enters regally with a tray of tea, a mod pot and matching set of retro cups and saucers.*]

Sit down, Susannah, make yourself at home. Like me cups? Present from Boy George. Sugar?

SUSANNAH: Two, please.

CRYSTAL: Bad for the skin.

SUSANNAH: Where's Frank?

CRYSTAL: He's lying down.

SUSANNAH: In the kitchen?

CRYSTAL [*bright*]: Mmm. Well? What d'you think?

SUSANNAH: I beg your pardon?

CRYSTAL: Of him . . . of me feller . . .

SUSANNAH: Sorry?

CRYSTAL: What did you think to him?

SUSANNAH: I didn't really get a good look.

CRYSTAL: Anyway, he's better with his clothes off.

Ooh, that's better. [*She puts down her cup.*] You back for good?

SUSANNAH: Yes.

CRYSTAL: Not going abroad no more?

SUSANNAH: No.

CRYSTAL: Packed it in, eh?

SUSANNAH: Yes.

CRYSTAL: What you going to do?

SUSANNAH: I haven't made my mind up.

CRYSTAL: There's not a lot about.

SUSANNAH: So I gather.

CRYSTAL: Still, you'll be able to pull something, eh? With your qualifications. Always room for your sort of work, eh?

SUSANNAH: Is he all right?

CRYSTAL: Sure. You don't look as if you've been having a good time.

SUSANNAH: You could say that.

CRYSTAL: Make up for it! You're only young once, that's what my Mum says. Tell you what, come down to the salon. I'll give you a peel . . . a skin-peel. For nothing. Cost you over fifty, you know . . . they vacuum your wallet as soon as you come through the door. What about the Dance Studio? Be good for your neck, that.

SUSANNAH: What's wrong with my neck?

CRYSTAL [*manipulates* SUSANNAH's *neck*]: There . . . you see? Stiff! You're all rigid! There's a lot of stuff now, dance, exercise, body-shaping . . . look . . . [*She displays her body, does a flip and the splits.*] I used to be ever so thick here. And here. I do this every morning. [*She demonstrates a floor exercise.*

FRANK *enters, stands watching her. She sees him.*]

Frank, how you feeling?

[*He does not reply. He finds an old grip behind his table, begins to throw things into it.*]

What do you think you're doing?

[*He glares at her, continues to pack.*]

Don't be so silly.

FRANK: Get out. [*As she tries to stop him*] Leave it!

CRYSTAL: Frank . . .

FRANK: Will you get out of my way?

CRYSTAL: What are you looking for, there's nothing in that drawer
– Frank! Look, don't be so stupid –
   [*They scuffle.*]

SUSANNAH: Please, stop it . . . look, this is ridiculous . . . ow!
[*She gets hit on the nose.*]

CRYSTAL: Now look what you've done, what do you think you're
doing . . . [*She helps* SUSANNAH *to her feet.*] . . . you shove
Harry down the stairs . . . just as well he was legless, he'd have
given you a right pasting . . . look at her nose, it'll be the size of a
marrow in the morning . . . Susannah . . . [*she shouts as if*
SUSANNAH *is unconscious*] . . . Susannah – you all right?

SUSANNAH: Oof . . . ooergh . . .

CRYSTAL: Oh Christ. [*She exits swiftly, returns with bowl, flannel
and the Listerine.*] Florence fucking Nightingale, I thought I was
going to have a quiet night . . . [*She looks at* FRANK.] . . .
crumbs, your eye!

FRANK [*to* SUSANNAH]: I'm sorry, I didn't mean to hit you.

SUSANNAH: Ooh . . .

CRYSTAL: Oh look, she looks terrible! Ah! Talk about Karl
Malden. She hasn't set foot in the country five minutes, first
thing you do – honest, I don't know. [*She ministers, with swift
competence.*] Lie back.

SUSANNAH: I'm all right. No really, I'm OK.

CRYSTAL: It'll be a week before she can see straight. Well, are you
going or stopping?

FRANK [*glares at her, sits abruptly, clutching his bag. To*
SUSANNAH]: I'm sorry, love.
   [SUSANNAH *nods, tries to smile.*]

CRYSTAL: No thanks to you. [*She takes the bowl off for a refill.*]

SUSANNAH: I should go.

FRANK: Where are you staying?

SUSANNAH: At the YW.

CRYSTAL [*returns, hears this*]: You kidding? She can't stay there!

FRANK: Stay here. At least for the night. [*To* CRYSTAL] OK?

CRYSTAL: Sure . . . up to you.

FRANK [*sitting firmly*]: I'm going.

CRYSTAL: Leave it out.

FRANK: I'm going!

CRYSTAL: You're not. He's not, is he, Susannah?

SUSANNAH [*speaking with difficulty, a tissue up her nose*]: Frank, you're upset – why not sleep on it?

FRANK: Fouling her own nest . . . I'm not having that.

CRYSTAL: Oh don't be so ridiculous, anyway where do you think you're going? You can't go anywhere, you can't afford it for a start, where's the bread coming from, you'd have to work!

FRANK: I do work.

CRYSTAL: Work?

FRANK: You try teaching kids –

CRYSTAL: I didn't mean that, I meant all your other stuff. [*Pause*] If it comes down to it, I'm the one to go. It's your place. Yours and hers. That's how it started. I'll go.

FRANK: Set you up, has he?

CRYSTAL: You kidding? If I get out of here, I'm finding something decent for me and the kids.

FRANK: You're not taking the kids.

CRYSTAL: I'm not leaving them.

SUSANNAH: Please. I'll go. Obviously I'm the one to go. I can't bear to see him unhappy!

CRYSTAL: Him?! He never even got me a decent house, all the girls I was at school with got a roof over their heads, one's living in Wimbledon! I should have gone in with Ray, I could of had me own salon by now, but no, dirty word, innit, business . . . no co-operation at all. It's all right for me to work me ass off seven days a week . . . we-ell, I'm rubbish, aren't I? I'm getting veins now. [*She displays an elegant leg.*]

FRANK: There's nothing wrong with your legs. You don't have to put in the hours. You do it because you want to.

CRYSTAL [*to* SUSANNAH]: You got any money?

SUSANNAH: Yes I have as a matter of fact. [*To* FRANK] Dad died.

FRANK: Oh. I'm sorry.

SUSANNAH: It was quick. Mark said he got up from the breakfast table, said 'I think I'll just stroll over to the links' and was dead before he hit the floor.

[CRYSTAL *stifles a giggle*.]

CRYSTAL: Leave a lot, did he?

SUSANNAH: Enough to put a roof over my head.

CRYSTAL: Yeah? [*Slight pause*] Tell you what . . .

FRANK: Shut up.

CRYSTAL: I was only thinking.

[*Pause*]

SUSANNAH: What? What were you thinking?

CRYSTAL: This girl I know. She's got a house. Some guy set her up – actually it's two houses knocked into one, so the garden's fantastic . . . you remember, Frank? I showed you.

[*He glares, and she pulls a resigned face.*]

It's a great house – she leaves dustbins and rubbish outside, you know, so's she don't get done over – but inside she's spent a fortune, it's all pale blue deco with a studio out the back.

SUSANNAH: She wants to sell?

CRYSTAL: Yeah, she's marrying an Arab . . . I introduced them. [*Flicks a glance at* FRANK.] We could get it for nothing, don't mean a thing to her and, like I say, she owes me a favour.

SUSANNAH: You mean I should buy it?

CRYSTAL: We could share. Frank, sit down.

SUSANNAH: Sit down, Frank. How do you mean, share, Crystal?

CRYSTAL: Well, the way I look at it . . . I mean, if Frank and you think it's a good idea. [*To* FRANK] I mean, let's face it, love, it's OK in bed but I bore the tits off you when I open me mouth . . . I mean, sometimes I don't but that's because I act up and make you laugh. Only you don't always feel like playing Betty Boop . . . know what I mean? [*To* SUSANNAH] Have you seen the kids?

[SUSANNAH *shakes her head.*]

Ah, you'll love them.

[SUSANNAH *gazes at her, mesmerized.*]

SUSANNAH: Will I?

CRYSTAL: They both look like Frank. [*Pause*] I've always felt bad about it. Taking him off you. I was potty for a baby. Frank happened to turn up at the right moment.

SUSANNAH: That looks painful. [*As* FRANK *favours his eye.*]

CRYSTAL: He'll be all right.

[SUSANNAH *wrings out a cloth in the bowl. He applies it to his eye.*]

SUSANNAH [*to* CRYSTAL]: You were saying?

CRYSTAL: What?

SUSANNAH: About the house . . .

FRANK: Forget it.

[*He tries to rise, they press him back.*]

CRYSTAL: It's perfect for sharing, there's lots of rooms. She's got them all done simple, the bedrooms are like little nuns' cells, I mean little cells for nuns, not little nuns . . .

[*They giggle.*]

. . . then there's this huge big kitchen, two sitting rooms, and another little room Frank could use as an office – it backs on to the cemetery so it's nice and quiet, for work.

[*The last flicked at* FRANK, *who looks at her without expression.*]

We've got *some* money, and we'll get something for the lease on this.

SUSANNAH: Frank?

FRANK: No.

SUSANNAH: Frank . . .

FRANK: Susannah!

[*She retires, defeated.*

Slight pause]

CRYSTAL: It could work, love.

FRANK: Fuck off.

CRYSTAL: Oh come on! What's all the sulking for? You know I've always had a bit on the side. Don't be so double-faced – what's the matter, are you afraid of being shown up in front of Susannah? Look, I'm not like you two. I don't want to get it out of books, I like living!

[*They look at her without response.*]

I just think it could work, that's all. The three of us.

[FRANK *looks from one girl to the other without reply.*]

Look at him, he wants the best of both! What a face! No good looking like you want to wring my neck . . . you done me out of a bit of hey diddle diddle, mate. You know what your trouble is – you think too much. Look, tell you what, why don't you have a talk about it? I'll push off, go to bed . . . you two have a talk, sort it out . . . OK?

FRANK [*low and furious*]: And you've got all the answers – what do you mean, sort it out? What's that supposed to mean? We're married! We are married. We have two children. You know what my plans are . . . you agreed! You agreed about chucking the teaching –

CRYSTAL: Sure . . . fine –

FRANK: I'm doing it off your back, and I know very well you've no idea, not the faintest idea what I'm about . . . any more than you ever have – I'm not blaming you, simply stating a fact, I take full responsibility for the marriage, for . . . Just the same . . . just the same . . . [*He puts his head in his hands momentarily.*] . . . it *is* a marriage. We have created a marriage. We are a family. There are your parents, my parents . . . [*To* SUSANNAH] . . . I know *you'll* understand . . . there are facts and truths and values here . . . I'm not prepared to overturn, not just *my* life, God knows that's worth little enough, it's unimportant enough, not a swallow would be affected, oh, I'm well aware of that, of what the world thinks . . . my mates . . . [*To* CRYSTAL] . . . you . . . nonetheless . . . nonetheless . . . [*He looks up at* CRYSTAL *without expression.*] . . . it is our marriage.

[*Pause*]

CRYSTAL: I know you've put a lot in. You don't want to waste it. Nobody wants to think they've wasted their life. But I'm not a fucking ornament. And I don't need you trying to tell me what to do. Why don't you work your own patch for a change? For Christ's sakes, can't you see? She's bloody grieving for you!

SUSANNAH: Crystal, please.

CRYSTAL: Right. Nothing to do with me, right? Only I'm not having my kids messed about. There'll be no splitting off out of it. Might do for some, not for me. We got a solution – [*To* FRANK] if you can just get your fucking jealousy out of it.

[*Pause*]

FRANK [*low*]: I'll kill you.
   And myself. And the kids.
   [*Silence*]
CRYSTAL [*mutters*]: It's what it's all about. What it's always been
   about. Watch it, Susannah. They're not going to change.
   [*Silence*]
FRANK: I . . . I don't know what to do any more. I try. But I don't
   seem to be able to –
   The women yell, and complain, and I see it . . . I accept the
   argument. And I wash the nappies, and the kids' drawers. And I
   wait at the school gate. And you don't respect me. If I were a
   bugger you'd respect me. But because I try to respect you, you
   don't.
CRYSTAL: I'm not yours. You don't own me. [*Pause*] If you want
   me to go, I'll go . . . but the kids come with me.
   [*He gives her a dangerous look.*]
SUSANNAH: No. I'll go. This is all my fault, I should never have –
   [*But she falters and begins to cry.*] It's just that I . . . I want . . .
   [*She cries.*]
CRYSTAL [*full of sympathy*]: Ah!
SUSANNAH: I'm sorry –
CRYSTAL: No, go on – have a good cry. [*She cuddles* SUSANNAH.]
   It's him, isn't it?
SUSANNAH: Does it show?
CRYSTAL: When you're with him. Always did. I done you out of it.
   I'm the one to go.
SUSANNAH: No –
FRANK: I'm bloody going.
CRYSTAL: We can't all go.
   [*Pause*]
CRYSTAL: Stay then.
   [*Pause*]
SUSANNAH: Frank?
CRYSTAL: Frank? Ah, look at his poor eye. Shall I see if Inez has got
   a steak?
FRANK: Stuff it. [*He rises, looms over her dangerously, then exits
   to the bedroom.*]

SUSANNAH: How big is the garden?

CRYSTAL: A hundred foot, *and* round the side.

SUSANNAH: Wow!

CRYSTAL: And there's a conker tree.

[FRANK *returns. He is stuffing clothes into his bag.*]
I said I'd let her know.

SUSANNAH: Frank?

[*He looks from one to the other. And goes.*]
Damn.

CRYSTAL: Don't worry.

SUSANNAH: His poor eye.

CRYSTAL: He'll be all right.

SUSANNAH: Do you think he – I mean, has he – ?

CRYSTAL: Nah. Don't think so. Do you?

SUSANNAH: I don't know. He does have a tendency to pop his cork.

CRYSTAL: He'll be back.

SUSANNAH: I wonder.

CRYSTAL: He's left his books.

SUSANNAH [*doubtful*]: Mmm.

CRYSTAL: Oh well, soon find out. More tea – oh, it's cold. I know, drop of the ruin – be good for your nose.

SUSANNAH: I doubt it but thanks, yes I will.

CRYSTAL: Put your feet up. [*She crosses to record player, puts on* How Long Blues *by Jimmy Yancey.*]

SUSANNAH: D'you think he –

CRYSTAL: Relax. Don't worry about it.

[*She gives* SUSANNAH *a drink, picks up her own drink, in a long glass, and sashays to the music, glass in hand.*

SUSANNAH *drinks, lies back and relaxes. She looks around the room she has thought of so often, taking it all in again. She feels comfortable, and warm, and where she wants to be. She sighs aloud, a long sigh.*]
What?

SUSANNAH: I mean . . . is it too much to ask?

CRYSTAL: What?

SUSANNAH: You seem to manage.

CRYSTAL [*with an eloquent gesture towards the door*]: You kidding?

SUSANNAH [*giggles*]: He always was an old chauve – well, they all are.

CRYSTAL: Yeah, and rapists.

SUSANNAH [*getting a bit drunk*]: Oh no – not Frank! No!

CRYSTAL [rueful]: No.

　　[SUSANNAH *laughs.*]

　　What's he been telling you?

SUSANNAH: Nothing.

CRYSTAL: No, go on – [*She makes to sit by* SUSANNAH *but jumps up*] – I'll bring the bottle.

SUSANNAH: Listen . . . was that the door?

CRYSTAL [*shakes her head*]: He'll be down the pub, drowning his miseries. Look, forget it, let him do what he wants.

SUSANNAH: But we need to talk this over.

CRYSTAL: Sod him, who needs him! Here, what's he been telling you? [*She adds gin to* SUSANNAH's *glass.*]

SUSANNAH: Nothing really – well . . .

　　[*She laughs and tilts slightly, then she and* CRYSTAL, *heads together, begin to gossip and giggle, their voices inaudible under the music of the blues.*]

MORE ABOUT PENGUINS, PELICANS, PEREGRINES AND PUFFINS

For further information about books available from Penguins please write to Dept EP, Penguin Books Ltd, Harmondsworth, Middlesex UB7 0DA.

In the U.S.A.: For a complete list of books available from Penguins in the United States write to Dept DG, Penguin Books, 299 Murray Hill Parkway, East Rutherford, New Jersey 07073.

In Canada: For a complete list of books available from Penguins in Canada write to Penguin Books Canada Ltd, 2801 John Street, Markham, Ontario L3R 1B4.

In Australia: For a complete list of books available from Penguins in Australia write to the Marketing Department, Penguin Books Australia Ltd, P.O. Box 257, Ringwood, Victoria 3134.

In New Zealand: For a complete list of books available from Penguins in New Zealand write to the Marketing Department, Penguin Books (N.Z.) Ltd, Private Bag, Takapuna, Auckland 9.

In India: For a complete list of books available from Penguins in India write to Penguin Overseas Ltd, 706 Eros Apartments, 56 Nehru Place, New Delhi 110019.

THE PENGUIN ENGLISH DICTIONARY

The Penguin English Dictionary has been created specially for today's needs. It features:

* More entries than any other popularly priced dictionary
* Exceptionally clear and precise definitions
* For the first time in an equivalent dictionary, the internationally recognised IPA pronunciation system
* Emphasis on contemporary usage
* Extended coverage of both the spoken and the written word
* Scientific tables
* Technical words
* Informal and colloquial expressions
* Vocabulary most widely used *wherever* English is spoken
* Most commonly used abbreviations

It is twenty years since the publication of the last English dictionary by Penguin and the compilation of this entirely new *Penguin English Dictionary* is the result of a special collaboration between Longman, one of the world's leading dictionary publishers, and Penguin Books. The material is based entirely on the database of the acclaimed *Longman Dictionary of the English Language*.

1008 pages   051.139 3   £2.50   ☐

PLAYS IN PENGUINS

A CHOICE OF PENGUINS

☐ *Small World* **David Lodge** £2.50

A jet-propelled academic romance, sequel to *Changing Places*. 'A new comic débâcle on every page' – *The Times*. 'Here is everything one expects from Lodge but three times as entertaining as anything he has written before' – *Sunday Telegraph*

☐ *The Neverending Story* **Michael Ende** £3.50

The international bestseller, now a major film: 'A tale of magical adventure, pursuit and delay, danger, suspense, triumph' – *The Times Literary Supplement*

☐ *The Sword of Honour Trilogy* **Evelyn Waugh** £3.95

Containing *Men at Arms, Officers and Gentlemen* and *Unconditional Surrender*, the trilogy described by Cyril Connolly as 'unquestionably the finest novels to have come out of the war'.

☐ *The Honorary Consul* **Graham Greene** £1.95

In a provincial Argentinian town, a group of revolutionaries kidnap the wrong man . . . 'The tension never relaxes and one reads hungrily from page to page, dreading the moment it will all end' – Auberon Waugh in the *Evening Standard*

☐ *The First Rumpole Omnibus* **John Mortimer** £4.95

Containing *Rumpole of the Bailey, The Trials of Rumpole* and *Rumpole's Return*. 'A fruity, foxy masterpiece, defender of our wilting faith in mankind' – *Sunday Times*

☐ *Scandal* **A. N. Wilson** £2.25

Sexual peccadillos, treason and blackmail are all ingredients on the boil in A. N. Wilson's new, *cordon noir* comedy. 'Drily witty, deliciously nasty' – *Sunday Telegraph*

A CHOICE OF PENGUINS

☐ *Stanley and the Women* **Kingsley Amis**   £2.50

'Very good, very powerful . . . beautifully written . . . This is Amis *père* at his best' – Anthony Burgess in the *Observer*. 'Everybody should read it' – *Daily Mail*

☐ *The Mysterious Mr Ripley* **Patricia Highsmith**   £4.95

Containing *The Talented Mr Ripley, Ripley Underground* and *Ripley's Game*. 'Patricia Highsmith is the poet of apprehension' – Graham Greene. 'The Ripley books are marvellously, insanely readable' – *The Times*

☐ *Earthly Powers* **Anthony Burgess**   £4.95

'Crowded, crammed, bursting with manic erudition, garlicky puns, omnilingual jokes . . . (a novel) which meshes the real and personalized history of the twentieth century' – Martin Amis

☐ *Life & Times of Michael K* **J. M. Coetzee**   £2.95

The Booker Prize-winning novel: 'It is hard to convey . . . just what Coetzee's special quality is. His writing gives off whiffs of Conrad, of Nabokov, of Golding, of the Paul Theroux of *The Mosquito Coast*. But he is none of these, he is a harsh, compelling new voice' – Victoria Glendinning

☐ *The Stories of William Trevor*   £5.95

'Trevor packs into each separate five or six thousand words more richness, more laughter, more ache, more multifarious human-ness than many good writers manage to get into a whole novel' – *Punch*

☐ *The Book of Laughter and Forgetting*
   Milan Kundera   £3.95

'A whirling dance of a book . . . a masterpiece full of angels, terror, ostriches and love . . . No question about it. The most important novel published in Britain this year' – Salman Rushdie

A CHOICE OF PENGUINS